Margaret

By

C J Bessell

Other Books by C J Bessell

<u>The Copper Road Series</u>
Pioneers of Burra
For the Love of Family

Jacob's Mob

ISBN: 978-0-6451051-4-8

The story and characters portrayed in this
production are fictitious. No identification
with actual persons (living or deceased), is
intended or should be inferred.

Based on the life of Margaret Chambers,
who was the daughter of Sir Samuel
Chambers and Lady Barbara Roper.

Chapter One

*The River Derwent
Onboard William Metcalf January 1837*

Gripping the ship's rail with one hand I tucked a few wayward wisps of dark hair back under my cap. The sweet scent of earth and trees was on the breeze, and after months at sea, I could hardly wait to step foot on solid ground. My skirts billowed in the wind and I pushed them back down with my other hand. I had to quickly grab my cap which nearly flew off in the meantime. I couldn't help but smile, not just at my unruly attire, but at the sea birds that squawked and skimmed the waves beside the ship.

The ship, 'William Metcalf' was making its way slowly up the river and I had ample time to take in the dusky green of the trees and sloping hills. The small township of Hobart Town was nestled on the banks of the Derwent River, and behind it, the land sloped upwards and upwards. A large mountain, like a sleeping giant, overshadowed the small settlement. Even from this distance, I thought I could see snow on the summit. How very odd. The day was warm, and getting warmer and the Captain had informed us that it was summer here. I really have to pinch myself. I can hardly believe I'm on the other side of the world, so far away from my family back in Kent.

I pressed my lips together at the thought of them and took a couple of deep breaths. I'd had months at sea with little else to do but think about them, or rather to reconcile myself with my father. Not that I was letting Mamma off so easily. She could've done something to stop him and didn't. I'll never forget, or likely forgive him for trying to sell me off like some prized broodmare.

Not being privy to the inner workings of my father's affairs, I'd been oblivious to his growing financial problems. My two dear sisters, Barbara and Charlotte, had long been married, but I was always the quiet one. I've always preferred my music or the quiet refuge of the rose garden. Marriage has never appealed to me. Anyway, I thought my family had given up trying to matchmake me. At thirty-one I was sure they viewed me as an old maiden aunt. So you can imagine my surprise when Papa came into the conservatory with a look on his face that required my immediate inquiry.

"Whatever is the matter, Papa?" I said putting down my secateurs. I placed my hand on his arm and guided him over to a wicker chair. "Sit. You look like you might have a fit." His red face and pale lips made my heart skip a beat. Uncle James often looked like that right before he had one of his fits. I hoped to God Papa hadn't developed some similar type of apoplexy.

He sat down and gulped in some air. "I'm fine, nothing to worry about."

I didn't like the look of him at all. "Stay here Papa," I said and hurried from the conservatory to find some help. I hadn't gone far down the hallway when I ran into one of the maids. "Papa's in the conservatory and he's unwell," I said with some urgency. "Please fetch the decanter of brandy."

"Yes Miss Margaret," she said giving me a slight bob before going off to do as she was bid.

I went back into the conservatory and sat in the chair beside him. I took his hand in mine and smiled at him. "Now Papa, what's the matter?"

He took a large handkerchief from his pocket and wiped his brow. "Margaret, I'm sure you're aware that since your Uncle's bankruptcy we've had to tighten our belts."

I didn't pretend to understand what Uncle James' declaration of bankruptcy had to do with us. Of course, I knew Papa had let several servants go. The number of grooms had been reduced as well, but I thought that was because he'd sold off a number of horses. I smiled at him and nodded. I honestly didn't know what to say. I didn't want him to think I was so self-absorbed that I hadn't noticed his financial difficulties. Anyway, I doubted they were serious.

"Well, then you'll understand why your mother and I have agreed to your betrothal."

He might as well have tipped a bucket of water over me. I stared at him. He must've seen the confusion on my face. What did he mean my betrothal? We both knew perfectly well I had no intention of marrying, and I was quite firmly sitting on the shelf. Anyway who'd want to take an old maid like me to wife? I quickly realised I'd stopped breathing, and gasped in a large lungful of air in a most unladylike manner. The maid chose that very moment to appear with the decanter of brandy and cut crystal glass.

"Put it on the table and leave us." I spoke more abruptly than I'd intended. She put the brandy down and scampered from the conservatory. "Thank you," I called after her.

"I knew you'd understand," he said smiling warmly at me. "Your mother was worried you'd take to the idea of marriage badly. But I knew you'd do your duty."

"My duty?" I said rising to my feet. Duty! He wasn't serious. I looked at his now beaming face as he looked up at me. I was speechless.

He poured himself a nip of brandy and took a mouthful. "Your soon to be fiancé will be joining us for dinner on Friday. I'm having the marriage contract drawn up this week. All you have to do is sign and set the date for your wedding." He placed the glass on the table and stood up. "It won't be a long engagement, he's anxious to be wed." He hugged me and kissed my cheek. "Congratulations my dear."

"You can't be serious," I said at last. "I don't care who it is. I won't be signing any marriage contract on Friday."

His smile evaporated and he licked his lips. "Now Margaret, I've just explained to you that we're in a financial squeeze. It's your duty to obey me in these matters."

"I don't understand." I couldn't see any point in pretending any longer. I didn't have the faintest clue about our financial situation. "What has Uncle James' bankruptcy got to do with us?"

"Well it's complicated, and I wouldn't expect you to fully understand," he said a frown creasing his brow. "That doesn't really matter. What matters is that you agree to marry Sir Richard Owens to help us recover our fortunes."

"I will not." Sir Richard Owens! He was old enough to be my grandsire, and I've never met a more repugnant old lecher in my life. The thought of him touching me made my skin crawl. I shuddered at the thought. How could my mother have agreed to this? Tears threatened to overwhelm me, but I swallowed them along with what care I had left for my father's feelings.

I swept from the conservatory with as much grace as I could muster. I heard him call me back, but I ignored him. I hurried upstairs to my bedroom. I locked the door and flung myself down on the bed and let my tears go. I sobbed uncontrollably for some time. I felt so betrayed. I couldn't believe that my own sweet mother had agreed to this match. It was abhorrent.

I had to think; I had to find a way out of this nightmare before it was too late. I knew my father - Sir Samuel Chambers had been the High Sheriff of Kent and a more determined man I'd never met. If he intended me to marry Sir Owen, then by God that's what I would do. I gulped in several large breaths and tried to stop crying. Tears were not going to help or stop my father from getting what he wanted.

The tears hadn't helped, but he couldn't marry me off to Sir Owen if he couldn't find me. I'd taken no chances. Running away to Charlotte or Barb's was my first thought, but he'd have found me immediately. So I'd taken more extreme measures, and here I was about to land in Hobart Town.

The smaller tugs had come alongside the William Metcalf and were attaching ropes to guide us safely into the dock. A feeling of nervous excitement swept through me at the thought of finally getting off the ship. I put my hand to my stomach to quieten the flutter. I wasn't like all the other women on board. For the most part, they were coming out to Van Diemen's Land to work as domestic servants, as was I. There was just one rather big difference between them and me. I'd never done a day's menial work in my life. The only way I could get free passage out here was to tell, what I hope will only amount to a small lie. I said I was a general servant, and Mrs Hector from Coal River had paid my fare. In return, I'm to work for her until my passage is paid. I imagine she's expecting me to be an experienced servant.

I sucked in my lower lip and sighed. I wonder what will happen if she finds out? I don't think they'd put me in prison for lying, would they? The flutter of nerves was now becoming a full-on anxiety attack. Panic threatened to overwhelm me and I sucked in some deep breaths to try and calm myself.

"Are ye alright Margaret?" said Ann Chapman coming along to stand at the rail beside me. She put her hand on my arm. "Is it the seasickness?" She peered at me and smiled kindly.

"No, just nerves," I said placing my hand over hers and smiling. She was such a kind girl. Ann had shared a compartment with me and although we had little in common, she'd always shown me such kindness.

"Oh, I know what ye mean," she said letting go of my arm and gripping the railing as the ship lunged. "I've not seen my Aunt in such an age. I hope she remembers me"

"Oh, of course, she will." I put my arm around her waist and hugged her close. "She wouldn't have paid for your fare otherwise now would she?"

"I suppose yer right."

A few hours later the ship was safely tied up at the dock, and the excitement onboard was palpable. Captain Philipson had told everyone to wait on board until their friends and family came to collect them, but it did little to stop the chaos. The women were frantically trying to get their trunks up onto the top deck. I'd packed my trunk that morning and I was now sitting on it while I waited. Women were rushing to and fro down the narrow corridor between the compartments, many in an absolute frenzy. Finally, Captain Philipson intervened and brought some order to the mayhem.

"Ye will remain below decks until ye're called for," he said at last. "Mr Jackson will see to ye trunk an' such when the time comes. In the meantime, I expect ye all to behave in an orderly fashion." He heaved a great sigh as went back up to the quarter deck.

I hoped Mrs Hector would come today or tomorrow at the latest. Now that we'd arrived in Hobart Town I was of the same mind as everyone else. I wanted to get off the ship as soon as I could. Ann came rushing down the corridor with her skirt hoicked up in one hand.

"Margaret, oh Margaret my Aunt's come for me," she said beaming at me. "I just wanted to say thank ye and goodbye." She grabbed me and pulled me into her embrace. "I hope we'll see each other again."

"Lucky you," I said hugging her close. "I wish you the best of luck Ann."

We let go of each other and I smiled at her. "I'm sure we'll meet again."

She smiled at me and sighed. "Well until then. I hope it all works out for ye with Mrs Hector."

"Thank you, I'm sure it will. Now off you go. You don't want to keep your Aunt waiting."

"No of course," she said as she leaned forward and kissed my cheek. "Goodbye." She gathered her skirt in her hands and hurried down the corridor.

I watched her go with a pang of sadness. Under normal circumstances, I would never have befriended someone like Ann. She would've been a maid in my father's house, and I would never have thought of sharing accommodation with her. And yet, we'd spent the past three months sharing a confined compartment with two other girls. I smiled to myself. Well, Margaret you just never know what you might do, or what lies ahead.

After a week of waiting on board the William Metcalf, there was still no sign of Mrs Hector. There were only a handful of us left to be collected, and I think Captain Philipson was just as frustrated as me. I'm sure he wanted to get underway to wherever he was going next, and I certainly wanted to get off his ship. Land was so close, and I spent my days on deck gazing at the houses and bustling docks full of people going about their business. The weather was warm and the ship's hold had become hot and stuffy. I sighed as I watched the gulls glide on the breeze. How wonderful to be so carefree.

Two days later the first mate, Mr Jackson called for me to join him on the quarter-deck. My heart skipped a beat. Mrs Hector must've finally come for me. I gathered up my skirts and climbed the ladder to the top deck. There was no sign of Mrs Hector. Rather, Mr Jackson was waiting for me with a man who was clearly a Reverend by his mode of dress.

"Mr Jackson you called for me," I said smiling at him. I gave the Reverend a nod of acknowledgement.

"Miss Chambers, this is Reverend Davies."

"Pleased to make your acquaintance," I said. A frown of puzzlement must have been evident on my face.

"Likewise Miss Chambers," said Reverend Davies. "I can see you're puzzled by my appearance." He smiled, and it wrinkled the corners of his chestnut brown eyes. "I'm afraid Mrs Hector's situation has changed drastically, and she's no longer in a position to take you into her household."

"Oh," I said rather stupefied by the news. I looked from the Reverend to Mr Jackson for some clue as to what might happen to me now. Their faces were unreadable.

"That's what brings me to Hobart Town, Miss Chambers," said the Reverend with a degree of impatience evident in his voice. "My wife and I have agreed to take you instead. We have a long journey ahead of us, so if you'd gather your belongings we'll be on our way."

"Oh," I said again. I'm sure he must think me an absolute imbecile, but I'm feeling quite lost for words. I don't suppose it's going to make any difference whether I go to Mrs Hector or the Reverend's, but I'd gotten used to the idea of working for Mrs Hector.

"Is your trunk packed Miss Chambers?" asked Mr Jackson turning his attention to me.

"I just need to pack a few last-minute items," I said, at last finding something sensible to say. "I'll go and see to it right away."

"Good," said Reverend Davies waving his hat in front of his face like a fan. "Please be quick about it Miss Chambers."

I hurried below decks to pack my last few belongings which were strewn around the small compartment. There was my fan and a volume of Reformation that I'd been reading. Well, not so much reading as skimming. My favourite shawl was poking out from under the narrow bunk and I folded it neatly and packed it. I scanned the small compartment for any other wayward items, but I couldn't see any. I closed the lid, pulled the straps tight and fastened the buckles. I wondered briefly if I should've kept my shawl out.

I picked up my violin case and was about to head back up when one of the crew arrived to collect my trunk. He dragged it along the corridor and with the help of another mate they carried it up onto the deck. I was right behind them. My heart fluttered nervously as I emerged and saw the Reverend waiting for me. This was it. My new life far away from the bosom of my family was about to begin. I took in a deep breath and slowly let it out. I was both excited and nervous at what it might lay ahead.

Chapter Two

The road to 'Ardmore House'

It was just after midday when I climbed into the Reverend's cart. It was an open wagon with just one seat for passengers and a curved canvas canopy. A young man dressed in an odd assortment of ill-fitting clothes jumped up onto the driver's seat. He'd been assisting the crew of the William Metcalf to load my trunk and I was surprised that he was the Reverend Davies' driver. I don't know what or who I'd been expecting, but he just seemed very unlikely.

The Reverend climbed up onto the seat beside me and sighed. "Are you ready Miss Chambers?"

"Yes Reverend, thank you," I said folding my hands in my lap. I smiled. I think it may have looked more like a grimace than the demure smile I was hoping for. I was nervous and unsure, and perhaps even a little fearful. Here I was, in a cart going to God only knew where with two men that were neither family members nor acquaintances. It would never have happened back in England. I consoled myself with the fact that I was with a man of God, and surely that made it acceptable.

The cart lurched forward catching me unawares and I grasped the side of the seat to stop myself from falling. We set off at a fast pace and I held on for dear life.

The settlement of Hobart Town soon gave way to rolling hills. We'd only gone a few miles when we came to a halt by the banks of the river. In the distance, I could see a launch making its way towards the shore being towed by a smaller vessel. I swallowed, before glancing at the Reverend, who was sitting very still and looking quite calm.

"Are we going to take the ferry?" I asked.

"Yes. It's the only way to cross the river."

"Oh." I couldn't swim, and while I'd been on a barge before on the River Thames, it was never far from shore. The river looked like it was nearly a mile across and the ferry appeared to be a flat decked punt. I took in several deep breaths and tried to calm my rising anxiety.

Ten minutes later I closed my eyes as we boarded the ferry. Reverend Davies placed his hand on my arm and when I opened my eyes he was peering at me.

"Are you alright?"

I took a couple of large breaths and smiled weakly at him. "Yes thank you. It's just...I've not been on a ferry like this before."

"Oh, well I can assure you it's quite safe," he said smiling. "John, help Miss Chambers down, will you. I find it better to stand by the railing than to sit up here."

I nodded, before placing my hands on John's shoulders while he helped me down. I had to agree with Reverend Davies, it didn't seem quite as frightening now that I was standing on the deck. He took my arm and ushered me over to the rail.

"I find it best to stand by the railing and watch the river go by."

I must admit he was right. As the punt started to cross the river I found myself starting to relax. I watched the currents and eddies in the river as they swirled and hurried to the sea. I sighed as the far shore came ever closer.

"May I ask you something?" asked Reverend Davies.

I was lost in my reverie and he caught me quite by surprise. "Yes, of course."

"I understand from Mrs Hector that you've been employed as a servant. How long have you been working as a general servant?" he said eyeing me with a quizzical brow. "You must excuse me, but I can't help but notice the quality of your attire, nor your refined speech."

I swallowed. "Oh," I said looking into his brown eyes. Did I imagine I saw kindness in their depths? Actually, they appeared more astute than kind. I decided another small lie was probably my best option right now. "I've been employed for some time, and my mother insisted on elocution lessons."

"I see," he said.

He continued to stare into my serene grey eyes – at least I hoped they weren't showing my inner turmoil. I wasn't sure I could trust him with the truth of my situation. What if he threw me and my luggage out when we landed on the other side of the river? What would I do then? I swallowed and nervously twisted my fingers together.

"And the violin? Am I to presume that you play, Miss Chambers?" he said glancing towards the cart.

My violin case was sticking up beside my trunk, and I wished I could push it down out of sight. His continued stare was unnerving me. I sucked in my bottom lip and looked away from him. He must've read my face. I was never very good at hiding what I was thinking. He put his hand on my arm, and I turned quickly to look at him.

"Yes I play," I blurted out. "My father always encouraged my sisters and me." I tried to keep my voice calm and composed. "I also play the piano."

His brows raised and his expression changed from inquisitor to one of genuine interest. "Would you consider playing the organ at Sunday's Service? I'm sure my parishioners would be most appreciative," he said studying my face. "We haven't had anyone to play for some time, and the hymns aren't the same without musical accompaniment."

"Of course," I said smiling. "I'll need some practice, but I'd be happy to."

He smiled and turned his attention back to the river. I breathed a sigh of relief. It would appear that the inquisition was over for the moment. I would need to be on my guard and ready though. I had a distinct feeling the Reverend Davies would want the truth eventually. I just hoped I'd have enough time to ingratiate myself into his household before then.

In no time at all the punt bumped against the shore and I climbed back into the cart with the Reverend. We set off along the narrow dirt road heading north away from the green of the Derwent Valley. The dusky green trees and scrubby undergrowth Reverend Davies told me they were gum trees, and their leaves were long and thin and a dark dusky shade of green. They were so unlike the oaks and elms that surrounded my home in Kent.

It was late afternoon when we came into a small village called Richmond, which was situated on the Coal River. We crossed a stone arch bridge and continued until John brought us to a halt outside the Lennox Arms Inn. It was a modest double-storey sandstone building with a long veranda. I was grateful to climb down from the cart. After hours of inactivity, my limbs were stiff and cramped.

"Miss Chambers," said Reverend Davies coming around to my side of the cart. "Won't you join me for supper?"

"Thank you," I replied. I glanced around, but John was already disappearing around the back of the inn with the cart. "Will we be staying here for the night?"

"Yes. We won't get to Ardmore for another day and a half," he said opening the door to the inn. "I assure you, it will be all very proper."

"Of course," I said feeling a flush of color sweep over my face.

It was cool inside the timber panelled hallway. A staircase went straight up to the second floor and a sign above the door on the right read 'Public Bar'. Reverend Davies opened the door on the left and gestured for me to enter. I was relieved to find myself in the ladies ordinary. Several other patrons were already seated and the Reverend led me over to a small table in the corner. I sat down and folded my hands in my lap.

"I'll be back momentarily," he said before walking back out of the ordinary.

I watched him go. I was nervous about spending the evening alone with him. He wasn't much older than me, and under normal circumstances, it wouldn't be appropriate for a single woman such as myself to spend an evening alone with a married man.

I'd worked out for myself that John wouldn't be joining us. When I'd first seen him this morning I'd just thought his clothes were odd and ill-fitting. But I'd observed during the day, that a lot of men were dressed just like him in canvas breeches, brown shirts and blue jackets. They were convicts. Actually, I was quite curious about them, having never been anywhere near a criminal before. I can't help wondering how many convicts Reverend Davies has working for him? I've also been wondering all day what Mrs Davies might be like. I didn't think the Reverend and I were quite so well acquainted that I could ask.

Reverend Davies returned about fifteen minutes later. "I've arranged our rooms for the night and supper," he said sitting down opposite me. "John's already taken care of your luggage."

"Thank you," I said and smiled. "You've shown me nothing but kindness. I only hope I can repay you."

"Well, I expect Mrs Davies will soon have you hard at work earning your keep."

"Of course." I didn't know what else to say. I can only hope Mrs Davies is a patient woman. I sighed. When I'd lied about myself to Mrs Hector I hadn't actually worked out how I was going to explain my lack of ability. Now that I was faced with the reality of being a servant, I was getting more than a little anxious. I didn't know what I was going to do.

A serving girl arrived at our table with two plates of roast beef and vegetables which she placed down in front of us. It smelled delicious. I hadn't realised until right this moment that I was starving.

"I'll be back wi' the tea," she said smiling at the Reverend.

"Thank you."

She turned on her heel and without giving me the slightest glance headed back to the kitchen. Reverend Davies placed his hands together and bowed his head. I did likewise while he recited grace.

The roast beef was delicious. I can't remember the last time I had fresh meat.

Onboard the ship it had been a monotonous diet of salt pork, so supper was a real treat. I ate with relish and didn't mind the lack of table conversation. At any rate, I wasn't anxious to reopen our earlier conversation. The serving girl came back to our table with a pot of tea and two cups and saucers. I poured us each a cup and added a little sugar to mine. I took a sip of the hot sweet substance and sighed with pleasure.

"Tell me Miss Chambers have you had any experience with babies?"

He took me by complete surprise. Not just the nature of the question, but he'd been so quiet through supper. "Ah no," I said putting my cup down. "Do you and Mrs Davies have many children then?"

A sadness descended over his eyes like a veil. "Mrs Davies is expecting our first."

"Well congratulations," I said smiling at him.

He didn't return the smile and he put his cup down. "If you'll excuse me I think I'll retire," he said rising to his feet. "Good night." He quickly walked from the ordinary.

I stared after him. I have no idea what just happened. If he didn't want to talk about his wife and child why did he raise the subject? I was confused by his demeanour and intrigued. Why would he look so sad when they are expecting their first child? It was perplexing.

I was just finishing my tea when the serving girl came back to my table.

"The Reverend asked me to show ye to yer room. Come wi' me." She marched across the ordinary to the door and stood with it open, clearly waiting for me.

I quickly got to my feet and followed her. She proceeded down the hallway passed the stairs and beyond the kitchen. She stopped and opened a door on the left and stood back to allow me entry.

"Ye'll be sharin' wi' me," she said following me into the small room. "Ye can have the bed under the window."

I looked around the small shabby room. There were two narrow cots; the one she'd said was mine had a grubby quilt thrown over it. I tried not to grimace or screw up my nose in distaste. I reminded myself that it would only be for one night. A stub of a candle was burning on the nightstand which bathed the room in its yellow glow. All it did was illuminate the peeling wallpaper and faded curtains. I shuddered.

I breathed a sigh of relief at the sight of my trunk. At least I had a warm cloak in there that I could wrap myself in for the night. I wouldn't have to touch the filthy quilt.

"Thank you," I said smiling at her. I hoped it was a friendly smile and not a scowl. "You are most kind to share your room with me."

"Ye best get some rest, ye'll be up at dawn." She slammed the door on her way out.

I let out my breath and threw back the quilt. I shuddered at the sight of the stains on the sheets and quickly tossed the quilt back on. I sat down on my trunk and wrapped my arms about myself. I wasn't sure I'd be able to sleep at all tonight. I sat there for ages not wanting to lie down on that cot or touch anything. Tears weren't far from the surface but I swallowed them. I realised that I'd mistaken Reverend Davies' kindness. I was his servant, nothing more. Of course, he'd made sure I was fed and had a place to sleep; I would've done no less for any of my maids. I let the large salty tears fall down my cheeks.

Finally, exhaustion drove me to pull my cloak from my trunk. I wrapped myself in it and lay down. I must've fallen asleep sometime during the night. I heard my companion come in at some late hour and the next thing I knew she was shaking me.

"Time to get up, the Reverend's waitin' for ye."

Chapter Three

Another long day on the road

Reverend Davies was distant over breakfast and appeared to be in a melancholic mood. I thought if I could draw him into some conversation it might improve his demeanour. The sun was just coming up as we departed the Lennox Arms Inn.

"Will we reach Ardmore today?" I asked as the cart lurched forward and we set off down the road.

"No."

"Oh," I said smiling. "So where will we stay tonight?"

"Campbell Town I expect."

"This is such an adventure for me," I went on. "All these new sights and places I've never seen."

"Hrmm."

After half an hour or so of similar unresponsive conversation I gave up and tried to make myself comfortable on the narrow seat. Getting comfortable was proving difficult. Last night I hadn't wanted to touch anything in that dreadful room, and there hadn't been anyone to help me out of my stays. I'd only removed my outer clothes and slept in my chemise. I managed to loosen my stays, but I hadn't had anyone to tighten them again for me this morning. They were still loose and they felt like they'd bunched up around my ribs. I wriggled and tried to get into a more comfortable position. Reverend Davies looked quizzically at me. I smiled weakly and stopped my fidgeting. I sighed. It was going to be a long day.

We made several stops during the day for various reasons. We had our midday meal in the small town of Oatlands which had a long strewn out Main Street. It was lined with small sandstone shops and cottages with shady verandas. It was so quaint. We continued onto the leafy village of Ross for afternoon tea. I was so thankful to stretch my cramped legs and I tried to wriggle my stays into a more comfortable position. I hoped someone would be able to unlace them for me tonight. I couldn't bear the thought of sleeping in them again.

I was so bone-weary by the time we arrived in Campbell Town. John pulled the cart up out the front of the Foxhunters Retreat. It was a double story red brick building with tall Georgian style windows set back a little from the main road. John helped me down from the cart.

"Thank you," I said and smiled at him. The lines on his face were etched with weariness but he gave me a weak smile in return. I knew how he felt. My limbs were stiff and cramped. The day of weary travel bouncing around in the cart must've been evident on my face.

"See to the horses and bring in the luggage John," said Reverend Davies in a brusque tone. "If you'll join me, Miss Chambers."

He didn't wait for my response, instead he headed straight into the inn. I hurried to catch up and whilst several retorts were going through my head I said nothing. I was perplexed. What had happened to the kind Reverend of yesterday? I knew it had something to do with his wife's confinement, but I hadn't raised the subject - he did. I sighed as I followed him into the cool interior of the inn.

We enjoyed our supper of pork pie and potatoes in silence before retiring for the evening. A very kind young servant girl by the name of Alice helped me out of my stays. I vigorously rubbed the nasty red welts on my sore ribs and sighed with pleasure at having the things off. I had a room to myself for the night and although it was small and airless, it was clean. Anyway, I was so tired I didn't care.

We set off at daybreak on what I hoped would be the last day of travel. Although I'd slept well last night, no doubt from sheer exhaustion, I was still weary. I sat quietly with my hands folded in my lap as the cart set off down the road. Reverend Davies had been quiet over breakfast again this morning, and so I wasn't expecting him to start up a conversation.

"I think you'll like Ardmore," he said with a look of longing on his face.

I wasn't sure if it was his house he missed, or perhaps he was longing for his wife's company. I thought it was the latter.

"I'm sure I will," I said and smiled at him. "I only hope Mrs Davies can find a use for me."

He nodded. "Without doubt Miss Chambers. She has a large household to run and is always in need of extra hands."

"Does she have a large garden?" I asked. I hoped there might be a small rose garden that I could disappear into occasionally.

"Yes. We have a very large garden, in fact, we're in need of another gardener," he said as though the idea had just occurred to him.

"Well, I'm not much of a gardener I'm afraid. Although I used to spend many hours in my mother's rose garden."

"Oh, I didn't mean you, Miss Chambers," he said with a slight scoff to his voice. "No, no. I'm sure Maria, that is Mrs Davies, will need your assistance indoors."

"Oh," I said. I was slightly disappointed. Goodness only knew what type of indoor work Mrs Davies would have me do. A flutter of nerves went through me and I sucked in my lower lip. I hope she wouldn't want me to do laundry. I didn't have the faintest idea of where to begin with a chore like that, and it always looked like hot exhausting work.

"Well we should arrive at Ardmore before midday," he said flipping open the cover of his pocket watch. He snapped it shut and put it back in his pocket. "Don't worry Miss Chambers. We'll find something suitable for you."

We veered off the main road as we came into the village of Norfolk Plains. I was a little disappointed that we didn't go up the main street. It looked like it was lined with shops and double story brick buildings. I was both excited and nervous as John turned the cart down the tree-lined driveway.

Up ahead I could see Ardmore House nestled in amongst tall gum trees and a well-manicured garden. It was a lot larger than I'd imagined it would be. The country clergymen back home generally lived in modest homes, nothing as grand as this.

It was a two-storey stuccoed dwelling with two wings. A large gable up one end with fancy bargeboards and a lovely brick chimney. The middle section had a charming dormer window and the west wing was double story with a large picture window on the ground floor. Along the front, it looked like it had a closed-in veranda, although I couldn't be sure.

I took in a large breath as the cart came to a halt. All of a sudden my heart started thumping madly and I was filled with apprehension. I took in several deep breaths and tried to calm my growing nerves. John helped me down and I smiled or rather grimaced at him. I knew my anxiety would be visible on my face. I've never been good at hiding my feelings. The Reverend came around the back of the cart and headed for the front door.

"Come, Miss Chambers," he called over his shoulder. "John will bring your luggage."

"Yes Reverend," I said as I followed him down the short path to the front door.

He held the door open for me to enter and after giving him a brief smile, I stepped inside. I found myself in a wide timber floored hallway with ornate cornices. I didn't get a chance to take in much more as a large woman in a white starched apron arrived on the scene. She had warm brown eyes and a rosy complexion and her presence seemed to fill the hall.

"Welcome home Reverend," she said smiling broadly at him. "Mrs Davies will be ever so glad to see yer. An' I see yer brought the lass."

"Thank you, Mrs Fitz, I'll attend to my wife immediately. Would you please see that Miss Chambers is settled in?"

"Aye of course," she said stepping aside to allow the Reverend to squeeze passed her. "Come with me, yer must be exhausted after such a trip."

I was still breathing heavily, almost panting in fact from sheer nerves, but I found myself relaxing in the presence of Mrs Fitz. She waddled off down the hallway and I found myself smiling despite my apprehension.

"Come this way. I'm Mrs Fitzpatrick, everyone calls me Mrs Fitz an' yer can too," she said gesturing with her hand. "We'll get yer settled an' washed up in no time."

She turned down another short hall and began climbing a narrow staircase. "The kitchen's through that door there at the end of the hall. Yer can always get a cup of tea from Martha. I'll introduce yer to her soon enough."

There was a small landing at the top of the stairs with two doors opening into it. Mrs Fitz opened the one on the left and went inside. I followed her into a large room that contained four narrow beds and two large wardrobes. I realised we were at the gable end of the house as the timber-lined ceiling followed the shape of the roof. Two narrow windows looked out into the back garden and a washstand stood against the opposite wall.

"Yer can have the bed on the end there," said Mrs Fitz indicating to the one nearest the wall. "John will be up with yer luggage afore yer knows it. Come an' I'll introduce yer to cook. Would yer like some tea?"

"That would be wonderful."

"Well yer freshen yerself up an' then come on down to the kitchen," she said pouring water into the basin on the washstand. "There's soap an' such on the shelf."

"Thank you."

She smiled at me before leaving the room. I sighed. I could only hope that Mrs Davies would be as kind. I took the soap and washed my face and hands. It felt so good to wash off the dirt and grime from the road. I would've liked a bath, but I realised that would have to wait. I took a moment to inspect the room before going back downstairs. The furnishings were simple and modest, but they looked clean and fresh. The beds all had patched quilts on them and the rug on the floor was a bit threadbare. Two worn, but comfortable looking armchairs completed the room. None of that mattered as long as I could ingratiate myself with my new mistress.

I went back down the narrow stairs and opened the door at the end of the hall. I found myself in a large country style kitchen with a long wooden table down the middle.

"Here's the lass now," said Mrs Fitz as I entered. She was sitting down one end of the table with a cup of tea in front of her. "This here's Martha. She's the head cook."

"Pleased to meet you," I said giving Martha a slight nod. "I'm Margaret."

"Nice to meet ye," said Martha looking me up and down. "Would ye like a cup of tea?"

"Yes thank you."

"Sit. Martha will pour yer one," said Mrs Fitz patting the chair beside her.

I took her queue and sat down beside her. The kitchen had a large wood stove on one side and several dressers full of crockery. I presumed I would be eating my meals in here with the rest of the staff. That was an odd thought, but I was one of the downstairs servants now. My days of being Miss Margaret of Bredgar House were well and truly over. I only had one small regret, and that was the not so small lie I'd told to get here. Martha put a cup of hot black tea down in front of me and I thanked her.

"I'm sure ye'll settle in soon enough," said Mrs Fitz sipping her tea. "Ye'll be sharing yer room with Martha here, as well as Liz who does laundry an' Annie. You'll do as I tell yer mind. I'm the housekeeper here an' Mrs Davies likes me to run things."

"I understand," I said taking a mouthful of tea.

"Good," she said putting her cup down. "Mrs Davies hasn't decided what yer to do yet, she wants to meet yer first. Have yer any experience with bairns?"

"No, I'm afraid not."

"More's the pity. She'll be needing a hand with the new bairn soon enough."

I smiled and nodded. "Will I be meeting Mrs Davies today?" I poked several stray wisps of hair back under my cap as I said this. I must look a fright. My clothes were dirt-stained and crumpled from days in the cart. I doubt I'd give anyone a very good impression.

"No not today," she replied. "The poor wee lamb's feeling most poorly. Anyways, I expect ye'd like to rest as well.

Yer must be verra tired after yer trip up from Hobart Town."

"Yes, I am rather. Thank you."

"Well, of course, that will count as one of yer afternoons off," she said taking another mouthful of tea. "Ye'll get two afternoons a week to attend to yer own affairs. An' yer expected to attend divine service on Sunday morning."

"Reverend Davies has asked me to play the organ on Sunday."

"Has he indeed," she said looking at me with raised eyebrows. "Yer play then?"

"Yes. I'll need to practice the hymns that he wants to me play though. I haven't played hymns in a long time."

"Well I'll have to talk to the Reverend about that," she said putting down her cup again. "There's a piano in the parlour. Would that do?"

"No, not really. I need to practice on an organ."

"Oh," she said looking thoughtful. "Well the Church is only a few doors down, an' there's an organ there sure enough. I'll have to talk to the Reverend about it though. I dinna think yer should go down there by yerself."

"I'm sure I'd be fine." I drained the last of my tea. I was looking forward to taking a nap and resting my weary bones.

"Hrmph," she said frowning at me. "Yer've only just arrived an' yer don't know these parts. Be patient until I've had a chance to discuss this proper with the Reverend."

"Of course," I said smiling demurely. "Well if you'll excuse me I think I'll go and get some rest."

"Oh of course yer poor wee lass. I'm sorry I've kept yer talking. Go on with yer."

Chapter Four

'Ardmore House', Norfolk Plains

Over the next few days, I settled into my new life at Ardmore House. Mrs Fitz proved to be as helpful and efficient as she was kind. My mother would've loved her running her household. She made arrangements for me to practice on the organ down at the church; albeit not alone. For an hour following our midday meal, she'd arranged for Annie to accompany me. She's very young, I'd say only about seventeen, with a London accent.

Apparently, she was caught stealing a length of calico and transported here for seven years. I was quite shocked when I discovered she was a convict. I can't help but wonder how many of the Reverend's servants are convicts? Certainly, John is, and Annie. I don't think Mrs Fitz is, but Martha could be. I'm not even sure if it should matter to me or not. This is a whole new world.

With Annie for company, I'd spent the last hour practising the hymns I planned to play this Sunday. Annie spent her time unenthusiastically dusting and generally cleaning the interior of the Church. It's in a very bad state of disrepair. In fact, I'm not sure it's even safe to be inside it. Several props are holding up the roof and the mortar's crumbling in between the bricks. It smells damp and musty. Obviously, the roof must be leaking somewhere.

"Are ye nearly done?" asked Annie flopping herself down on the front pew.

I stopped playing and twisted around on the stool to look at her. "Just one more. Do you mind?"

"No. I'll just sit 'ere an' listen."

I smiled and went back to playing *'Christ is our Corner-Stone'*. It wasn't a long hymn and I finished playing in no time. I was happy with my arrangement and thought I'd be able to play it on Sunday without making a mistake. I folded the music sheet, pushed in the stop knobs and closed the organ.

"Come on then, let's go."

It was only a short walk back to the house through the Church grounds. There was a gate in the side fence that opened straight into the back garden of Ardmore House. Once through the gate, there was a large orchard with several potting sheds off to one side. A narrow winding path led passed several flower beds and an arbour overhanging with wisteria. A large shady gum tree was almost in the middle of the yard with several benches situated around its trunk. Closer to the house was the kitchen garden. All manner of vegetables were growing here along with a few medicinal herbs.

I opened the back door and we both went inside. Annie would no doubt have any number of chores to do, but I didn't know what Mrs Fitz had lined up for me. Yesterday she had me working in the kitchen with Martha. Poor Martha. It took me all afternoon to prepare a few potatoes and turnips. I don't imagine she'll ask for my assistance again.

"Oh good, yer two are back," said Mrs Fitz coming down the hall towards us. "Annie, yer needed in the wash house. Margaret ye come with me."

She looked me up and down and frowned. I looked myself up and down as well. I half expected to find something stuck to me. I was fine. I was wearing a simple cotton dress, but it was clean and in good repair. I tucked a wayward curl back under my cap and ran my hands over my skirt, smoothing any imagined wrinkles.

"The mistress wants to see ye."

I swallowed as a flutter of nerves swept through me. I could only hope that Reverend Davies would find my organ playing essential because I doubted Mrs Davies would have any kind things to say about my abilities as a servant. I sucked in my lower lip and followed Mrs Fitz as she headed up the hall to the main stairway. At the top of the stairs was a sunny landing and a short hallway. Mrs Fitz opened the door at the end of the hall and gestured for me to enter.

I found myself in a large airy room with a large double tester bed in the middle. Several comfortable chairs were situated under the window along with a low ornate table. A young woman was seated by the window with an easel in front of her. She looked up as we entered, and I was struck by how pale and thin she was. Everyone has been telling me how she's expecting her baby in another month, so I'd expected her to be more rounded. She had dark smudges under her pale blue eyes which made her angular cheekbones seem even more pronounced.

"Thank you, Mrs Fitz," she said putting down her pencil. "You must be Margaret. Please won't you join me?" She indicated to a floral wing back chair opposite her.

I smiled and perched myself on the edge of the chair. I heard Mrs Fitz retreat and close the door behind her. I fidgeted nervously as I waited. I only hope this young woman doesn't throw me from her house. She smiled warmly at me. No doubt she's noticed I'm nervous, and I appreciate her trying to put me at ease. I sucked in my bottom lip as I waited for her to speak.

"Robert tells me you're playing the organ for him this Sunday. Wherever did you learn to play?"

I swallowed. "My father insisted that my sisters and I learn to play a musical instrument of some kind."

"Forgive me Margaret, but that's rather unusual for someone of your standing. Don't you think?"

Maria Davies might be young but she was obviously astute. I tried to calm my growing anxiety as I drew in several deep breaths. I quickly realised that I had two options, and even the lowliest of servants could poke holes in the first one. I could stick to my story, or I could tell her the truth. My grey eyes met her pale blue ones, and I saw a determination in their depths. I lowered my eyes and sighed.

"Mrs Davies I can assure you that I'll work hard and do my best."

She smiled, but it didn't quite reach her eyes. "I don't doubt it, Margaret. It has come to my attention, however, that your experience in the kitchen is rather limited. And as for the laundry, well I think we both know you've never done that before."

"Ah yes," I said entwining my fingers together. "I've not had much experience in those areas."

She wrapped her robe more firmly about herself. "I presume your experience in other areas will also be lacking? Please tell me if I'm wrong."

Her eyes seemed to bore into me and I was surprised. I was at least ten years her senior and yet I felt like a child in her presence. I decided in that instant that I had little choice but to confess. If she threw me out, well I'd work something out.

"You presume correctly Mrs Davies," I said blinking as tears pricked my eyes. I didn't want to cry for God sake. "I never meant to deceive anyone, and I promise you I'll learn to do whatever chores you want. Only don't dismiss me." I was starting to feel a little hysterical, and I gulped some air into my lungs in a most unladylike way.

She reached out a thin hand, her long fingers just touching my skirt. "Margaret, you can trust me." She took a deep breath and sat up straight in her chair. "You've never worked as a servant before have you?"

I swallowed. "No."

"There you are," she said smiling at me. "Doesn't that feel better?"

She was right, I did feel better. The weight of the lie I'd told to get away from Kent had been playing on my mind. I sighed and waited for her to continue. If she wasn't going to dismiss me, what was she going to do with me?

"Now, all we need to do is find something for you to do."

She got to her feet and gazed out the window. She was awfully thin I thought, and her pregnant belly was very pronounced. She ran her hand absently over it.

"Do you knit or sew Margaret?" she asked turning to face me.

"Yes, although I must confess I've never actually made a dress or anything. I'm better at embroidery and fancy work." Perhaps I could help sew for her new baby. I remember when my sister Charlotte was expecting her first baby she sewed nightgowns and smocks. Barb and I helped by knitting booties and shawls. "I could help sew for your new baby."

A shadow passed across her face as she sat back down. "I have everything ready," she said. She looked at me as though deciding if I could be trusted. She sighed. "Robert and I lost a son last year. He was born too soon and there was nothing we could do to save him."

"I'm so sorry." I was genuinely sad to hear of their loss. It also explained Reverend Davies odd behaviour on our journey from Hobart Town. One minute he had been so kind and the next cold and distant. It was only after discussing my experience with babies that his demeanour had changed. Now I understood.

"Thank you," she said rubbing her stomach. "This baby is so important to us. Not only because we lost our boy last year, but I had several miscarriages before that." She gazed momentarily out the window. "I can't risk losing this one."

I wished I could've reassured her, but when I looked at her I found myself unable to utter the words. She was so thin and pale. I sucked in my bottom lip while I thought of something comforting to say.

"I'm sure, God willing, your baby will be fine and healthy."

"Thank you, I do hope so," she said looking down at her belly. "Enough about me. Do you read and write?"

"Yes."

"Oh well, I'll be sure and tell Robert. He needs help with his correspondence and such."

"I'd be happy to help."

"Good," she said and she smiled at me. "I expect you've also had some experience with ladies maids. Not being one of course, but did you have a ladies maid back in England?"

"Yes. My mother and I shared one. Would you like me to be your maid Mrs Davies?"

"Well, I've never had a personal maid as such, and I don't know what I'd do with one. I was thinking of you being more like a companion. Would you consider that?"

She must've seen the surprise written on my face. I never expected such an offer. This was something I thought I could do easily. She was a personable young woman, and maybe under different circumstances, we might have been friends.

"I'd be happy to," I said smiling. "I was so worried when you found out the truth about me you'd dismiss me. I can't thank you enough for showing me such kindness."

"Nonsense," she said waving her hand at me. "To be honest with you, I very much need some female companionship. I can't very well befriend my servants, but you Margaret; you're from my world."

I smiled and tears pricked the back of my eyes. Not from fear or sadness, but from sheer relief. "Thank you."

"When we're together, just the two of us, I'd like you to call me Maria."

I nodded "Alright."

She smiled and stood up. "I need to rest now, Margaret. We'll talk more tomorrow."

I stood up and went to the door. "Thank you once again. Can I get you a cup of tea or something?"

"Yes, that would be lovely. Send Martha up with some tea and cake."

I nodded and stepped out into the hall and quietly closed the door behind me. I stood there for a moment while I gathered my thoughts. I had to pinch myself. I would be staying here as Maria's companion. I never would've imagined this morning that my position here would be sorted out so easily.

Chapter Five

'Ardmore House', Norfolk Plains

I was just finishing my breakfast when Mrs Fitz came bustling into the kitchen. Her face lit up when she spied me sitting at the table. I put my cup down and looked up at her.

"Can I help you, Mrs Fitz?"

"Margaret, I've been looking for ye," she said putting her hand to her ample bosom and catching her breath. "The Reverend wants to see ye in his study."

"Of course," I replied and I smiled at her.

"Right away."

"Oh."

I immediately sprang to my feet. The rest of my breakfast of poached eggs and toast would have to wait. I wiped my face with the corner of the napkin before heading off to the Reverend's study. I presumed he wanted to discuss Sunday's hymns, but surely he could've waited until I'd finished breakfast. There was no point in complaining. I hurried down the hall to his study and knocked on the door.

"Come," came the muffled reply from the other side.

I opened the door and went inside. The Reverend's study was quite large but cluttered with all manner of books and documents. He was the local registrar for births, marriages and deaths, and a large ledger for recording those events was open on his desk. He looked up at me from behind a pile of letters.

"Margaret, I need you to copy the registrar entries for the past month so I can send them off," he said pushing the ledger towards me. "I'm sorry for the late notice but it must be done this morning."

"Of course, I'll get to work right away."

I took the ledger and placed it on the other small desk which had been crammed into the corner of his study for my use. I prepared a quill and ink and set to copying the entries onto a clean sheet of parchment. I enjoyed the quiet of Reverend Davies study, but I preferred it when I was alone. Over the past few weeks, I'd been copying his letters and other correspondence. On those days he generally wasn't in his study, and I enjoyed those precious hours of being by myself.

The time flew by as I scratched away with my quill. The Reverend muttered to himself occasionally as he wrote his letters, but otherwise, we spent a few quiet hours working. I stretched my cramped hand and finished writing the last entry. I glanced at the clock sitting on the mantle; it was just after noon. No wonder I was hungry, and right on cue, my stomach gave a noisy grumble.

"They're all done," I said closing the ledger and standing up. I stretched and placed my neatly written entries on his desk.

He glanced at the pages and looked up at me. "Thank you. You can go," he said going back to his writing. "Oh, would you tell Martha I'll take my midday meal in here?"

"Yes of course."

I left the study and quietly closed the door. I briefly wondered if Maria had been looking for me. If that was the case I hoped I'd be able to have dinner first. I made my way down to the kitchen and gave Martha the message from the Reverend. She was in the middle of dishing up the midday meal of cold ham with peas and potatoes, so I sat down and waited.

Dinner was a noisy affair with all the servants and convicts eating together in the kitchen, presided over by Mrs Fitz. I'd learned over the past few weeks that Annie was the only female convict assigned to the Reverend. There were three men, one of whom was John who drove the cart for the Reverend and Mrs Davies. Another was employed to bring in the water and wood for the house; his name was Henry. I hadn't had much to do with the other one; I think his name's Sam – he's the gardener.

The convict men didn't sleep in the house. They had separate accommodation in a small bungalow situated down the back of the garden passed the stables. I hadn't ventured that far down the garden myself, but Annie had told me that's where they slept. I suspect she might go down there after dark. I've woken on more than one occasion in the middle of the night and Annie hasn't been in her bed. I haven't mentioned this to anyone, because she's back in her bed by morning. However, I think she might be sweet on Henry. I should perhaps mention it to Maria, but I wouldn't want to get either of them into any trouble.

It was nearing the end of March and the midwife had proclaimed Maria's baby would arrive in about a week. The whole household seemed to be fizzing with excitement at the prospect. I was no less excited, but I was also worried for her. I wondered if all the bed rest and inactivity had sapped her of strength, but Doctor Salmon had insisted upon it.

I was enjoying a few moments of quiet solitude in the garden under the pretext of digging dandelions for Martha. It was a cool autumn morning and there was something wholesome about digging for roots in the earth. I already had several large roots in my basket, but Martha wanted at least half a dozen. She was making some medicinal concoction. I was surprised by Reverend Davies who rarely, if ever, came down to this part of the garden.

"Oh Margaret you're just the person I was looking for," he said pausing to look in my basket. He gave the dandelion roots an odd look. "I'm giving a sermon in Ross this Sunday and I'd like you to accompany me. We leave at dawn, and we'll be gone for two nights."

I stood up and wiped my hands on my apron. "Of course Reverend." My voice sounded calm even to my ears, but inside my mind was whirring like an overwound clock. It would take an entire day to get to Ross and then the same back again. In that horrible spring cart. I nearly groaned out loud but managed to stop myself in time.

"Oh, you'll need to bring your music sheets. Pick out three or four hymns to play."

"Of course," I said again and nodded.

I spent the remainder of the day with Maria in her room. She was adding the final touches to a painting she'd done of the view from her window. She was a talented artist, and she'd captured the gum tree with the benches around the base perfectly.

I thought she looked better today than she had in a while. There was a faint glow to her cheeks and a sparkle in her eye. I supposed she must be tired of being confined and waiting for her baby to come. She was no doubt even more excited than the rest of the household at the impending birth.

I awoke early the following morning and dressed in a warm skirt and jacket. The mornings were starting to get quite chilly, and I wrapped myself in my woollen cloak. I'd packed an overnight bag with a nightgown and other necessities the night before. At the last minute, I put in my favourite paisley shawl. I picked up my bag and went downstairs. I hoped I'd at least be able to get a cup of tea before leaving for Ross. I'd noticed Martha wasn't in bed, so she was probably already in the kitchen preparing breakfast.

The warmth hit me as soon as I entered the kitchen. Martha turned from the stove and smiled at me. Reverend Davies and John were already seated at the kitchen table with cups of steaming hot tea in front of them.

"Sit down I'll get ye some tea," said Martha over her shoulder. "Breakfast won't be long."

"Thank you," I said and sat down opposite the Reverend. "Good morning Reverend, good morning John."

John gave me a grunt and a nod.

"Good morning Margaret. Are you all ready to go?"

"Yes. I've left my bag out in the hallway."

"John will load that for you," said Reverend Davies sipping his tea. "How much longer will breakfast be Martha? We've got a long day ahead."

"Comin' right now," she said placing a plate of sausages and eggs in front of him.

"Hrm thank you."

Breakfast was a quiet affair, and I gulped down the last of my tea as the Reverend got to his feet.

"I'll go fetch the cart," said John standing up and wiping his mouth with the back of his hand.

Reverend Davies nodded before heading towards the kitchen door. "I'll just bid farewell to Mrs Davies," he said over his shoulder. "Meet me out the front Margaret."

"Alright," I said as he disappeared. I doubt he heard me. "Thank you for breakfast Martha."

"You're welcome."

I went out of the kitchen and down the hall to the front door. There was no sign of Reverend Davies so I stepped outside to wait. A pale autumn sun was just peeking above the trees and a chilly breeze was blowing. It would be cold in the back of the open spring cart. It had a curved canvas top that was only large enough to provide some protection from the weather for the two passengers. Up in the driver's seat, John would be at the mercy of the wind and rain. I looked at the sky, there were a few scudding clouds, but it didn't look like rain.

A few moments later John arrived with the cart and I climbed up onto the seat. I pulled my cloak around me to try and keep out the cold wind. I pulled the hood up over my cap and waited. I shivered and thought with dread how miserable I would be in a short while. I was not looking forward to the day ahead in the back of the dreaded cart at all. I sighed.

A few minutes later Reverend Davies emerged from the house and climbed aboard. "Let's go, John. We'll need to make Campbell Town by noon." He tucked a blanket around himself and gave half to me. I smiled thankfully.

"Aye sir," said John immediately urging the horses forward.

There was no escaping the chilly wind that blew in our faces as we headed down the road. I pulled my half of the blanket around myself and huddled as close to the Reverend as I thought was appropriate. The seat was narrow and we were already rubbing shoulders.

We made good time and arrived in Campbell Town in time for our midday meal. It was only a short stop, however, as the Reverend was anxious to be on the road again. By mid-afternoon, I was beyond cold. My legs were cramped and I doubted I'd be able to move by the time we reached Ross. I groaned as I thought about the return journey on Monday. I hoped the weather might be kinder to us and the cold wind might have eased by then.

We arrived in the leafy village of Ross late in the afternoon and John pulled up out the front of the Man O'Ross Hotel. It was a handsome two-story sandstone building with a wide veranda situated between two tall gables. Reverend Davies stepped down from the cart and waited to assist me. I held on firmly to his forearm as I climbed down. My legs were so stiff from hours cramped in the cart and my lower back was aching. I stretched and wondered if there might be some chance of a hot bath to help ease my pains.

"See to the horse's John and then bring in our bags," said Reverend Davies.

"Come, Margaret, we'll see if we can't get a cup of tea to warm us."

"That would be wonderful," I said, and I couldn't help but smile hopefully at him.

I followed him into the hotel. As soon as I stepped inside the pressed tin panelled hallway I felt the warmth from a fire somewhere nearby. Two doors at the end of the hall opened into a large dining room and there was a fire blazing in the hearth. I made a beeline for it and spread my fingers before it. I stood there for several minutes just waiting for the warmth to seep into my bones. It had been such a dreadful trip down from Norfolk Plains.

A few minutes later Reverend Davies joined me by the fire and smiled at me. "I've arranged a nice hot bowl of soup for us both."

"Oh that sounds heavenly," I said and smiled at him.

The dining room was currently deserted except for the two of us. I expect more patrons will arrive closer to supper time. I remained by the fire warming myself until the Reverend suggested we sit down at the nearest table. I removed my cloak and sat down. Not more than ten minutes later a young serving girl came into the dining room. She was carrying a tray which she put down and served us each a bowl of hot vegetable soup and some crusty bread. I smiled at her as I breathed in the aroma. It smelled so good.

By the time I'd finished my soup I was feeling warm and relaxed. I hoped whatever accommodation the Reverend had arranged for me tonight would be clean. As long as it was warm I probably wouldn't care.

Chapter Six

Ross, March 1837

I was up at dawn the following morning, knowing the Reverend would want an early start. He was giving his sermon today and I expected there to be a number of baptisms to conduct as well. I dressed in my best blue dress and pulled my unruly hair back into a tight bun. I always had wisps of dark curls that escaped my best attempts to subdue them. I put my cap on and shoved them under as best I could.

There was a small mirror on top of the tallboy and I peered into it. I looked a little pale so I pinched my cheeks until the colour came into them. I thought my grey eyes were my best feature. They looked large and luminous, as for the rest of me – well I've always thought I was plain. My mouth is just a bit too wide to be considered pretty, and my nose just a little too pointed. Still, I was presentable. I grabbed my cloak and tossed it over my arm and picked up my music sheets. It was a cool morning, although I didn't think it would be as cold as yesterday.

The Reverend was already halfway through breakfast when I arrived in the dining room. A bowl of porridge was sitting in my place and a pot of tea was on the table.

"Good morning," he said as I sat down opposite. "I took the liberty of ordering you breakfast."

"Thank you," I said reaching for the pot and pouring a cup of tea.

"It's only a short walk to the Church from here," he said in between mouthfuls of porridge. "But I'd like to get there well ahead of the congregation."

"Of course." I knew very well that he'd want to be there at the door to greet his parishioners. He did it every Sunday without fail. "You can go on ahead if you like."

"You wouldn't mind?" he said taking a mouthful of tea. "I could ask John to escort you."

"No, I'm sure I can find my way," I said and smiled at him.

"Well if you're sure. It's just across the road and up the hill. You can't miss it," he said waving his arm in the general direction. "Don't be late Margaret. I'd like you to play the opening hymn as soon as everyone's seated."

"I promise you I won't be late," I said before spooning a mouthful of porridge into my mouth.

"Well, in that case, I'll be off," he said wiping his mouth with the napkin and standing up. "See you soon."

I sighed as I watched him hurry from the dining room. I was glad to be left on my own to finish breakfast. Sometimes he made me nervous, particularly when he was anxious. He seemed to have the uncanny ability to share his anxiety with those around him. I finished my porridge and poured another cup of tea. I had plenty of time to get to Church.

When I'd decided I couldn't delay any longer I put on my cloak and headed out of the hotel. It was a fine morning and I glanced up and down the street to get my bearings. I could see the church steeple through the trees and headed up the road in the general direction. It was only a short walk once I'd crossed the main road. I walked up the short hill under the branches of several young oak trees. They reminded me of home. I sighed and wondered when I'd get news from my mother. I still didn't understand why she'd supported my father's decision to marry me off.

Following the conversation with my father that fateful day in the conservatory, I'd tried to think of a way to escape my fate. Friday had come and I still had no idea what to do. I'd dressed for supper without paying much attention to how I looked. I caught a glimpse of myself in the hall mirror as I passed and I paused. Mary had pulled my hair up into a tight bun but had left several tendrils to fall around my face. I liked the effect. It softened my otherwise pointed nose. I sighed. I doubted Sir Richard would care about my presentation, and I certainly didn't.

I continued on down the hall to the parlour. I could hear my mother's voice above the men. She sounded nervous. Her voice often became shrill when she was anxious and I imagine she's quite unsettled this evening. I'd voiced my disapproval at being sold off and she's no doubt worried I won't sign the stupid contract. I, on the other hand, can't see how I can get out of it. I took a deep breath and stepped into the parlour. My father immediately came to my side and kissed my cheek.

"You look lovely my dear," he said taking my arm. "Of course you remember Sir Richard."

He guided me over to the fireplace where Sir Richard Owens was standing, leering at me.

"Good evening," I said giving him a slight nod.

He took my hand and bowing over it placed a wet kiss on it. It took all my will power not to snatch it from his grasp. I sucked in a deep breath and tried very hard to smile demurely. I rather think I failed dismally.

"Such a delight to see you again my dear," he said straightening up and finally letting go of my hand.

I rubbed it vigorously in the folds of my skirt, all the while I wanted to turn and run. The man was hideous. His partially bald head was shining in the light and long wisps of grey hair were poking out in all directions. His thin lips appeared to be in a permanent scowl and his pale bulbous eyes stared straight through me – like he could see me in my underclothes. I sucked in my lower lip and swallowed.

"Shall we go into the dining room?" said my mother standing up and taking my father's arm. "After you, Sir Richard."

He offered me his arm, and I could do nothing but smile politely and take it. We went through to the dining room and I sat down. Supper was a complete blur. I drank too much wine, but it helped to calm my nerves and dull my senses. After supper, we retired to my father's study, where the marriage contract was laid out on his desk. I have no idea what it said. It didn't matter. I signed it, and Sir Richard, the ghastly little man placed a warm kiss on my cheek. I thought I was going to die.

My father and Sir Richard relaxed with brandy and discussed the wedding date. I was numb and on the verge of tears. I could feel them pricking the back of my eyes, but I'd rather die than cry in front of them. I just sat there while my parents made all the arrangements. It was only when they'd made all the decisions that my mother turned to me.

"So we're all agreed then, Margaret. You'll be wed in a month. That should give us plenty of time to make the arrangements, and for you to be fitted for your gown," she said smiling happily. "Men don't worry about such things, but it's important for any young woman to have her wedding gown made," she said smiling warmly at Sir Richard.

A month. Honestly, it was more than I could've hoped for. I nodded and smiled. My wedding gown – now there was a thought. "I'll need to go up to London," I said coming out of my wine stupor for a moment. "Miss Smidden will need several weeks to make my trousseau."

Father nodded and Sir Richard drank down the last of his brandy. "I'll leave the details to you, my dear," he said standing. "In the meantime have the contract sent to my lawyer will you?"

"Of course," said my father smiling warmly at his soon to be son-in-law.

They shook hands and Sir Richard bowed politely to my mother. "I was hoping you'd take a walk in the garden with me Margaret."

How could I say no?

Two days later I arrived at my sister Barb's house in London. She lived with her husband John in a three-story Georgian style house in St Giles. The main purpose of my visit was, of course, to be fitted for my wedding gown, but I was also looking forward to spending time with Barb.

"I don't know what you're going to do, Margaret. The situation is just hideous," said Barb putting down her cup. "I can't believe Mamma has agreed to this."

I appreciated her support. "I know. But what I don't understand is what Uncle James' bankruptcy has to do with us," I said taking a sip of my hot chocolate. "It's all got to do with that somehow."

"Oh well I'm not exactly sure," said Barb getting up from the table. She picked up a copy of the London Times that was sitting on the sideboard. "But, it's all in the newspapers that he's been declared a lunatic."

"What?" I said putting down my cup.

"Yes it's on page four I think," she said handing me the paper. "It also says in there that Papa was his heir. I wonder if that's got something to do with you having to marry Sir Richard?"

I gaped at her. I spread out the paper, turned to page four, and scanned the page for the article. Sure enough there it was. Uncle James was being openly referred to as a lunatic. "He's in Bedlam."

"That's right," said Barb shaking her head. "Poor Uncle James."

I went back to reading the article. I had no idea what all this had to do with me, but somehow my father's affairs were tied up with Uncle James'. I finished reading the piece and was about to close the paper when I noticed a small advertisement. Free passage to Van Diemen's Land for all female servants – apply to Mr John Sinclair at the Immigration Department. My heart started racing as I read it. Free passage to the other side of the world – it seemed too good to be true.

"Barb, look at this," I said pointing to the advertisement.

She read it and stared at me. "You're not seriously considering it, are you?"

"What would you do? Marry that ghastly little man?"

"No, I think I'd rather die," she said with a shudder. "But how Margaret? You're not a servant, and I expect they'll want some guarantee that you'll work when you get there."

"You could write me a reference," I said looking into her oval face and soft grey eyes, so like my own. "Please Barb you have to help me."

"You're serious?"

"Yes, I'm serious. Please you're my only hope."

The following morning I was fitted for several outfits at Miss Smidden's, including my wedding gown. I could hardly contain myself while her seamstresses measured and prodded and poked me. Barb had written me a glowing reference which I fully intended to present to Mr Sinclair at the Immigration Department this afternoon.

I finally escaped their attention and after a quick bite to eat at a nearby cafe, Barb and I climbed back into her carriage. She gave her driver the address in London and we set off. Twenty minutes later I climbed out of the carriage outside a rather imposing Government building.

"Wish me luck," I said to Barb.

"I do wish you luck, Margaret. But I also wish you'd reconsider."

I smiled. "Thank you. You know I would if there was any other way," I said closing the carriage door.

I sucked in a deep breath and ran my hands over my skirt. I dressed with care this morning, and I was wearing a rather simple brown skirt and jacket. I hoped Mr Sinclair wouldn't notice that it was a good cut of cloth. I went inside and found myself in a wide oak panelled hallway. I wandered along it looking for any signs of Mr John Sinclair or a clerk or someone. At the end of the hall, I noticed a brass plate on the door which read Sinclair - Immigration I knocked and went inside.

A young man behind a desk looked up as I entered. He was busy writing in a large ledger. "If you're here to see Mr Sinclair, then take a seat," he said going back to his work without giving me a second look.

I smiled to myself and sat down on one of the hard wooden chairs which were sitting along the wall. It was only a small office with barely enough room to walk between his desk and the chairs. I waited somewhat anxiously for Mr Sinclair to appear. I didn't have to wait long. He emerged from his office about ten minutes later accompanied by a young woman, who I presumed was also applying for free passage. As soon as she left he gestured to me to follow him, which I did.

"Please take a seat Miss," he said indicating a chair opposite his desk. He went around the other side of it and sat down. "Now I presume you wish to apply for free passage? I only have a few places left and unless you have particularly good references then I'm afraid you're likely to miss out."

I hoped to God Barb's reference would be good enough. "Well I only have one reference from my current employer," I said handing him the envelope.

He slit it open and unfolded the crisp parchment. He was silent while he read the letter, and I held my breath. If this didn't work I didn't know what I was going to do. Probably jump off Tower Bridge.

"Well, Miss Chambers, Mrs Hart seems most sad to lose you," he said folding the letter and tucking it under some other papers on his desk. "I have a position that I think will suit you most admirably, Miss Chambers. Mrs Hector of Coal River is after the services of a general servant with your experience. What do you say?"

"Yes. That sounds wonderful," I said.

"Excellent. You'll need to present yourself at the Immigration Depot in

Portsmouth three weeks from now," he said. "Do you read Miss Chambers?"

"Aye."

He handed me several sheets of paper. "This lists everything you can take on board ship. Don't worry if you can't find any marine soap, you'll be able to get that at the depot. Any questions?"

I quickly scanned the sheets he'd given me. It all looked quite straight forward. It listed what clothing I should take, and that I could only have one sea trunk and no liquor. I nodded as I finished reading the list.

"Now you understand that you're getting free passage as a bounty immigrant. You'll be expected to work for Mrs Hector until you've repaid your fare."

"I understand," I said nodding.

"Excellent Miss Chambers, I wish you the best of luck," he said standing up. He opened the door and gestured for me to go ahead of him. "My clerk, Mr Jones will give you a letter to give to the Immigration Depot. They'll be expecting you."

I nodded once more before he disappeared back into his office. Mr Jones indicated for me to take a seat while he wrote the letter. I couldn't believe how simple it had been, or that it was going to work out so perfectly. I'd be in Portsmouth in three weeks and before anyone knew it

I'd be far out to sea. I couldn't help grinning as I left the building and climbed back into Barb's waiting carriage.

I sighed and wondered if I'd ever see my dear sister again. I prayed I'd hear news of my mother. I'd written to her almost as soon as I'd arrived at Ardmore House to tell her I was safe and well. I didn't expect she'd have even received my letter yet – it would take months to get there.

Since arriving in Van Diemen's Land I'd tried hard to put my family and my former life behind me. It was moments like this though that made me realise how much I missed them. I wondered if my brother Osborn's wife had given birth yet. She'd been expecting their third child when I left England. I don't suppose I'll ever see any of them again. I shook myself out of my melancholy as I approached the church.

It was a lovely building of sandstone set among the oak trees. The front doors were open ready to receive the worshippers and I stepped inside. I was pleased to see it was not in such disrepair as our church in Norfolk Plains. It was lined with pews and the high timber ceiling was whole and intact. I smiled as I made my way up the aisle. Reverend Davies was at the pulpit and he looked up and smiled as he saw me approaching.

"Oh Margaret you've made it in plenty of time," he said. "I hope the organs in tune, I don't remember the last time anyone played it."

"Well, we'll soon see."

The organ looked like it had seen better days. It was badly scuffed and scratched and covered in dust. I sat down and opened the lid, and was pleasantly surprised to see that it was in much better condition on the inside. I put my music sheets down and played a few chords. It sounded just fine. I played a few more practice notes while Reverend Davies positioned himself at the door ready to greet his parishioners.

I wondered how many people generally attended when he gave a sermon here. I didn't have to wonder very long. A stream of people started arriving. Reverend Davies greeted each one as they arrived. I smiled and nodded at them as I waited. It took a good twenty minutes for everyone to come in and sit down. The Church was full and I wasn't sure the Reverend would be heard over the hum of voices. It was a larger congregation than we normally got at Norfolk Plains. We'd be lucky if there were twenty or so, unlike here. I suppose it's a treat for them to have Reverend Davies come.

The Reverend's sermon went over well I thought, and they sang the hymns with enthusiasm. Actually, their voices reverberated around the Church and sounded beautiful. Afterwards, Reverend Davies conducted five baptisms and read banns for three impending weddings. I wonder if we're going to come back to do the marriage ceremonies. As much as I detested the journey to get here, I'd very much enjoyed playing the organ and being a part of it all.

Several parishioners invited Reverend Davies to their homes for dinner, and he even had offers to stay the night. He finally agreed to a very insistent invitation from Mr and Mrs Powell. I assured him I would return to the hotel and would be perfectly fine. I was very much looking forward to a few quiet hours on my own. I intended to visit the shops and peer in their windows.

Reverend Davies didn't return to the hotel for supper and so I dined alone. Several people were staying at the hotel, and I'm sure I could've sought their company if I'd wanted to, but I was enjoying being alone. Nowadays I get so few opportunities to enjoy the solitude of my own company. I retired early. It would no doubt be another long arduous day tomorrow as we headed back to Norfolk Plains.

I rose early, packed my bag and dressed warmly for the day ahead. I expected the Reverend to already be waiting for me at the breakfast table, and so I was rather surprised that there was no sign of him in the dining room. Perhaps he'd accepted the invitation to stay over at the Powell's for the night? I shrugged. I'm sure he'd be along in good time to collect me. I ordered breakfast and put the Reverend's social affairs out of my mind.

I'd finished my breakfast of poached eggs and was enjoying another cup of tea when he arrived. He looked a little flustered, which was most unusual for him. He hurried over to my table.

"I'm so sorry Margaret, I thought I'd be back before you came down for breakfast."

"That's quite alright Reverend," I said smiling at him. "I knew you'd come back for me eventually."

"Yes, well...quite right," he said quickly regaining control of himself. "I've been making arrangements for our new gardener. He'll be returning home with us today."

"Oh, you were saying you needed another gardener, You must be pleased," I said as I drained the last of my tea and rose from the table.

"Yes, well he's most recently been employed on one of the chain gangs," he said as he opened the door for me. "But I think we can straighten him out. His name's William. William Hartley."

"Oh," I said. Honestly what else could I say - a convict straight from the chain gang to our back garden? That seemed a little optimistic even for the Reverend. Surely he could've found someone less troublesome.

I stepped out of the hotel and climbed aboard the spring cart. All I could see was the back of William Hartley's head as he was sitting up front with John. I couldn't tell what he even looked like from here. I hoped the Reverend would not regret his decision to bring him into his household.

The trip back to Norfolk Plains was uneventful. We stopped for a late dinner at Campbell Town before continuing on. It was getting dark by the time John pulled the horses up in front of Ardmore House. I was tired and wanted nothing more than a nice hot cup of tea and then to retire for the night.

The front door opened and Mrs Fitz came hurrying out with her lantern held high. "Oh blessed be," she said smiling broadly at the Reverend as he climbed down from the cart. "Mrs Davies has delivered a fine healthy boy. She'll be ever so glad yer back."

"A boy?" he said staring at her. "I have a son?"

"Aye that ye do Reverend, come, come. Ye'll want to see him. A fine an' healthy bairn ye have."

Reverend Davies disappeared inside the house with Mrs Fitz at his heels. I was grinning stupidly. I was so grateful Maria had delivered a healthy baby. After her miscarriages and losing her baby last year, she deserved this happiness. I went to climb down from the cart and William grabbed my arm and helped me.

"Thank you," I said smiling at him. Even in the dim light, I could see he was tall with wide shoulders. His hazel eyes locked briefly with mine and I felt a very odd quiver run through me.

"You're welcome ma'am," he said letting me go.

"I'll bring the luggage in, ye needn't worry," said John twisting in the driver's seat to look at me.

"Thank you," I said again. I realised I was still staring into William's face and quickly looked away and headed into the house. He looked much younger than me, but there was no doubt he had a certain something. I wouldn't have said he was overly handsome, but I think a lot of young ladies would give him a second look.

The house was buzzing with excitement - it felt like lightning in a thunderstorm. I headed straight for the kitchen in the hopes of getting a cup of tea and nearly ran into Annie as she came around the corner.

"Oh, Margaret did ye 'ear? Mrs Davies' had a boy. Isn't it exciting?"

"Yes I heard, and yes it is."

"I'm just on my way upstairs with her supper," she said indicating to the tray she had in her hands. I was surprised she hadn't dropped it in her haste. "Would ye mind taking it instead? I always gets so nervous around her."

I sighed. "Well I suppose it will give me the chance to offer my congratulations," I said as I removed my cloak and hung it over Annie's shoulder.

"Thank ye, Margaret, I owe ye one," she said handing me the tray.

I turned and walked back down the main hall to the stairs. I navigated my way carefully up the stairs balancing the tray. I wasn't particularly adept at such things, but I made it to the top without dropping or spilling anything. I heaved a sigh of relief when I saw Mrs Fitz emerging from Maria's room. I don't know how I was going to open the door otherwise.

"I thought young Annie was doing that?"

"I don't mind," I said smiling. "Anyway, it will give me a chance to see the new baby."

"Oh an' he's bonnie," she said beaming. Anyone would think she had something to do with it by the look on her face. "Don't stay too long Margaret, Mrs Davies needs her rest."

"I promise I won't stay long. I'm rather looking forward to bed myself."

"Oh well, of course, ye are after yer long trip from Ross."

She went off down the stairs and I hurried into Maria's room. She was sitting up in bed surrounded by pillows. Reverend Davies was sitting in one of the wing chairs, a look of rapture on his face as he gazed at his newborn son asleep in his crib.

"Oh Margaret you didn't have to do that," said Maria as I approached and placed the tray across her knees. "You must be exhausted."

I smiled warmly at her. "Not as exhausted as you I expect. Congratulations Mrs Davies. We're all so pleased with the news of your new son."

"Thank you," she said as she lifted the lid on her supper. "Oh, I'm famished. You'll have to excuse me Margaret. Would you come and visit in the morning? I would so like to hear all about Ross."

"Of course I'll come up right after breakfast." I retreated and went back downstairs. I didn't see anyone else, so I decided to go straight to bed. I'd ask Martha for an extra big breakfast tomorrow. I just wanted to go to sleep.

Chapter Seven

Rowland Robert Davies

My life at Ardmore House changed drastically with the arrival of young Rowland Davies. For one thing, Maria was now up and about and far more demanding of everyone; me included. Whereas the Reverend had been happy to eat his meals in his study or even in the kitchen on occasion, Maria expected every meal to be served in the dining room. Martha was run off her feet. I expect they all knew what life was like before, but of course, I didn't.

Maria and I were in the parlour where she was busy making plans for Rowland's christening. If Maria gets her way it will be the event of the year.

"How many have you got on the list for dinner?" she asked as she gave the pram a slight push back and forwards. Rowland wasn't quite asleep yet and was making little mewing noises.

I quickly scanned the list of names before me. "Eight so far, including you and the Reverend," I said raising my eyes back to her face. "Will your parents be attending?"

A shadow cross her thin face. "No, they're still in England," she said and sighed. "None of my family are in the country at the moment."

"Oh well, that is disappointing."

"Yes it is, but still I wish to invite some of our local families to the christening," she said turning her attention back to me. "We must include Thomas Archer and his lovely young wife Elizabeth. Oh, I've just had a thought, Margaret. Would you play your violin for us after dinner?"

I hadn't had much opportunity to play my violin in recent times. I would need some practice, but I couldn't help but smile at the prospect. "Yes, I'd love to."

"Oh, wonderful. I think our guests will really enjoy a recital," she said smiling. "Of course you'll play the organ in Church won't you?"

"Yes, Maria you know I will."

"Well, I think we're all arranged then. Please make a copy of the list for Mrs Fitz, and I'll write out the invitations."

"Alright," I said rising from my chair. I couldn't help notice she had a daydreamy look on her face. "Is there something else?"

"No, not for the christening. I really want to get outside to sketch and I'm itching to do a painting of you," she said and her pale blue eyes looked enquiringly at me.

"A picture of me?"

"Yes, would you sit for me, Margaret? I rather like the idea of painting you under the arbour. Please say yes."

I was more than a little surprised by her request, but how could I deny her when I could already see the light of excitement in her eyes. I groaned inwardly. I'm not sure I fancy the idea of me hanging on a wall somewhere in the house. I'd look at myself every time I went by. I can't imagine how odd that would be.

"Please Margaret."

"Of course," I found myself saying.

We were well into autumn and the mornings and evenings were cooler however, the days were still lovely. Maria and I had taken her easel and pencils out into the garden while Mrs Fitz kept a close watch over baby Rowland. I was currently sitting as still as I could under the arbour of wisteria while Maria sketched.

"Turn your head just a little further to the left Margaret," she said holding her pencil between her small white teeth and eyeing me with intensity.

I obliged, although I did wonder if my jawline was quite as attractive as Maria thought it to be. I sighed and tried to hold the position. I noticed the gardeners working in the flower bed just down the path. I couldn't help but admire the figure

William made. He had his shirt sleeves rolled up and I could see the muscles and tendons flexing under his skin as he worked. I blushed as I thought about him and would've looked away but Maria was still sketching me. I swallowed and took in a couple of deep breaths.

"Keep still Margaret. Not much longer I promise."

"Sorry."

I must admit he seemed to have settled well into life as a gardener here. I'd initially had misgivings, but I'd obviously been wrong. I do think he's got an eye for the ladies though. I've spied Annie giggling and flirting with him on a couple of occasions. I wonder how Henry feels about that? Not that there's anything spoken between them, at least not that I knew of. I've just realised that I've become a real gossip. All this speculation about Annie and her admirers - it's none of my business. Still, my eyes and my mind keep wandering back to William. He's such a handsome young man.

Mrs Fitz came hurrying down the path with her voluminous skirts billowing all around her. She was panting by the time she arrived at Maria's side.

"Rowland needs his Mamma," she said putting her hand to her ample bosom. "It's his feed time poor wee lamb."

"That will have to do for now Margaret," said Maria as she put down her pencil.

I stretched and smiled at her. "Did you finish the sketch or will we have to come back tomorrow?"

"Just about. If the weather's good I'll finish the sketch tomorrow. I'm sorry Margaret but I'll have to go and attend to Rowland."

"Of course," I said waving my hand in her direction. "You go on ahead, I'll bring your easel and pencils."

"Thank you," she said as she started up the path towards the house with Mrs Fitz right behind her.

"Oh Margaret," called Mrs Fitz as she stopped and turned towards me. "Would ye ask William to dig some sweet bucks for supper?"

"Yes of course," I called back to her.

I've no doubt William heard her himself she'd yelled so loudly. I put Maria's pencils back in their box before heading down the path to where William was working. He was on his hands and knees weeding and he stood up when he saw me approaching. I couldn't help but notice how large and solid his hands were.

"Good afternoon. Are you out for a walk in the garden then?" he said and smiled at me before glancing up and down the path. "You look like you're in need of a companion. I'm at your service."

"How very kind of you," I replied smiling.

His hazel eyes were shining and I wondered if he was teasing me. I saw a flash of his white even teeth as he grinned before proffering me his arm. I'm neither practised in the art of love or men so I couldn't be sure – but I thought he might be flirting with me. I gaped stupidly at him while my heart raced and I felt like I'd just run out of air. I was flustered, and it must have been obvious to anyone, but particularly to William.

"I'm sure Mrs Davies won't miss you for a few minutes," he said still with his arm out inviting me to take hold. "You should at least take a closer look at the dahlia. They're in flower right now."

I didn't know what to say so I placed my hand in the crook of his arm. He pulled me closer to him. Closer than I felt comfortable with. I went to pull away but discovered he had a firm grasp of my hand.

"You needn't be afraid of me, Margaret," he said as we started walking down the path. "I don't bite."

"Well I should hope not," I said finally coming to my senses. "Mrs Fitz wants you to dig some sweet bucks for supper."

"Aye I'll get onto it right away," he said and he smiled at me. "How long have you been working for the Reverend and his wife?"

"Only a few months," I said sidestepping a hydrangea that was taking over half of the path.

"And do you find them to be fair taskmasters? I only ask because I've been assigned to a couple of people before who were neither kind nor fair."

"I'm sorry to hear that." My concern for his welfare in the past was genuine. I knew he'd been on the chain gang, but I wasn't quite brave enough to ask him what he'd done to deserve such punishment. "I've found them both to be demanding, but fair. They've shown me nothing but kindness. I don't think you need worry on that account."

"That gives me some comfort," he said and smiled at me.

I blushed and looked away. His stare unnerved me and I found myself gasping for air again. I wasn't comfortable being in such close proximity to him. I could feel his muscles under my fingers and his solid presence beside me. He smelled of earth and the musky scent of a man who'd been working. I breathed in the scent of him and swallowed. What was I doing? I pulled my hand out from the crook of his arm.

"I really must be getting back. Mrs Davies will be looking for me."

He stopped and looked at me. I sucked in my lower lip and breathed in through my nose. I've never been attracted to a man before. Even the young men I used to dance with at parties and balls never had any effect on me. I'd even kissed one once. I couldn't see what all the fuss was about. The kiss was just soft and wet and he'd tried to poke his tongue into my mouth. How ghastly. I remember I'd pushed him away and told him never to do that again.

"Well it's been nice talking to you Margaret," he said taking a step back. "Perhaps we can do it again?"

"Yes of course," I said taking in a deep breath.

I turned and hurried back up the path to the arbour. I was breathing heavily and I could feel my blood thrumming through my veins. I gathered Maria's pencils and canvas and headed back to the house. I'd have to come back for the easel.

We didn't get a chance to get back out in the garden to finish her sketch. With the impending christening, the whole household was busy. The house was dusted and cleaned and even I was required to help polish the silverware. I was thankful I hadn't been allocated kitchen duty. Annie and Liz had been assigned to help Martha prepare and serve dinner for their guests. Martha had been busy baking for the event for days.

They were still preparing vegetables for the roast dinner as I was getting ready to leave for Church. The beef was in the oven and I breathed in the smell of roasting meats as I left the kitchen. I was dressed in my best blue dress and I wrapped my woollen cloak around myself as Mrs Fitz and I went out the back door. I didn't see Maria. She'd be going down to the Church in the spring cart with baby Rowland all dressed in his christening gown and wrapped in a shetland shawl.

"Blessed be that it's a fine day," said Mrs Fitz as we went through the back gate and into the Church grounds.

She was right. The morning was cool but the sun was peeking through the clouds and there was no sign of rain.

"Yes we'll be able to remove the pots and pans," I said grinning at her.

"Hrmph," she said. "Ye'd think the Reverend could do something about that."

The roof of the Church had developed so many leaks that several pots had been placed to catch the water. It was most unsightly, and I was pleased for

Maria's sake that we'd be able to remove them for the day.

We were not the first to arrive. Several carts and wagons were already out the front and Reverend Davies was at the door greeting his parishioners.

Mrs Fitz and I hurried inside and she immediately set to removing the pots. I positioned myself at the organ ready to play the opening hymn. Maria had chosen today's arrangement and I'd be starting with *There is a Fountain*. The pews were filling quickly and I craned my neck to see if I could catch a glimpse of Maria and Rowland. There was no sign of them yet.

I spied William, Sam and Henry arriving. My heart skipped a beat and I sucked in a deep breath. I really needed to get a hold of myself. I've never experienced anything like what happens whenever I see William or think of him. And I've been doing a lot of that lately. My body seems to take on a mind of its own regardless of what I might want. I pushed thoughts of him aside as I watched the last of the congregation file inside.

I finally caught sight of Maria as she came down the aisle with Rowland in her arms. I smiled at her and locked eyes with Reverend Davies. A moment later he gave me a nod and I turned my attention to the music. I waited for him to make his way down to the pulpit before pulling out the stop knobs and pumping the treadle. As soon as I played the first chord all other thoughts evaporated from my mind. I immersed myself in the music and the singing.

Reverend Davies gave a lovely sermon on baby Jesus, which was most appropriate for the occasion. That was followed by the baptism itself. I played the final hymn before the well-wishers came forward to speak with Maria and Reverend Davies. I closed the lid of the organ and glanced around. People were milling around, cooing over baby Rowland, and I doubted if anyone could be heard over the rising hum of voices. I got to my feet and wrapped my cloak about myself before surveying the scene. I looked up just in time to see Mrs Fitz with Martha, Annie and Liz disappearing through the front door of the church. Of course, they had to get back to the house to prepare dinner, whereas my services weren't needed until later.

I carefully made my way through the throng and out into the churchyard. I took a deep breath as I made my way to the gate in the side fence. I'd just put my hand on it when it was pushed open by another. I looked up and found myself staring into a pair of hazel eyes.

"Oh William, you gave me a start."

"Sorry Margaret," he said smiling widely at me as he stood back to allow me to go through the now open gate. "I thought we might finish our walk. You never did get to see the dahlias."

"Oh not now," I said turning my head towards him. "I'm needed up at the house." It was only a small lie. I wouldn't be missed until after dinner, but I wasn't sure I wanted to spend my time with him. My heart was racing and I sucked in my lower lip.

"Come it will only take a minute," he said grabbing my hand and tucking into the crook of his arm. He set off down the path with me in tow.

"William please...I."

"I promise I'll have you back up at the house in plenty of time."

I stopped protesting and smiled at him. It was probably more a look of exasperation because that's how I was feeling. I wasn't in the habit of going for walks with men. He led me down the path passed the stables. I'd never been to this part of the garden before. I knew it led to the men's quarters and I came to an abrupt halt. It was quiet and secluded and unless one of the men happened to be going to their cottage I doubt anyone would see us down here.

"What's the matter?" he asked.

"I shouldn't be down here," I said glancing back along the path. I licked my lips and eyed him nervously. "I have to go."

I turned and had taken one step back towards the house when he grabbed me. I swivelled around with every intention of berating him for manhandling me in such a way. Instead, I found myself in his arms, his face mere inches from mine and a look of intensity in his eyes that I'd never seen before. He lowered his head and kissed me. Not a soft wet kiss, but a firm insistent kiss that my lips responded to in kind. I felt like my body was betraying me as my arms wrapped around him and I kissed him back.

A surge of excitement went through me like a bolt of lightning and I pulled myself from his arms. I stared at him. My lips were throbbing and I had no idea what had just happened. I gathered my skirts in my hand and I ran. I heard him call after me, but I didn't stop until I felt his arms go around my waist and he pulled me against his firm body.

"William, please let me go." I was panting and on the verge of tears, although I have no idea why. He hadn't hurt me. On the contrary. I just wasn't sure I wanted to acknowledge what had just happened between us.

"Margaret, I'm sorry," he said and I could feel his hot breath on my neck. "Please forgive me."

I sucked in several large breaths while I tried to calm myself. "There's nothing to forgive. Please release me."

He slowly let me go and I turned to face him. His face was flushed and his eyes still had a burning intensity in them. I wondered if my normally soft grey eyes had the same look. I swallowed. He was so handsome and so much younger than me. I reached up and ran my fingers down his clean-shaven face - and then I kissed him. It was a soft slow kiss. My lips parted and I melted into his arms. I'd never in my life done anything so brazen. My heart was racing as our kiss came to an end.

"Oh Margaret, I've wanted to kiss you since the first time I saw you."

I didn't know what to say - I swallowed hard. "I have to go."

Chapter Eight

Rowland's Christening Day

My mind was a whirl of thoughts slipping and sliding over one another as I hurried up to the house. I never imagined a kiss could feel like that. I touched my lips - they felt swollen and my stays felt like they'd been laced too tight. I didn't know where to begin with how I felt about William. I blushed as I thought of him. What must he think? I'd brazenly kissed him; thrown myself at him. A small part of me was mortified at the thought; the rest of me was zinging as if my nerve ends had been laid bare.

I opened the back door and stepped inside. I could hear voices coming from the dining room where no doubt the Reverend and Maria were entertaining their dinner guests. I went down the short hall to the kitchen. It was a buzz with people. Martha was directing the kitchen staff like an orchestra conductor. The bowls were all lined up ready to receive the first course. Annie was slicing crusty bread to go with the soup while Mrs Fitz had started ladling it into the bowls. Martha placed them onto large serving trays ready to go to the dining room.

I stood to one side where I thought I'd be out of the way. The soup smelled so good and I hoped I'd be able to get a bowl. I was famished. I opened the door for Annie and Liz as they headed out, each armed with laden trays. Martha heaved a sigh.

"Ye best get dinner while ye can," she said to those left in the kitchen. "Mrs Fitz would ye mind cuttin' more bread. Get the bowls, Margaret."

Annie and Liz returned for more trays full of soup and I laid out the bowls for our midday meal. Sam, William, Henry and John would no doubt be joining us soon, and my heart did a little skip and a flutter. How was I going to behave sensibly? By the time Annie and Liz returned I was seated at the table enjoying my bowl of soup. It was delicious. The men arrived moments later and in no time we were all seated and eating as fast as we could. We didn't have much time. Martha would need to get the main meal out to the dining room soon.

William seated himself across the table from me, and I tried hard not to look at him. I didn't have much luck with that tactic. My eyes kept glancing at him. He appeared to be doing a much better job of ignoring me. He looked perfectly composed as he ate his soup and chatted with Sam about the weeding down behind the potting shed that needed to be done. I was more than a little infuriated that I couldn't turn my attention away from him. I sighed.

"So what are ye playing on ye violin Margaret?" asked Annie as she reached for another slice of bread. "Will ye be playing what ye were practicing yesterday?"

"Yes," I said grateful for the distraction. "It's a sonata by Beethoven, and one of my favourites. Did you like it?"

"Oh well I don't know nothing about music," she said screwing up her face. "It was alright."

I smiled inwardly. "Well, I think Mrs Davies liked it and that's the important thing."

She nodded and went on slurping her soup.

"Ye two best hurry," said Martha getting up from the table. "Go an' clear the dining room table."

Liz and Annie hurriedly finished their soup and leapt from the table. I finished mine and collected the dirty bowls and plates. My hand brushed William's as I reached for his bowl and he looked up at me. His hazel eyes were unfathomable and had gone a shade of sea green. Our gaze locked for the briefest moment, but I was left breathless by the desire I saw in their depths. I'd never had a man look at me like that in my life.

My hands were trembling as I piled the crockery on the bench ready for washing up, but I wasn't about to do that. I was still dressed in my Sunday best and didn't want to slop myself with dishwater. I would've liked the distraction though.

"I'll wash up," said Mrs Fitz coming to my rescue. "Ye can help Martha dish up. Get the plates from the dresser."

"Yes." I sucked in my lower lip and proceeded to line the plates up ready for Martha to serve dinner.

I was having difficulty concentrating and would've liked nothing better than to escape the kitchen. I needed some time to myself to get my thoughts in order. William and Sam left the kitchen leaving Henry behind. He was needed to stoke the fire in the parlour and fetch fresh water for the kitchen. I heaved a sigh. Maybe now that William had gone I'd be able to think sensibly.

Dinner was served with a minimum of fuss and I waited patiently to be called into the parlour. I'd had plenty of time to freshen myself up and make sure I was presentable. I was feeling a little anxious. It had been such a long time since I'd played my violin for anyone, and I hoped I wouldn't make a mess of it.

"They're ready for ye," said Mrs Fitz bustling into the kitchen.

I took a deep breath and swallowed. "Thank you."

My violin was already in the parlour waiting for me. I went down the hall and knocked softly on the door before stepping inside. Maria immediately smiled reassuringly at me, and I gave her a tremulous one in return. Nearly every seat in the parlour was taken and every pair of eyes was on me.

My violin was in its case sitting on a small chaise lounge and I opened it and took a deep breath. I ran my fingers down the smooth wooden surface before lifting it from the case. I love the smooth feel of it under my fingers - it's almost like my violin speaks to me and I can't wait to play it. I took the bow and turned to face my waiting audience. My music sheet was already on the stand and I put my violin to my collar and smiled at everyone.

"This is one of my favourite sonatas," I said placing the bow against the strings. "I hope you like it as much as I do."

As soon as I struck the strings with the bow and played the first note I was transported somewhere else. The music surrounded me and I let it take me away. It took me back home. My sister Charlotte and I loved Beethoven's sonata number three. She would play the piano part and I the violin. It always sounded so beautiful when accompanied by the piano. I hoped Maria and her guests were not disappointed that they only had me on the violin. I played the last note and took a deep breath.

They enthusiastically applauded my playing and I smiled. I was so relieved that I hadn't made a mistake.

"Oh Margaret that was wonderful," said Maria jumping to her feet.

She came over to me and gave me a warm hug. I was a little surprised by her actions but I returned the hug, albeit with only one arm.

"I'm so glad you enjoyed it," I said as we separated.

"Oh I did," she said as she turned to her guests. "Would you like to hear another one?"

I don't think I was able to hide my surprise this time. I'd practised several pieces, but Maria had said I'd only need to play one. The room of people appeared to be just as enthusiastic about another tune.

"Would you mind playing another one Margaret?" said Reverend Davies smiling happily at his wife. "Maria does get carried away sometimes."

"I don't mind in the least," I replied.

I quickly flipped through my music sheets and decided to play sonata number one. I could play the shortened version. I smiled warmly at Maria as she sat back down and I began playing. The one good thing about the music is that it pushed all thoughts of William from my mind. The kiss we shared earlier in the garden almost seems like it was a dream. Maybe I'd imagined the whole thing. I finished playing to a round of applause and I bowed to my audience.

"Thank you so much, Margaret," said Maria. "You've really made Rowland's christening memorable for all of us."

"You're welcome," I said as I put my violin back in its case and closed the lid. I quietly left the parlour and made my way back down the hall. I decided I could probably escape for the rest of the day. I went out the back door and down the garden path. I needed some time alone to think.

Perhaps the garden wasn't the best place to try and get some time alone. No sooner had I found myself a secluded bench down by the potting sheds than William arrived. I'd forgotten about the conversation over dinner between him and Sam. They'd discussed at length the weeds that needed pulling down here.

"Margaret, I didn't expect to find you down here," he said sitting down beside me. "Have you finished the recital then?"

"Yes." My nerves were raw and on edge. William was about the last person I wanted to see right now. He was a solid presence beside me and I could almost feel the heat of his body emanating towards me. I shuffled along to the end of the bench.

"If you want I'll leave." He spoke softly and his voice rumbled with gentleness. I didn't know what I wanted. I shook my head.

"No, it's not you exactly." I pushed some stray curls back under my cap and looked at him. He was looking at me as if he was trying to decide what to do about me. "I don't understand what it is between us."

"Ah," he said as though that made perfect sense to him. He gave me an almost shy sideways glance. "I like you Margaret, and I think you like me."

Well, I couldn't deny that. But it didn't explain my heart flutters or the quiver that shot through me when he touched me. It also didn't explain why he always seemed to be on my mind.

"Yes that's true, but it's not exactly what I meant."

He grinned. "So you like me?" Then he turned serious. "Well, I think it's a perfectly normal thing between a man and a woman. Who knows where it might lead if we let it."

Several things raced through my mind all at once. My first impulse was to give him an annoyed look and leave. He might find it amusing that I like him, but I didn't. I've got no idea what to do with feelings like that. The other thought that immediately came to mind was – well, he's a convict. What possible future could there be between us? I know nothing about him. I don't even know how he came to be in this predicament, or how long he's going to be in it.

I shook my head. "But William you're a convict."

"I won't be a convict forever," he said indignantly. He sounded slightly annoyed and his hazel eyes looked at me from beneath his furrowed brow. "I'll be able to get a ticket of leave and then I can work for myself."

"How much longer before you can do that?"

"I don't know. If it all works out well here with the Reverend I think he'll recommend me."

I nodded. This still left me wondering how he thought we could have any kind of relationship – particularly one that might lead to marriage. He couldn't earn any money to keep a wife. I realised he was so young and didn't truly understand why I had serious misgivings.

"Well if that happens perhaps I'll think about it."

He shuffled along the bench closer to me and before I could even react had taken my hand in his. "Don't be afraid, Margaret."

He turned my hand over and placed a kiss in the middle of my palm. It was so soft and intimate and I gasped. All the sensible thoughts that had been in my head evaporated. None of that mattered as I gazed into his eyes and lost myself in their depths. He leaned forward and kissed me. My lips responded of their own accord and I kissed him back. It was a long slow kiss that left me gasping. I was completely out of my depth with him. I was like putty in his hands.

"I have to go," I said and stood up. I smoothed my dress with trembling fingers and sucked in a deep breath.

He grabbed my hand. "Meet me tonight, down here by the shed."

"What!" I turned and stared at him. He touched my fingers to his lips.

I didn't know what else to say. I grabbed my hand from his grasp and gathered my skirts in my other as I headed up the path.

Margaret

"I'll be waiting," he called after me.

Chapter Nine

Murder at Norfolk Plains

I was late down for breakfast. I'd delayed as long as I could reasonably do so in the hope of avoiding William. I took one last look at myself in the mirror before heading down the narrow stairs. I took a deep breath as I opened the door to the kitchen and then heaved a sigh. There was no sign of any of the men; they'd already had breakfast and left.

"You're late this morning. Are ye feelin' alright?" asked Martha turning from the trough to look at me.

"I'm fine thank you," I said smiling at her. Even though I was a bit late I hoped I'd be able to get breakfast. I glanced around and noticed a newspaper sitting on one end of the table. I raised a brow. That was unusual; I didn't think any of them could read.

"Sit down. Will tea and toast be alright?"

"Yes, that will be wonderful."

"Mrs Fitz was lookin' for ye earlier," she said as she poured me a cup of hot tea. "Did ye see her?"

"No," I said shaking my head. "I'll go and find her as soon as I've had breakfast."

"Well ye've not heard the horrible news then," she said sitting down beside me. "Poor young Joe Wilson's been murdered."

"Murdered?" I choked on my tea and stared opened mouthed at her. The Wilson family were members of the Reverend's congregation – I was horrified at the news. "Do they know who did it?"

"Aye. They've got two men I believe. The Reverend's gone to see Mrs and Mrs Wilson and no doubt will offer them some consolation. That's why Mrs Fitz was lookin' for ye. To see if ye'd read the newspaper for us, it's all in there."

"Oh, well, of course, I will," I said reaching for it and scanning the front page for any mention.

"I'll get ye some toast," said Martha getting to her feet.

It was all in the newspaper in graphic detail. I was shocked at how specific the article was about the murder. Apparently, he'd been set upon on his way home. He had a number of head injuries including a fractured skull. But the most horrific injury was a gunshot wound.

"Oh Margaret yer here," said Mrs Fitz as she hurried into the kitchen. "I see ye're already reading the paper. What does it say?"

"It's quite awful Mrs Fitz. The poor man was shot."

"Oh, dear heavens above. I heard tell Doctor Salmon attended to him."

"Yes that's right," I replied and smiled at Martha as she placed a plate of toast down in front of me. "He was taken to Mr Heaney's public house in Perth."

Mrs Fitz sat down at the table opposite me and looked at me expectantly. She obviously wanted all the details. I swallowed. The details were quite ghastly.

"Well, it says here that he was shot in the belly just below the ribs. By the time they got him to the public house he was vomiting blood," I said screwing up my face as I read further. He was also losing blood from the bowel, but I didn't think I should enlighten Mrs Fitz with that bit of news. "It sounds like he bled to death."

"Oh poor man," said Mrs Fitz. "And to think that Mr and Mrs Wilson are part of our small church."

I nodded.

"And what about them who did it?" said Martha.

"Oh, well they've arrested two men. A John McKay and John Lamb as his accomplice."

"I don't recognise either of their names," said Mrs Fitz with her brow furrowed. "What about ye Martha? Have ye heard of them?"

"No."

"It says here they don't know their residence, but McKay's been seen a few times in Norfolk Plains," I said reading the last paragraph. I folded the paper and pushed it aside. I expect a murder such as this in our small community would have everyone talking. I wonder if the Reverend will conduct the funeral service. I suppose so.

"Well I'm glad we don't know them," said Mrs Fitz getting to her feet.

I finished my breakfast and hid myself away in the Reverend's study. I loved being in here alone, it was so quiet and secluded, and no one ever came in. I was pleased to find he'd left me several letters to copy so I happily set to work. It gave me a chance to not think about my own problems.

The morning flew by as I carefully transcribed the letters. I found it so relaxing, but thoughts of William kept creeping into my mind. I tried hard to push them aside, but it was impossible. I hadn't gone down to the potting shed to meet him. How could I? The mere fact that he'd made such an outrageous suggestion made me wonder what his motives were. Or did I already know? The man was a scoundrel and I'd do well stay away from him.

I wasn't completely naive in matters relating to men, but that wasn't the real problem. I couldn't trust myself – that's what's scaring me the most. I can tell myself all the sensible things in the world, but once I'm in his presence, they evaporate. My lips want to be kissed by him, and I suspect my body wants him to touch it as well. I blushed at my own thoughts and turned my attention back to the letters. Well, at least I tried to.

It was nearly midday when the door to the study opened and Reverend Davies entered. He looked drained and exhausted.

"Oh, Margaret I didn't expect to find you here," he said as he sat down at his desk. "Thank you for doing the letters." He moved them to one side.

"That's quite alright." I hesitated, unsure how to even begin to ask about William and Sarah Wilson. "I was so shocked to hear what happened to Joe Wilson. How are Mr and Mrs Wilson?"

"As you can imagine, utterly devastated," he said rubbing his face with his hands. "It's hard to know where to begin to try and give them some comfort."

I nodded. "There's probably no comfort anyone can give them right now."

"No," he said and heaved a huge sigh. "The funeral's tomorrow. They want a graveside service and we'll be hosting the wake here."

I nodded once more. Martha would be exhausted having only just gotten over Rowland's christening. "Is there anything I can do?"

"I don't know," he said flatly. "Maria will know what's to be done."

"Of course. Well, I'll leave you to your business." I quietly left the study and closed the door softly behind me. I sucked in a deep breath and slowly let it out. My problems were so insignificant in light of the Wilson's losing their son.

I needed to visit the privy before washing up for dinner. I headed out the back door and down the path by the kitchen garden. It was a cool overcast day and I pulled my shawl around my shoulders as I hurried down the path.

My visit to the privy completed I had every intention of seeking out Maria. There must be a hundred things that needed to be done for tomorrow's funeral, and I wanted to be busy. The more I had to do the less time I had to think about William.

I went back inside and checked the parlour for Maria. She wasn't there, or in the dining room. I hadn't seen her out in the garden. In fact, I realised I'd been tucked away in the study all morning, and I hadn't seen her today at all. I went upstairs and knocked softly on her bedroom door. I heard a muffled reply and so opened it and went inside. She was sitting up in bed with baby Rowland at her breast. She looked up at me as I entered. She looked tired and drawn.

"Margaret, come in. Do sit down."

I sat in one of the floral wing chairs. "Are you alright? You're looking quite pale and drawn."

"I'm fine," she said and smiled weakly at me. "I'm just so very tired. I think a day of rest will do me the world of good."

She was probably right, although I thought she looked even more frail than usual. Rowland let go of the nipple with a small popping sound. He looked so fat and satisfied – I couldn't help smiling at him. Maria put him over her shoulder and began gently patting and rubbing his back.

"Did you hear about poor Joe Wilson?" she said.

"Yes. What a ghastly business. And I can't begin to imagine how his poor parents are dealing with it."

"Oh, I don't want to think about it," she said as Rowland let out a soft belch. "If anything should happen to Rowland I don't know what I'd do. I believe they're inconsolable."

I nodded. "Reverend Davies told me you're hosting the wake here tomorrow. Is there anything I can do to help?"

"I honestly don't know where to begin," she said guiding Rowland back to her breast. "Mrs Fitz will know."

"Alright," I said nodding. "I'll speak with her, don't you worry about a thing. Get some rest and take care of yourself."

"Thank you, Margaret."

I quietly left her room and went back downstairs to the kitchen, where I would no doubt find Mrs Fitz. The kitchen was crowded with everyone in for their midday meal. Martha looked frantic. No doubt she'd be baking for tomorrow's afternoon tea. If that's what it would be. I wonder how many will come? I expect most of Norfolk Plains. All the womenfolk will come here to the rectory, of course, they won't go to the graveside.

"Margaret, I dinna ken if you've heard, but we're to host the wake tomorrow morning for Joe Wilson. Ye'll be on tea service and ye'll need to help in the kitchen as well," said Mrs Fitz as she counted out cake forks, passing them from one hand to the other. "I've got no idea how many will be coming, and neither does the Reverend. I dinna ken how he thinks we can feed everyone if we dinna ken who's coming."

"Of course," I said nodding. Kitchen duty? I seriously doubt I'd be of any use, but I didn't say anything to the contrary. It was so unlike Mrs Fitz who took most things in her stride. She appeared to be completely flustered and gave an exasperated sigh as she began counting the forks again. "Perhaps I can do that for you?" I said.

"Thank ye, Margaret," she said dropping the forks and wiping her brow. She glanced around the kitchen looking harassed. "Annie, did ye clean the parlour?"

"Aye Mrs Fitz," she replied placing bowls of hot soup on the table as Martha filled them. "I'll do the dining room after dinner."

"Good. Henry make sure ye set the fireplaces afore the day's out," said Mrs Fitz as she sat down to a bowl of soup.

"Aye, I will."

I sat down and reached for a bowl of soup. William was sitting at the end of the table, and I glanced at him from under my lashes. He appeared to be so relaxed - he hadn't noticed me. A pang of disappointment went through me. Seriously, Margaret, you need to get a hold of yourself. It doesn't seem to matter how he behaves I'm not satisfied. If he pays me too much attention I run and hide, if he ignores me, like he's doing now, I want to draw his attention. I swallowed and stirred my soup.

"Sam, will ye make sure the front of the house is in order. Ye know, sweep the path and such and give the front a spruce up," said Mrs Fitz putting down her spoon. "We dinna want folks thinking ill of the Reverend and Mrs Davies now."

Sam was a quiet sort of man. I'd hardly spoken two words to him the whole time I'd been here. He nodded at Mrs Fitz and went on eating his soup. I glanced at William to see if he was looking, but he wasn't. How infuriating. I took another mouthful of soup and decided to ignore him as well.

After dinner, everyone had chores to do, even me. Mrs Fitz had me arranging platters and crockery for the dining room. Cups and saucers had to be put out on the sideboard with teaspoons and side plates. Cake stands and plates for sandwiches were decided upon and laid out ready to be laden in the morning. Martha and Liz were busy in the kitchen all afternoon baking pastries and other sweet treats.

I gratefully climbed into bed early. Tomorrow was going to be a long and busy day. I expect it's also going to be a rather awful day. Joe Wilson was only in his early twenties and his life had been cut off so abruptly. Not only were his family obviously devastated, but the whole community was still in shock. One of our own had been murdered. It was going to take some time for the people of Norfolk Plains to come to terms with such a dreadful occurrence.

I rolled over and pushed all thoughts of tomorrow from my mind. I didn't want to think about what a dreadful day it was going to be. No sooner had I managed to do that than thoughts of William crept in. I pressed my lips together and groaned. Why couldn't I stop thinking about him? Whenever my mind was unoccupied I started to think about him. I relived our first kiss down by the stables over and over again. I could almost feel his mouth on mine. I think I want him, but I'm not brave enough to admit it even to myself. Is this what love is? Or am I just infatuated with him because he paid me some attention? Am I so shallow? None of this is helping me get to sleep. On the contrary, my mind is a whirl of unresolved feelings. I feel like some activity might help me push him from my mind. Perhaps a walk in the garden in the cool night air.

Chapter Ten

The Rectory, Norfolk Plains

The entire household was up early the following morning. Breakfast was a hurried affair of porridge and black tea, along with Mrs Fitz barking orders at everyone. I was so frazzled by the time I'd finished my breakfast I barely even noticed William. I swallowed the last of my tea and set off on my first chore of the day - get Maria up and dressed for the day ahead.

I knocked softly on her door and called out as I entered. She was sitting in one of the wing back chairs and she looked up at me.

"Are you alright Maria?" I asked hurrying over to her. She looked so pale and there were dark smudges under her eyes. "Should I call for Doctor Salmon?"

"No, no," she said weakly. "I'm just so very tired. I don't know what's the matter with me."

I didn't like the look of her at all. Her normally pronounced cheekbones appeared to be more angular than usual. I peered at her and frowned. I couldn't imagine how she was going to host the wake today. She looked so frail.

"I think I should call the doctor, Maria."

"No please don't. I'm sure he'll be here for the wake later anyway. I'll see if he can take a look at me then," she said. She went to stand up and put her hand to her head and groaned. She promptly sat back down.

"What is it? Have you got a headache?"

"No, I just came over all giddy."

I sucked in my bottom lip. "Maria you can't possibly host the wake today, you're not well enough."

"The Wilson's are depending on me, Margaret. I can't let them down."

"Now that's just silly. You won't be letting anyone down. Anyway, I doubt you'd be able to make it down the stairs."

She put her head in her hands and I thought I saw her shoulders tremble. I knelt down and took her hands in mine. When she looked at me her pale blue eyes were awash with tears.

"Oh Maria," I said hugging her to me. "It'll be alright, but you need to rest."

She clung to me and gulped in some deep breaths and sobbed. I held her until they finally subsided and she pulled from my embrace. "I know you're right, Margaret. You'll have to host the wake for me."

I hoped my face wasn't giving away my thoughts. I hadn't hosted anything in such a long time. In fact, it felt like a lifetime ago that I was Miss Margaret of Bredgar House. I wasn't sure I could do it. She must have seen the doubt in my eyes.

"Oh, Margaret you'll be fine. I'm sure you can do it better than me."

"I doubt it. It's been such a long time since I've been a hostess."

"Well, there isn't anyone else. Mrs Fitz can't possibly be the hostess, but I know you can."

I nodded. "Alright. I'll make your apologies to Mr and Mrs Wilson, and as soon as Doctor Salmon arrives I'm sending him up to attend to you. No arguments."

"No arguments," she said smiling weakly at me.

"Can I get you anything before I go?"

"No, you've enough to do without worrying about me."

I nodded and got to my feet. "Perhaps, but we'll all be worrying about you nonetheless. I'll check in on you in a little while."

She smiled and nodded. I left and hurried back down the stairs. I was panting by the time I reached the study door. I knocked softly. There was no reply. I opened the door just wide enough for me to peek inside. There was no sign of the Reverend. I closed the door and continued onto the kitchen.

"Oh good you're back," said Mrs Fitz as soon as she spied me. "Can ye help Liz arrange the flowers in the parlour, and I think a vase on the hall table will be nice as well."

"Yes of course," I said smiling at Liz. "Do you know where the Reverend is?"

"He's gone a'ready," said Mrs Fitz looking at me with a raised brow. "Is something a matter?"

"Yes. It's Mrs Davies, she's not at all well and she won't be able to host the wake today. She's asked me to take her place."

"Oh, glory be, poor lamb," said Mrs Fitz immediately heading for the door. "I'll go see to her, you two get on with the flowers."

I nodded and followed Liz from the kitchen. She was such a quiet shy girl, who'd barely spoken to me in the whole time I'd been here. I knew she was from one of the local families and had been born in Van Diemen's Land, but that's about all I knew. We headed down passed the kitchen garden and I wondered if she knew what sort of flowers Mrs Fitz expected us to arrange.

"Are there any late roses do you think?" I asked as we went under the arbour.

Liz shook her head. "I don't think so. I thought we'd pick some lilies an' dahlia."

I was surprised. She was absolutely right. Lilies were far more appropriate for a funeral than roses. I smiled at her. "Good idea."

She turned her head sideways to look at me and gave me a shy smile. "Why don't you pick the dahlia an' I'll get the lilies? We'll need enough for three vases."

"Alright," I said and hoped my face didn't show the thoughts that were racing through my mind at the mention of dahlias. I wondered if she knew about me and William. She'd given me such an odd look.

"You'll find some nice ones down beyond the stables," she said pausing and handing me one of her baskets.

I took the basket and noticed there was a pair of scissors in the bottom of it. I smiled at her. "I'll meet you back in the kitchen then?"

"Aye."

I watched her saunter down the path to collect the lilies before turning in the other direction. The garden appeared to be quite deserted as I went down the path towards the stables. I glanced around and licked my lips nervously. I half expected to see William lurking down here among the garden beds somewhere. What would I do? I sucked in a deep breath and continued on until I spied the dahlias. I smiled as I remembered William wanted to bring me down here to see them.

They were large blooms with long stems and I cut what I hoped would be enough to fill the vases in the parlour and hall. I tucked the scissors back in the bottom of the basket and was about to head back up to the house when I was startled by a familiar voice.

"Well, this is a pleasant surprise," said William coming to stand beside me. He had a wheelbarrow full of mulch.

"Oh," I said looking at him. We hadn't spoken for several days, not since he'd suggested I meet him down by the potting shed the other night. My heart was racing and just being close to his very solid presence was making me gasp for air.

"I'm glad we've got a moment alone, Margaret," he said letting go of the wheelbarrow. "I waited for you the other night."

I swallowed and sucked in my lower lip. I didn't know what to say. I wasn't about to tell him how scared I am of myself when I'm with him. I couldn't tell him that I didn't trust myself to meet him in the dead of night. I'm like a leaf tossed in a river at the mercy of the currents when I'm near him.

"Margaret," he said taking a step closer to me. I could feel his breath and smell the musky scent emanating from him. "I thought you knew how I felt about you."

"I," I said. I had no idea what else I was going to say until it just sort of tumbled out of me. "I'm sorry. I was scared."

"You need never fear me," he said looking earnestly into my eyes.

I pressed my lips together and took in a deep breath. "It wasn't you I was scared of." My stays felt like they'd been laced too tight and I wanted to grab my basket and run.

He heaved a great sigh and smiled at me. "I'm glad. Will you meet me later? I just want to talk. Please."

"Alright," I said picking up my basket. "I'll meet you down by the potting shed after the funeral." Was I mad? I was so confused. I wanted him - I didn't want him. I really had to get a grip of myself.

He nodded and picked up his wheelbarrow. "Thank you."

I turned on my heel and hurried back up the path to the house. I was just approaching the kitchen garden when I saw Liz just up ahead of me. I called to her and she turned and waited for me to catch up.

She had a lovely lot of lilies. I smiled at her as we went back into the house.

The women of Norfolk Plains began arriving at around half-past ten. I greeted them at the door; explained that Maria was unwell and settled them into the parlour. Annie and Liz served them cups of tea while I handed around a plate of sweet biscuits. I licked my lips and tried to remain calm. I was relieved that they were more concerned with Maria than my shortcomings as a hostess. I'd decided to wait until the men arrived before opening the glass doors to the dining room. Most of the cakes, sandwiches and other pastries were already laid out in there.

It was nearly eleven before Sarah Wilson and her daughter arrived. They were both dressed in black with veils covering their faces. I didn't know what to say to them. I offered my condolences and ushered them into the parlour. I was hopeful that the other ladies would attend to them, which they did. Ten minutes later the Reverend arrived with the menfolk who'd attended the graveside service. He looked drained and forlorn.

"Reverend, can I have a quiet word please," I said putting my hand on his arm to prevent him from following the other men into the parlour. He looked quizzically at me but remained in the hall. "It's Maria. She's rather unwell and has asked me to take her place this morning. I think Dr Salmon should attend to her."

His face immediately turned to alarm. "I'll go straight up to see her. Would you send Dr Salmon up?"

"Yes, of course," I said, and without delay, he headed straight up the stairs. I went into the parlour, as sedately as possible. I didn't want to arouse anyone's undue concern. I caught sight of the good Doctor – he was currently giving his condolences to Sarah Wilson. I sucked in my bottom lip and waited for him to step away.

In the meantime, I caught hold of Annie's arm as she went by. "Annie, I think it's time to open the dining room and hand around some cakes and sandwiches."

She nodded. "Aye, Margaret."

"Ah, Dr Salmon," I said approaching him as soon as he turned his attention away from Mrs Wilson.

"Yes?" he said turning his rather dour face in my direction.

"I wonder if I might have a private word, out in the hall?"

He nodded and followed me out of the parlour, and away from prying eyes and murmuring voices. I quickly told him about Maria's dizzy spell this morning and he looked at me and nodded.

"Hm, go fetch my bag. It's under the seat of my cart. The Reverend's man knows which one," he said turning to go up the stairs.

I nodded and went out the front door. I presumed he was talking about John. There were a number of carts and wagons out the front and I hurried down the driveway looking for any sign of him. I finally spied him by a small cart with a chestnut horse that he was stroking and appeared to be whispering to.

"John," I called to him as I approached. He turned and smiled at me.

"Aye."

"John, I need to get the Doctor's bag. Could you please show me which cart's his?"

He nodded and pointed to a black spring cart parked under a shady gum tree. "That one over there."

"Thank you." I hurried over to it and reached in under the seat.

Sure enough, I pulled out the doctor's black medical bag. I was surprised at the weight of it as I hauled it from the cart. I could only imagine what was inside it – but it felt like rocks. I raced back inside and took a quick peek into the parlour. I

heaved a sigh; everyone appeared to be quite unaware that the Reverend and Dr Salmon were missing. They were talking and eating and I was glad to see Annie flitting among them with cups and plates.

I went upstairs and knocked on Maria's door. I could hear voices coming from inside, but I waited to be let in. I didn't want to intrude. Moments later Reverend Davies opened the door. He looked pale and drawn.

"Thank you, Margaret," he said taking the doctor's bag from me. "Please keep our guests entertained until I get back."

"Of course," I said with a nod.

He closed the door and I heaved a sigh. I could only hope that Maria would be alright, and whatever malady she was suffering from could be cured. I went back down to the parlour to supervise Liz and Annie. I checked the hall clock as I went by – it was already nearing midday.

I sighed. I realised I was anxious for the guests in the parlour to leave so I could meet with Will. A quiver of nerves went through me as I thought of him. I wonder if he'll kiss me again today? My lips tingled and I felt my face redden. My God I can hardly believe my own thoughts – what's happening to me?

Chapter Eleven

The Potting Shed, Ardmore House

I checked myself one last time in the tiny mirror in the room I shared with the other women above the kitchen. I let a few dark tendrils escape from beneath my cap. I thought they helped to soften my otherwise sharp features. I ran my hands over my dress, smoothing the folds of woollen fabric until I was finally satisfied with my appearance.

The afternoon had turned a little cool so I wrapped my paisley shawl around my shoulders before going downstairs. There was still a lot of noise coming from the kitchen. No doubt Martha and the girls would be cleaning up after the wake. I was glad I'd managed to escape that task. I went out the back door unnoticed and proceeded down the path towards the arbour. I spied Will waiting for me on the bench beside the potting shed well before I got to him. He looked so young and handsome. I sucked in a breath as I slowed my pace.

He looked up and noticing me gave a little wave and grinned. I smiled back as I approached the bench and sat beside him.

"I'm so glad you came, Margaret. I wasn't sure you would."

I smiled demurely. "You said you just wanted to talk," I said folding my hands in my lap. I tried to compose my face into a calm facade, but I wasn't sure I was succeeding. My heart was fluttering and as usual, I felt like my stays were too tight. I have no idea why I get so breathless and silly when I'm near him.

"Yes, well I'd like to explain to you that I'm not what you think," he said looking at me in a most unnerving manner. "I'm from a good family who must be so disappointed in me."

"Well I expect so," I said a little taken aback. I thought for a moment and then decided to dive right in. "So if you're not what I think, then who are you, Will Hartley?"

"Ah, well there's the thing," he said glancing nervously up and down the path. He took my hands in his and looked earnestly into my eyes. "My name's not William Hartley, but you must promise not to tell anyone."

The surprise must've been evident on my face. Not William Hartley? It only took a moment for me to regain my composure and I nodded. "I promise."

"Right, well my name's really William Hatley Penny. When I got arrested I changed my name so as not to shame my family," he said letting go of my hands. His head drooped. "I don't think they even know what's happened to me."

"What, you mean they don't know you got transported?"

"No, I don't think so. Well, they might know by now," he said turning to face me again. "So you see, Margaret, I can't even give you my name."

Well, now I thought he was getting way ahead of himself. I don't recall agreeing to marry him. "So how did you come to be in this predicament?" I thought I was being a bit bold, but if we were telling truths, then I needed to know if he was a murderer or not.

"It's a long stupid story. Let me just say that my mate, John, and I got caught stealing washing from the line."

Laundry? Well, it probably didn't matter – at least theft wasn't as serious as some other crimes. "So, were you sentenced to seven years or fourteen?"

"Seven."

I think he knew what my next question was going to be because he answered it before I even asked it.

"I've still got five to go."

"Oh." As much as Will excited me and I liked him very much, I wasn't sure there was a future with him. Five years was such a long time to wait before we could start our lives together.

"I reckon I'll get a ticket soon though," he said looking at me hopefully.

I nodded and shrugged. "It's such a big maybe, Will."

"If we were married the Reverend might recommend me sooner."

"Well, that's not very likely, is it? I mean you can't marry me can you?"

"No, not right now, not in the eyes of the law," he said. "But we could be married in the eyes of God."

I had no idea how he thought that was going to work. I sucked in a deep breath and slowly let it out. "Are you asking me to marry you?"

"I know I've no right to ask you such a thing," he said standing up. "I'm not free to be my own man."

He took my hands in his and drew me to my feet. I looked into his hazel eyes, which stared straight into mine and through to my heart which was quivering under the intensity. He lowered his head and kissed me. I instinctively wrapped my arms around him and held him close. The kiss seemed to go on forever and I finally broke away, breathless. All sensible thoughts deserted me as I allowed myself to bathe in his warmth.

"Marry me, Margaret," he said breathing heavily. "We could be handfasted until I'm free."

Handfasted? I'd heard of the custom, but that would be so uncertain. What kind of marriage would that be? We wouldn't be able to tell anyone, and I'd still be sleeping above the kitchen and him in the men's quarters. I couldn't see how it could work, but my heart melted at the sight of him.

"I promise you I'll be a true and faithful husband," he said still holding me. "And as soon as I'm able we'll be married proper."

"I," I said stammering. "I don't know."

"Would it help if I kissed you again?" he said grinning at me.

"No," I said and laughed. "I don't think that would help at all."

"Margaret," he said looking into my eyes and bringing my hands to his lips. "I love you."

I melted. I stared into the fathomless depths of his eyes and saw in there honesty and desire – a desire for me. No man had ever desired me before. In that split second, I saw the truth of my own heart and desires. I wanted him – actually, I wanted him quite badly.

"I love you too," I said stepping into his arms.

We kissed long and hard and he pulled me tight against his firm body. I could feel the full length of him pressed up against my soft flesh which seemed to mould to his. He ran his hands down my back and my lips parted as I drank him in. When we parted we were both breathless and gasping for air.

He held me still as he gazed down at me. I'm sure he saw the same burning desire in my eyes that I saw in his.

"So, Margaret Chambers. Will you handfast with me until we can be legally wed?"

"Yes." I couldn't believe what I was agreeing to, but it felt so right. I smiled at him and slowly kissed him again. "I have no idea how this will work, Will Penny, but together I'm sure we can do it."

He grinned down at me. "Yes, we can. I promise we'll have a proper handfast ceremony. When's your next afternoon off?"

"Sunday, but you don't get any afternoons off, so how will that help?"

"Don't you worry about that. I'll sort it with Sam, he'll cover for me."

I smiled. "Alright. Where will I meet you? Not here, someone will notice us for sure."

He nodded. "Down by the dahlia patch."

I smiled and stood on tiptoes and kissed him quickly. "Until Sunday."

"Yes. We should go before someone notices us," he said looking up and down the path. "I'll be waiting for you."

I nodded before turning and walking back up the path to the house. I glanced back over my shoulder, but he'd already disappeared around the side of the potting shed. I continued up the path until I came to the arbour. I sat down on the bench there to gather my thoughts. I'd just agreed to marry Will, and I'd told him that I loved him. I wonder when I'd realised that? I smiled to myself and sighed. There was no going back now, anyway, I didn't want to.

⁂

I spent the next few days cooped up with Maria, who was still feeling poorly. Doctor Salmon had given her a tonic and I actually thought it was helping. She certainly seemed to have more energy, and although we'd spent the last few days in her room, today she decided we should go down to the river so she could sketch. Martha had packed us a picnic and with Rowland's pram strapped to the back of the spring cart, we headed off.

The days were getting cooler, and I knew winter would be truly upon us soon. I'd heard that we wouldn't even get snow in Norfolk Plains, unlike back in Kent. I gripped the edge of the seat as John urged the horses into a trot. It wasn't far to the Macquarie River, and there was a lovely shaded flat area not far from the road. John pulled the horses up under a large gum tree and Maria looked around.

"This should do nicely, thank you, John," she said as she gazed up and down the river flat. "Here, hold Rowland while I get down."

I smiled and took Rowland from her. I was surprised at how heavy he was getting. At nine weeks old he was becoming quite a handful. He was tossing his little arms about and I was enthralled when he smiled at me.

"Maria, he just smiled at me."

"Oh really. He's only been doing that for about a week. He must've recognised you," she said as John helped her from the cart. "Here, hand him to me."

I handed him to her and she hugged him close. "Did you smile at Margaret? You clever boy," she said as she kissed his forehead.

I climbed down from the cart while John unstrapped the pram and positioned it ready for Rowland to be tucked inside. It was a cool morning but the sun was trying hard to peek out between the clouds. Armed with Maria's canvas and pencils, and with the basket Martha had packed perched precariously on the pram with Rowland, we headed off along the river. We didn't go far before Maria spied a fallen tree overgrown with creeper which was half in the river. The riverbank was covered in ferns which were dipping their fronds in the water.

"This will do perfectly," she said coming to a halt.

I had to agree the setting was perfect for one of her landscape watercolours, which were her favourite. I spread out the rug and Maria settled herself down with her canvas and box of pencils. I decided to wander a little further along the river on my own.

"Don't venture too far, Margaret. Stay within eyesight."

"I will," I called to her over my shoulder as I began meandering along the riverbank.

I'd barely had five minutes to myself since I'd agreed to marry Will, and I really wanted some time alone to think. I was anxious about marrying him in secret. Eventually, someone would surely find out, and then what would happen? My worry wasn't so much for myself as it was for him. He was still a convict, and not free to marry without permission. I reminded myself that it would only be a handfast marriage - still, what would the Reverend do if he found out about it? Or Maria for that matter? I glanced back along the river to where I could just see her through the trees. I would hate to make life difficult for her, she'd been so incredibly kind to me. I sighed.

The sun finally managed to break out between the clouds and spread its wintry warmth along my back. I perched myself on a tree stump and watched the river currents hurry by. I wished my sister Barb was here; she would surely have some good advice for me. Not that I'd probably take any notice. I loved Will, and regardless of the risks or the dangers, I would be handfasted to him on Sunday. A quiver ran through me at the thought. Not of the ceremony, but of what would happen after that. I felt my face blush and my heart race. Oh my goodness.

Chapter Twelve

Handfasted

Sunday morning dawned overcast with a chill wind blowing. I wrapped my cloak around myself as I made my way up the aisle to the door of the church. Maria looked up as I stepped outside. She was busy tucking Rowland into his pram and covering him with a warm shawl.

"Will you walk with me back up to the house?" she said smiling at me.

"Of course."

It was only a short walk across the churchyard to the gate which led directly into the backyard of the rectory. I opened the gate for her and waited while she pushed the pram through. I closed the gate and caught up with her.

"I can't help but notice, Margaret that you seem preoccupied these days. Is everything alright?" she said coming to a halt beside the potting sheds.

She caught me quite off guard and I'm sure the surprise showed on my face. "Yes, of course. Everything's just fine." I smiled and hoped that would be enough to allay her concerns.

"You know you can trust me," she said sitting down on the bench by the shed.

She patted the seat beside her. "Sit for a moment."

I swallowed and took in a deep breath before sitting beside her. I wondered how much she knew or suspected about me and Will. I couldn't possibly tell her. As much as she'd been kind and understanding in the past, I couldn't imagine how she'd react to the news that I intended to marry Will Hartley today. My heart gave a flutter and I lowered my eyes.

"I know something's bothering you," she said pushing the pram back and forth. "Is someone harassing you?"

"No, not at all. I'm really very happy here."

"Well I'm glad," she said eyeing me sideways. "I like to think that we've become friends, and I'm here to help if you need it."

"Thank you," I said relaxing a little. I smiled at her. "You have been more than kind and generous to me Maria, and I consider you my closest friend."

She smiled and her pale blue eyes crinkled at the edges. She took my hand and squeezed it. "Please come to me if you find yourself in trouble, or just need a friend. Promise me, Margaret."

I nodded. "I promise I will."

"Good," she said standing up. "Let's get up to the house, it's freezing out here."

We went back up to the house and as soon as I stepped inside I was greeted with the aroma of freshly baked bread. I breathed in and smiled at Maria.

"Ooh Martha's been baking," I said. "I hope there's some for our dinner."

"I'm sure there will be," said Maria and she laughed. "Enjoy your afternoon off."

"Thank you," I said and then headed for the kitchen. I was famished and hoped there'd be some hot soup to go with the bread.

I spent the afternoon mending my stockings and trying to not think about tonight. I chatted aimlessly with Annie over supper and did my best to ignore Will. Every time I caught sight of him my heart started racing. I could barely think straight by the time I went to bed. I put on my best nightgown and feigned sleep until I was sure everyone else was fast asleep. I had no idea what time it was when I crept out of bed. I wrapped myself in my cloak and grabbed my boots before tiptoeing down the stairs.

The house was all quiet, and I put on my boots and stepped out of the back door and headed down the garden to meet

Will. I was so nervous, yet excited as I made my way down passed the arbour. I'd brought a length of ribbon with me to use to fasten our hands. At least, that's what I understood the handfasting ceremony would require. I wasn't sure what words we'd say to one another, but I thought they'd be fairly simple. I reached into the pocket of my cloak and felt for the coin. It felt warm and smooth and I smiled as I thought about giving it to my new husband.

There was no sign of him as I went down the side of the stables. The dahlia patch was just beyond, and I glanced around. Although it was dark I thought I'd see the shadow if someone was waiting in the garden. There was no sign of anyone. There was a chilly wind blowing and I pulled my cloak more firmly about myself as I prepared to wait. I'd expected Will to be here before me, and I was quite surprised that he wasn't.

I wrapped my arms about myself and sheltered beside the stables. I'm not sure how long I waited, but I do know I was nearly numb with the cold before he turned up.

"I'm sorry," he said and he gave me a quick hug. "You're shivering."

"Well, yes, I've been waiting a while and it's freezing."

"I'm so sorry," he said again.

Leading me by the hand we stepped into the relative warmth of the stables. It smelled of hay and horses and the outside sounds seemed to be muffled. Maybe it was the hay and all the equipment hanging from the walls. There were spare cart wheels, reins and bridles, in fact, all manner of horse related paraphernalia. Between the stalls was a ladder which clearly led up to a small loft. Will stopped at the bottom of it and gestured that I should go first.

I raised my brows. "What are you suggesting?"

"Somewhere quiet and private where we won't be disturbed."

I glanced nervously around the stables. Did I want to go somewhere quiet and private with him? I sucked in a deep breath and slowly let it out. Yes came the immediate reply. "What about John?"

"He won't be bothering us," he said shaking his head. "Come, I promise you no one will bother us here."

I hoicked my nightgown up with one hand and carefully climbed the ladder. Two lamps were illuminating the loft which was larger than I'd imagined. It was covered in a layer of fresh hay with a woollen blanket laid out over the top. Several hay bales were positioned around the walls, and an old blanket was also thrown over two of them. I noticed a bottle of wine and two goblets sitting on one of the bales. I smiled to myself. It was to be a proper celebration then.

"What do you think?" said Will coming to the top of the ladder and stepping over.

"I'm amazed," I said sitting down on one of the bales. "I see you've put a lot of thought into today."

He grinned at me. "It wasn't easy finding somewhere suitable," he said looking around the small cosy loft. "But I think this will do perfectly."

I nodded. I had to agree. I had no idea we could find somewhere at the rectory where we could be so alone. Will sat down beside me, and I could feel the warmth radiating from him. He was so big and solid beside me. I drew in a deep breath and tried to calm the nervous flutter in my stomach.

"Have you changed your mind?" he asked looking serious. "Because if you have, that's alright."

"I wouldn't have come if I'd changed my mind."

"Good."

He reached into his pocket and drew out a length of green cord. I watched him as he wrapped it around his left wrist before taking my left hand and placing it on top of his. He then wrapped the cord around my wrist, binding us together.

"I believe you'd normally tie both hands, but that isn't possible with just the two of us. I think this will suffice."

I nodded and sucked in my lower lip.

He took my other hand in his. "I don't know what the proper words should be, but I hope these will do." He paused and took a breath. "I, William Hartley take you, Margaret Chambers to be my wife and I pledge you my troth," he said looking earnestly into my eyes.

This was it then. No preamble, no questioning whether we should or shouldn't handfast ourselves. On one hand, I was glad he hadn't given me any time to think about it or back out. I swallowed.

"I, Margaret Chambers take you, William Hartley to be my husband and I pledge you my troth."

I let go of his hand and reached into my pocket and withdrew the coin. I took his hand in mine and turned it palm up and place the coin in the middle of it. I closed his fingers over it and kissed them.

"A token of my love and commitment."

"Thank you," he said smiling at me. He put it in his pocket and then reached in and drew out a small folded handkerchief from his breast pocket. "Please take this as a token of my love and commitment."

I smiled and took the handkerchief. He unbound our hands and tossed the cord aside.

"I wish I had a ring or something of more value to give you," he said taking my hands in his. He raised them to his lips and kissed them before turning them over and placing a soft kiss in the palm of my hand. It sent a quiver through me that I hadn't expected.

"I don't care," I said. And I meant it. Baubles wouldn't make our marriage any more meaningful than it already was.

He smiled. "One day, Margaret, I'll give you all that you deserve."

He then took my face in his hands and kissed me. It was a long slow passionate kiss, that left me breathless and wanting more. My lips were tingling as he pulled away, but I grabbed him and kissed him back. He ran his hands down my back and pulled me closer before abruptly letting me go.

"Not yet," he said reaching for the two goblets and handing them to me. He poured us each a cup of wine and then took one. "To us. To many happy years together," he said and then took a mouthful of wine.

I smiled and took a sip. It was good wine. It was only now that I wondered where he'd got it. Perhaps it was better that I didn't know. I took another mouthful and let it slowly go down my throat. I realised I was trembling, and not from the cold. I looked at the blanket all laid out on the hay and sucked in a deep breath. I glanced at Will. He was looking intently at me as he drank his wine. His gaze made me shiver and I realised I was breathing heavily. I gulped down the last of the wine.

He took my empty goblet from me and put them down on the hay. Taking me by the hands he stood up and pulled me to my feet. I looked into his face, and he bent his head and kissed me as he pulled me close. My lips parted as I returned his kiss with equal fervour. He hugged me close and I could feel him pressed against me. A surge of excitement ran through me and I pressed myself up against his firm chest. He groaned and deepened the kiss. When we finally parted he hugged me close and I breathed in the musky male scent of him.

"Are you scared?" he asked his hot breath on my neck.

"A little."

He smiled at me as he untied my cloak and it dropped to the floor. "Don't be."

My heart was hammering as I gazed at him. I was only in my nightgown and all of a sudden it seemed too flimsy. I shivered – both from the chilly air and the feel of his large warm hands on my bare flesh. I felt so exposed and I wanted to hide. I pressed myself against him and hugged him close as we kissed again. He lowered me gently onto the blanket before standing up to remove his clothes.

His body was silhouetted in the lamplight and I gasped as he removed his breeches and turned to face me. I could see the outline of his muscles, firm and taut. His lean body was like an ancient sculpture. I barely had a moment to admire him before he joined me on the floor. He took me in his arms and we kissed as he ran his hands down my back and grabbing my bottom pulled me to him. I could feel him through my thin gown and I moaned.

I copied him, and ran my hands down his back to his bare bottom. The feel of his skin was intoxicating. It was so firm under my fingers and furry in places. He ran his hands up under my nightgown, pushing it up around my thighs. I gasped as his fingers found the soft cleft between my legs and then a long moan escaped my lips as a spasm of pleasure went through me like a lightning bolt. When he entered me I gasped, but the pain was short-lived. It was quickly replaced by a growing feeling of pleasure as I thrust my hips into his.

Later, we lay in each other's arms wrapped in the warmth of my cloak. I was exhausted and would've liked nothing better than to sleep in his arms in the loft all night. However, the longer we lingered the more likely it was that we'd be discovered. I finally pulled myself from his arms and got up. I grabbed my cloak and wrapped myself in it.

"Don't go," he said grabbing my hand.

"We'll get caught if we stay any longer," I said bending down and kissing him softly. "I'll come and find you tomorrow."

"Alright."

I gave him one last look and then climbed down the ladder. All was quiet in the stable and I opened the door a crack before glancing up and down the path. It was cold and dark, and I hurried up to the house and in the back door. I crept up the stairs and was relieved that all the women were breathing rhythmically. I tossed off my cloak and climbed into bed and within moments I fell asleep.

Chapter Thirteen

Good News and Bad News

I'm deliriously happy and madly in love with my husband. He's so kind and gentle with me, and over the last few weeks, I've really got to know him. After making love last night we talked until the early hours. He told me he's originally from a small village called Margaretting in Essex. I couldn't help the smile that crept across my face as I dipped the quill in the inkpot. How funny he's from Margaretting and he's married to me - Margaret.

I was in the study with Reverend Davies. He was reading his correspondence while I transcribed the births, deaths and marriages for the past month. Apart from the clock ticking on the mantle it was quiet and cosy. I stretched my hand which was starting to cramp when the door opened. I looked up at Maria as she came in. It was most unusual, as she rarely came into the study.

"Maria," said Reverend Davies looking up from the letter in his hands. "Did you want something?"

"No, no," she said waving her hand in the air. "Some mail's just arrived for you." She placed several letters on his desk.

"Thank you," he said.

"You're welcome," she said before turning her attention to me. "How much longer will you be, Margaret?"

"Not long, I'm nearly done."

"Good. I want to see you as soon as you've finished."

"Alright," I said and I smiled at her.

"I'll most likely be in the parlour."

I nodded, and she turned and left. I went back to my writing, but I was curious to know what she wanted. She'd seemed rather excited about something. I sucked in a deep breath as I wondered if she'd somehow found out about me and Will. I shook my head as I dismissed that idea. No, we'd been so careful not to be seen.

Half an hour later I left the study and went to find her. I found her sitting in the parlour with Rowland playing on a rug on the floor. She looked up and smiled at me as soon as I entered.

"Oh, Margaret. Come and sit," she said indicating the seat beside her on the sofa.

I smiled at Rowland on the floor and sat down. "Is everything alright?"

"Yes, everything's just fine," she said opening the small drawer in the table beside her. She took out a letter which she handed to me. "It's from Bredgar House."

A flutter went through me at the mention of my old home. I looked at the envelope and immediately recognised the writing. "It's from my mother."

Maria grinned. "I thought so. If you like I can leave you alone to read it?"

"No, that's not necessary," I said and I smiled at her. "She must've written it as soon as she got mine." I tore open the envelope and began reading, or more like devouring every word.

Dearest Margaret,

I cannot begin to tell you how relieved I was to receive news that you were safe. We were worried sick for you when you disappeared. Barbara didn't tell us for several days that you'd run away to Van Diemen's Land. Of all places Margaret.

The situation has very much changed here. Sir Richard Owens was, of course, furious at your father for letting you escape. However, I believe he managed to smooth things over with the help of your Uncle Abraham. Anyway, Sir Richard has now married Amelia Forsyth. You'd remember her I'm sure. A rather plain girl, but from a good family.

Your Uncle Abraham has also managed to somehow disentangle your father's affairs from Uncle James'. It was looking like debtors prison there for a moment, but it has all been straightened out.

Your father's been most unwell and has been bedridden for the past few weeks. Margaret, he forgives you and would very much like you to come home. I promise you, there will be no schemes to marry you off. We would all just be so relieved to have you back amongst us.

Our family is growing, with Osborn and Eleanor having another daughter who they've named Eleanor. Charlotte and John are returning from Edinburgh at the end of the month. I can hardly wait to see them again. John's taking up a position with your Uncle Abraham at his law firm in London. It's quite a prestigious move for him and I believe Charlotte's quite delighted.

Please do consider returning home, won't you? If you find yourself short of funds then take out a small loan. We will repay it when you get here. I beg you to think about it, for your father's sake if not for your own.

As always I am your own dear mother, Barbara.

Large salty tears were leaking from my eyes and I wiped them away with the back of my hand. I hadn't realised until right this minute how much I was missing my family. In particular, my own dear sweet mother.

"Is it bad news?" said Maria placing her hand on my arm.

"Oh no. Not at all," I said and I smiled at her through my tears. "I just miss them all so much."

"Well of course you do."

"My mother wants me to come home. My father's not well and he'd like me to come back," I said as I folded the letter and put it back in the envelope. I would read it again later when I was by myself.

"What will you do?" asked Maria peering at me.

I shook my head. "I don't know. I never considered going back when I came here," I said running my fingers over the envelope. "But, my father's forgiven me."

Maria bent down and picked Rowland off of the floor. He was starting to fuss and immediately quieted when she put him over her shoulder and rubbed his back.

"Of course I'll miss you dreadfully if you decide to go," she said and a shadow passed over her pale blue eyes. "But you should definitely consider it. Family is family after all."

I nodded. She was right, and I did miss them all so much. But what about Will? If only the letter had arrived a month ago, then I'd have gone home without a second thought. I sucked in my bottom lip and sighed. I honestly didn't know what to do.

"You're right. Family is family, but I'll have to think about it."

"Well I'm sure Robert won't mind you using the desk in his study to write your reply," she said getting up from the sofa. "I need to go and attend to this little one."

"Thank you, Maria."

She smiled at me. "You're welcome," she said as she left the room.

I sat there on the sofa for a few more minutes. I wasn't sure I was ready to write a reply, anyway what would I say? I was so torn between my new life here with Will and my family back home. I was going to need to take some time to really think about what I wanted to do.

We were well into winter now and the mornings were cold and frosty. It seemed very strange to me to not have snow flurries at the door and tree branches laden with it. It wasn't like winter at all. With the colder weather, Maria and I had been cooped up inside for weeks. It gave her a chance to paint some of her earlier sketches while I watched over Rowland. He was now five months old and liked nothing better than to roll on the floor and kick his legs. He was a lovely baby with big blue eyes so like Maria's.

I was glad for the quiet hours spent with them both. For the past week or so I'd been feeling quite unwell. I don't know if I've eaten something that's disagreed with me or if I've picked up some sort of illness. Either way, I've been feeling quite queasy and the thought of food makes me feel even worse.

"Margaret, I really think we ought to get Dr Salmon to take a look at you," said Maria turning from her painting and peering at me again. "You're awfully pale and sickly looking."

I smiled at her. "No, I'm sure it's nothing. I'll be better in a day or two."

"Well at least try some of that tonic he made for me. It's done wonders for me, I think I've even put on some weight." She paused and looked herself up and down and patted her stomach.

I had to agree, Maria was looking so much better. She was still a bit too thin but she had some colour in her cheeks. She was also more energetic and hadn't spent a day in bed in a long while.

"Yes, I must agree it has done wonders for you."

I bent down and rolled Rowland back onto his stomach. He was able to roll from there onto his back but had not yet worked out how to do it the other way. Maria smiled at him and he cooed and kicked his legs in response.

"If you don't mind, Maria I might go for a walk in the garden and take in some fresh air."

"Yes, that's a good idea it might make you feel better. You go, Rowland and I will be fine."

"Thank you," I said and I smiled at her. She was so kind and while some fresh air might help me feel better, I was also feeling a little teary. How very odd. I wanted nothing more than to bury myself in Will's arms.

I went and grabbed my cloak before stepping outside. It was a grey overcast day with a chilly wind blowing. I shivered and pulled the hood of my cloak up over my head. I had no idea where Will would be working today, but he wouldn't be hard to find. I headed down passed the kitchen garden and the arbour. I spied him immediately, working under the large gum tree in the middle of the garden.

He looked up and smiled as I approached and my heart leapt. I glanced around for signs of Sam or anyone else, but the garden appeared deserted. I hurried to him and threw myself into his arms, and then I buried my head into his shoulder and sobbed.

"Meg, what's wrong?"

I heard the alarm in his voice but I just clung to him until finally, my tears subsided. I sucked in a deep breath and released him as I wiped them away with my hand.

"I don't know," I said at last as I pushed my hood off. "I'm not feeling well."

His hazel eyes were full of concern as he looked into my face. "Come and sit for a minute," he said guiding me to the nearest bench. "When did this start?"

I sighed. "A week ago, maybe, I'm not sure."

He put his arms around me and pulled me close. I sighed as I rested my head on his shoulder and felt his presence calming me. He was so warm and solid and smelled so familiar. Now that I was in his arms I felt so silly. Why had I needed him so desperately, and what was with the tears? I sighed and snuggled closer to him.

"Perhaps you should see Dr Salmon."

"That's what Maria suggested," I said sitting up so I could look at him. "But I'll be fine in a day or two, I'm sure."

He sat silent for a minute or so like he was carefully weighing his words. "Do you think this has something to do with the letter from your mother?"

I shrugged. "I don't know. I don't think so."

"Perhaps you should consider going home, just for a visit," he said and then he pressed his lips together. "Not that I want you to go."

"Maybe," I said and sighed. He might be right. I'd written to my mother and told her I wouldn't be coming back, I had a new life here now. I missed them all so terribly though, and maybe that was why I was feeling this way. "I've already written to her and told her I won't be coming." I took his face in my hands and kissed him softly. "I love you, Will, and I don't want to leave."

He hugged me close, kissing my neck and ear lobe. "I love you so much, Meg, but if it will make you happy, perhaps you should reconsider."

I shook my head. "No." I took in a deep breath and slowly let it out. "You make me happy. I'm sure I'll be fine, I'm just being silly."

He smiled at me and it wrinkled the corners of his eyes. My heart just melted at the sight of him. "You're not being silly," he said and he kissed me long and slow until I was gasping for air. "And I'm glad you came to me."

We sat there on the bench under the gum tree for ages, just being with one another. It was only when I saw Annie coming down the path that I quickly shuffled along the bench away from him. He noticed her as well and got to his feet and pretended he was weeding under the bench.

"Oh Margaret, there ye are," she said flopping herself down on the other bench.

She gave Will an odd look which made me wonder if she'd seen us. I sucked in my bottom lip and pulled my hood back over my head. I've had my suspicions for a while now that she's infatuated with Will. She often manoeuvres herself into sitting beside him at supper, and I've seen her flirting with him more than once.

I smiled at her. "Is something wrong Annie?"

"Oh, no," she said finally taking her eyes off Will. "I just wondered if ye'd like to go down to the church to practice on the organ today? It would help me get out of helping Liz in the wash house."

I smiled to myself. Annie was always thinking about Annie. "I'd be happy to. Come on we'll let Mrs Fitz know we're going, then we'll go for an hour or so." I got to my feet and wrapped my cloak more firmly around myself.

"Oh thank ye, Margaret," she said jumping up and starting up the path. "Bye Will."

"Oh, goodbye," he said pulling his head out from under the bench.

I grinned at him, before following Annie back up to the house. My conversation with Will had left me feeling so much better, although I was still feeling nauseous. I can only hope I'll be feeling better in another day or so.

Chapter Fourteen

Spring of 1837

I hung onto the washstand while Annie tugged at my stays. I'd put on weight and she was having trouble lacing them.

"Breath in," she said as she attempted to pull the lacings tight.

She finally got them laced, but I thought I'd probably die. "Oh no, you'll have to loosen them, I can't breathe," I said holding my stomach and gasping for air.

"Alright, but I don't know how ye are gonna get ye skirt on," she said as she loosened them off.

I sucked in a deep breath. "I'll work that out. Thank you, Annie."

She looked me up and down as I stood there in my chemise. "Ye've got bigger all round."

"I know," I said looking down at myself. "Too many of Martha's cakes I think."

She nodded. "Maybe. Anyways, I'll see ye downstairs. I'm going off to get breakfast. Mrs Fitz'll be after me otherwise."

"Yes, she will. Thank you, Annie."

She headed out the door and I looked down at myself. I wasn't sure how much longer I'd be able to hide my growing belly. I ran my hand over it and sucked in my bottom lip. It had taken me a while to put all the clues together, but it had finally dawned on me last week – I was expecting. Any thoughts I'd had of going home for a visit were now quite out of the question. I wasn't even sure how I was going to tell Will, let alone Maria.

I took my brown skirt out and tried it on. Thankfully it had a large loose waist with a tie so it didn't matter that my stays weren't as tight as usual. I settled it a little above my waist for comfort and then put on my blouse. I tried the jacket on over the top. It was a little tight but no one would likely notice. I tucked a few wayward tendrils back into my bun and put on my cap.

I took one last look in the mirror. I actually looked rather well. My cheeks were full of colour and the dark shadows under my eyes had all but vanished. They'd had dark smudges under them for weeks, but now that the nausea had passed they were fading as well. All I had to do was figure out what to do about my impending motherhood. A nervous flutter went through me at the thought and I pushed it from my mind; I'd think about that later.

By the time I got down to the kitchen for breakfast, everyone else was already seated. I smiled at Will who was sitting down one end of the table opposite Annie. I don't know how she always manages to position herself close to him. I took one of the last vacant chairs and a moment later Martha popped a bowl of porridge down in front of me. I thanked her before pouring on a little milk.

I was chatting with Mrs Fitz who was full of news about the new church.

"Tis about time something was done, and I hear tell it will fit a thousand people," she said waving her spoon about. "Imagine that. And no leaky roof."

I couldn't help but smile at her enthusiasm. "It sounds wonderful," I said spooning another mouthful of porridge into my mouth. "Do you know when they'll start building it?"

"Och no," she said scoffing. "Twill be a while for sure. The good Reverend will need to raise some money first."

I nodded and continued eating my breakfast. I heard part of a conversation at the other end of the table that caught my attention. Annie was chatting away and Will was staring at me. He looked as though the colour had drained from his face.

"So what did ye say her name was?" said Annie and she gave me a very smug look.

I frowned as I tried to work out what they were talking about.

Will looked from me to Annie and swallowed before replying. "Fanny."

"An' do ye think ye'll ever see ye wife again?" asked Annie.

Wife? What was she talking about? I stared at Will who all of a sudden had found his bowl of porridge particularly interesting. I stared at him as I waited for him to reply.

"No," he said and then he looked up at me.

His hazel eyes bore into me, but I barely noticed. I dropped my spoon and gaped at him and then Annie. She was sitting there with a very satisfied look on her face. I felt like my whole world had just shifted beneath my feet. Married? Will was married to some woman named Fanny. My mouth went dry and I felt sick. I stood up.

"I'm sorry, I'm not feeling very well," I said and I hurried from the kitchen.

My eyes filled with tears as I ran out the back door and down the garden path. I had no idea where I was going or what I was going to do. I just knew I had to get away from Will and Annie. I found myself down near the orchard and so I continued through the gate to the church. I knew I shouldn't be down here on my own, but I needed to be alone. I went inside and sat down in the back row.

I can't believe Will's lied to me. We were handfasted; he told me he loved me, and yet here he is with a wife already. I put my head in my hands and sobbed. What an idiot I'd been to believe him, to trust him, to think that he loved me. He'd used me, and now I was carrying his child and there would be no marriage. Oh my God, what am I going to do? I can't go home, and very soon everyone will know that I'm expecting, and unmarried.

My heart was racing and I was gasping for air as panic overwhelmed me. I was ruined, utterly disgraced and I had no one to blame except for myself. The door opened and I looked up at Will as he came inside. I didn't want to see him.

"Meg," he said as he sat down beside me.

I shuffled along the pew. "Go away."

"Meg you must believe me, I never meant to hurt you. Fanny means nothing to me."

"That doesn't really matter now does it," I replied glaring angrily at him. "The fact is you never told me, and your promise to marry me is rubbish."

He looked down at his hands which were resting on his knees. "Please I love you, Meg."

I sucked in a deep breath and continued to glare at him. Did he honestly think me so stupid or naive? "Go away."

He licked his lips and moved closer to me. I stood up and went to the end of the aisle. "You must think I'm a complete idiot," I said breathing heavily. I gave him one last look before I hurried to the door. I paused and turned. He was already on his feet ready to follow me. "Go back to your wife."

I heard him calling my name but I ignored him as I hurried back to the rectory. I wouldn't be giving him another chance to treat me like a fool. I was near the arbour when he caught up to me and grabbed me by the arm.

"Please let me explain."

I turned abruptly and tried to wrench my arm from his grasp. "Let me go. I don't want to hear any more of your lies."

He grabbed hold of my other arm and held me firmly in front of him. I wriggled and pulled but he had a tight grip on me. I finally stopped struggling and sighed. My eyes filled with tears – I couldn't help the hurt from showing in my eyes.

"Alright, explain."

"Unhand her this instant," said Maria giving Will a shove. He immediately let me go and I stumbled slightly before Maria grabbed my arm and steadied me. "Are you alright?"

I nodded. "Yes. He didn't hurt me or anything."

"Well I should hope not," she said before turning her formidable gaze on Will. "Get back to work."

"Mrs Davies, I can explain," said Will looking frantically between us. "Please Margaret."

"Oh, you will most certainly explain yourself to the Reverend when he returns," said Maria wrapping her arm around my shoulders. "Come Margaret."

She turned me around and we began walking back to the house. I didn't dare turn around to look at Will. I had a sick feeling in the pit of my stomach, as I suspected my situation had just worsened. How could I begin to explain myself to Maria? As much as I was hurt and angry at Will I didn't want him to get into more trouble. Maria not only had the power to send him back to the Government but could also order him to be punished. I swallowed the rising bile in my throat as she guided me into the house and down the hall to the parlour.

"Sit down," she said and looked so kindly into my face. She popped her head out of the door and called down the hall for Mrs Fitz. She arrived moments later huffing and holding her hand to her bosom.

"Aye Mrs Davies?"

"Oh I'm sorry to hurry you, Mrs Fitz," she said looking apologetically at her. "Would you please ask Martha to bring some tea for Margaret and me?"

"Aye," she said trying to peer into the parlour at me before heading off to the kitchen.

As soon as Mrs Fitz had gone she turned her pale blue gaze on me. It wasn't that she looked at me unkindly or anything, but I dissolved into tears anyway.

"Oh Margaret," she said hurrying over to my side and sitting on the sofa beside me. "Whatever is the matter? And don't go telling me nothing, because I don't believe it."

She handed me a clean laundered handkerchief and sat quietly looking at me while I sobbed uncontrollably. Where was I going to begin? I couldn't tell her about Will and I. And I certainly couldn't tell her that we were married, or at least promised to be married. I took in a couple of deep breaths and tried to stop crying. I dabbed my eyes and finally looked at her.

"I don't know where to begin."

She smiled kindly at me and laid her hand on top of mine. "At the beginning, and don't leave anything out."

Oh God, I couldn't do that. Tears threatened to overwhelm me again, but there was a knock on the door and Martha came in with a tray. I did my utmost to present myself normally until she went.

Maria poured us both a cup of hot black tea and I sighed after the first mouthful. It's amazing how soothing tea can be.

"I don't want to get Will into trouble or anything. He didn't do anything to me - really."

She raised her brows at me. "Really? That's not how it looked to me."

"He was just worried for me that's all."

She nodded. "Alright, let's leave Will out of it. I won't mention it to Robert if that's what you want."

"Oh, I do, very much so."

She nodded. "I still need to know what's wrong though. You haven't been yourself for weeks and I've been worried sick about you. Please, Margaret, you can trust me."

Tears leaked out of the corner of my eyes unbidden and I sucked in my lower lip. I had to tell her something; she wasn't going to let it go this time.

"Um. I..I'm," I said stuttering over my words. Oh my God, I can't believe how stupid I've been. I sucked in a deep breath. "I'm expecting."

"Oh," she said putting down her tea. "Oh, this complicates matters. Expecting?"

I nodded."I don't know what I'm going to do."

"Is Will the father?"

She must've seen the panic on my face at the mention of his name. I quickly glanced at her. "No," I said shaking my head. I hoped she couldn't read my face. I was never a very convincing liar.

"Well I'm glad about that," she said looking at me intently. "We'll work something out. You can stay here, at least until you baby's born, then we might have to work something out."

"Stay here? Everyone will know soon enough Maria, I can't stay here."

"Nonsense, of course, you can," she said waving her hand at me. "It might just be a little difficult once your baby comes. Perhaps you should consider going home?"

"I can't do that," I said aghast at the idea. "I'm utterly ruined."

"They don't need to know that," she said sipping her tea. "You could lie about that. Tell them your husband died or something."

"I can't believe you, Maria," I said staring at her.. "Anyway, I should've mentioned that in my last letter to my mother." I leaned over and I kissed her cheek. "Thank you. I can't believe how kind and understanding you are."

She smiled at me and sighed. "I'm a Reverend's wife, it's my job to be kind. And anyway, you and I are friends. I'll do whatever I can for you, Margaret."

Chapter Fifteen

The Crown Inn

I packed my bag with sorrow and a heavy heart. I couldn't believe how happy I'd been here at Ardmore House. I'd actually been happier than I'd ever been in my life. I sighed as I packed the last of my belongings that would fit in the carpetbag. I'd have to leave most of my clothes behind but I couldn't do much else.

Maria had told the Reverend of my situation and then they'd argued. I'd heard them on more than one occasion and I couldn't allow Maria to continue to defend me. I ran my hand over my growing stomach and sucked in my bottom lip. I was on my own. I really hadn't planned this very well; I had no real clue as to where I was going to go or what I was going to do. All I knew was that I had to leave the rectory. I couldn't allow Maria to continue to argue with her husband over me.

"Don't worry little one," I said rubbing my stomach. "I promise I'll protect you."

I took one last look around before picking up my bag and violin case. I couldn't leave that behind. Tears threatened to overwhelm me but I swallowed them as I made my way downstairs. It was early in the morning, and while most of the house was already up they would be in the kitchen. I hurried down the hall to the front door and quietly opened it.

I heaved a sigh as I stepped outside and closed it behind me. It was misty raining and I pulled the hood of my cloak over my head as I started down the driveway. At least I'd managed to save some money over the past few months, and I'd have enough to pay for lodgings for a few nights. From there, well I didn't know what I'd do after that.

It was only a short walk to Main Street where there were several Inn's situated quite close to one another. There were three to choose from, but I was quite undecided. I wandered up and down Main Street for at an hour while I tried to decide. In the end, I settled on the Crown Inn which was situated on the corner.

It was a double-storey stuccoed Georgian style building, and I hoped I'd be able to get a modest room that wouldn't cost too much. I opened the heavy oak door which set off a little tinkling bell which was obviously there to alert the Innkeeper that a customer had arrived. The hallway looked a little shabby with a threadbare runner and some rather dreary wallpaper on the walls. I'd only taken a couple of steps down the hall when a middle-aged woman came hurrying towards me.

"Good morning lovey," she said looking me up and down with a critical eye. "how can we help ye then?"

"I'm looking for a room for a couple of nights."

"Are ye now? Well, come this way then."

Turning on her heel she led me along the hall to the stairs and up to the second floor. It was even shabbier than the hallway, but as long as the room was relatively clean I didn't mind. She stopped outside one of the rooms and unlocked the door. I went inside. It was small and cramped with a bed shoved against one wall and a chair. A washstand with a jug and washbowl took up the rest of the available space. The quilt on the bed looked worn and faded, but at least it appeared to be clean. I glanced around the gloomy interior; the only light coming in was through a dirty narrow window.

"Well what do ye think?" she said eyeing me with some suspicion.

"It'll do just fine," I said smiling at her. "Thank you."

"Right well that'll be two shillings an' ye'll need to pay now," she said holding out her palm.

I sucked in a breath and reached into my bag and withdrew my purse. I found two shillings and handed them to her. She looked from me to the money and then she gave me a toothless smile and handed me the room key.

"I'm Mrs Kent. Ye'll find the ladies ordinary down the back near the kitchen," she said going to the door. She paused and turned back to face me. "Does I know ye from somewhere? What's ye name lovey?"

"Margaret. Margaret Chambers."

She shook her head. "No, the name don't ring a bell. Ye sure is familiar though."

I had no intention of enlightening the suspicious Mrs Kent. News of my departure from the rectory would no doubt be all around Norfolk Plains in no time. But, I wanted to be far away from here before anyone found me. And by anyone, I meant Will. An anxious flutter went through me at the thought of him, and I swallowed.

Mrs Kent gave me one last look before leaving and shutting the door firmly behind her. I heaved a sigh of relief at her departure and dropped my bag and case on the floor. It was a dreary room with very little in the way of comfort, but I wouldn't be here long. As soon as I could arrange some transportation I'd be gone. Where?

Well, I had no real idea as yet. I sat on the one and only chair and my tears came unbidden. I'd been such a fool and made such a mess of things. Now, I had no idea how I was going to take care of myself, let alone my baby. I ran my hand over my stomach and pressed my lips together. Well, I wasn't going to solve my problems by sitting here and crying.

I wiped my tears away and got to my feet. I grabbed my purse and put it in the pocket of my cloak before stepping out into the hallway. I locked the door behind me and proceeded downstairs. I went out the front door and looked up and down the street. There must be a coach service somewhere in town. Of course, I'd never needed a public coach service before. I'd always gone with Maria or the Reverend in their cart. I started down the street with no real idea of where to go.

I was near the blacksmiths when I saw a familiar figure walking down the street towards me. My heart leapt and a quiver ran through my stomach. I sucked in a deep breath and ducked into the smithies. I didn't immediately notice the blacksmith until he poked his head up from behind a carriage.

"Oi won't be but a minute."

I was momentarily startled but managed to contain myself. "Oh..um..take your time."

I wasn't sure if John had seen me or not, and I dared not peer out the doorway to see if he was coming. I wandered over to the carriage and leant on the wheel. I sighed as I wondered how long I'd have to hide in here. I didn't have to wonder for long – John came into the smithy's and glanced around. His face registered with recognition when he saw me.

"I thought that was ye, Margaret. What are ye doin' here?"

"Oh, hello John," I said in what I hoped was a casual tone. "I'm just running a few errands for Mrs Davies."

"Oh," he said and he smiled at me. "Ye best see to the lady first Joe. I can wait."

Joe the smithy poked his head up again. "Oi won't be long." He grinned at me before disappearing again.

I smiled at John and hoped my face wasn't giving away how I was feeling. My heart was racing and I sucked in a breath to try and calm myself. I had no errands to run and I couldn't very well order up some candlesticks or whatever for Maria. I swallowed and wandered over to Joe's workbench.

"You know, I'll think I'll come back later. I've got more errands to run."

"Alright," came the muffled reply from Joe. "Sorry 'bout that."

"See you later John."

He nodded and I went out of the door. I heaved a sigh of relief as I walked down the street. That had been a close call, but I still didn't know where I was going to get a coach to Launceston. I wandered up and down the street looking for any signs of a coach service. I saw none. It was dinner time before I went back to the Crown Inn feeling rather dejected.

Mrs Kent's cook gave me a bowl of soup which was watery and lacking any flavour. I ate it because I was hungry, but I yearned for some of Martha's home cooking.

"Is everything alright lovey?" asked Mrs Kent as she came bustling into the ordinary.

"Yes thank you," I said smiling at her. "Oh, actually, Mrs Kent do you know if there's a coach to Launceston?"

"Oh aye," she said taking my empty bowl. "It'll come Thursd'y."

"Thursday. Can you tell me where I'd be able to catch it?"

"It pulls up right across the street," she said eyeing me. "So will ye be wanting to stay another night then?"

I smiled at her. "Yes."

"Right well that'll be another shilling."

"Of course," I said reaching for my purse.

I paid her before retiring to my room for the afternoon. It was such a dreary room, but I'd packed my copy of Reformation and although I wasn't really in the mood for it, I settled down to read for a few hours.

I must've fallen asleep because I awoke with a start with someone knocking on my door.

"Just a minute," I said as I leapt from the bed and wrenched open the door. "Oh, Mrs Kent. What can I do for you?"

"There's a gentleman to see ye."

"A gentleman?" I wasn't expecting visitors and could think of only one person who might have tracked me down. Will. And I wasn't sure I wanted to see him.

"Aye. He's in the ordinary," she said over her shoulder as she headed back down the hall.

I shut the door and leant against it as I sucked in a deep breath and slowly let it out. It could only be Will. He must've found out where I was somehow. Of course, running into John earlier today at the blacksmith's was the obvious answer. I ran my hand over my stomach. No, I didn't want to see him. There was nothing he could possibly say to me that would make a difference. He was married, and I was carrying his child. Damn him.

I sat down on the one and only chair and tried to not think about him. Of course, no matter how I tried my thoughts strayed to him, waiting for me downstairs. They just kept going around and around in my head until I thought I'd scream.

"No," I said out loud. "No."

I don't know how long I sat there staring at the door trying to think of anything but Will Hartley. It was getting dark when I finally rose from the chair and lit the small oil lamp. Surely he'd have given up and returned to the rectory by now.

I nearly jumped out of my skin when there was a loud knock on my door followed by a male voice whispering my name. My heart leapt and started hammering like a lunatic at the sound of Will's voice. I sucked in my bottom lip and stared at the door. What was I going to do now? If I didn't open the door he'd likely try others and disturb all the patrons. I could feel the panic starting to grip me.

"Go away," I said as I opened the door and stared into a pair of very familiar hazel eyes. "Leave me alone."

"Meg, please you must listen to me," he said forcing his way passed me. "I'm not leaving until you hear me out."

I glanced up and down the hallway, which much to my relief was deserted. I'd half expected Mrs Kent to be on his heels, and wondered how he'd managed to get up here without her noticing. I shut the door and turned to face him.

"Alright. You're obviously not going to go away, so say what you came to say and then leave."

He sat on the bed and indicated for me to sit in the chair which I'd not long ago vacated. I sighed as I sat down. Just being near him was making it difficult for me to think straight. I'd missed him the last few days, but I wouldn't allow him to treat me like a fool again. I steeled myself to send him away.

"You're right to be angry about finding out I'm married," he said looking me straight in the eye. "I should've told you about Fanny, but truly she means nothing."

"That's not really the point though is it? You're already married so you can't possibly marry me. Your promises were empty words, Will, nothing more."

"No, they weren't. I meant every word, and I'll marry you," he said earnestly and he got off the bed and knelt in front of me. "You see when I married Fanny I was

William Penny. Now I'm William Hartley. They don't know I'm married and so there's no reason I can't get permission to marry you."

I stared at him while several thoughts raced through my head. He was right. William Hartley wasn't married. Tears prickled the back of my eyes and I sucked in a breath to try and make them go away.

"I love you, Meg, and you're my wife. Truly."

"Oh, Will I love you too," I said and I fell into his arms.

I sighed as I breathed in the smell of him and felt his strong arms around me. I was home. He kissed me long and hard and my lips responded. I drank him in like I was dying of thirst. We only parted when the door to my room unceremoniously crashed open and Mrs Kent came barging in.

"I don't know what kind of establishment ye think I'm running," she said staring horrified at us. "Get ye things an' get out."

I pushed Will aside and jumped to my feet. "It's not at all what you think, Mrs Kent. This is my husband."

"Ye must think I came down in the last shower. Get ye things an' go afore I call for the constable."

"You must believe my wife. You can't kick her out," said Will getting off his knees and facing the formidable Mrs Kent.

She glared from him to me and back again. "I run a respectable establishment, an' I know exactly what this is," she said before turning to me. "I want ye out of my house...now."

I burst into tears and fumbled around on the bed for my book and shawl which I'd tossed on there earlier. With shaking hands, I shoved them into my bag. Will grabbed me and gently pushed me aside and finished packing for me. I was trembling from head to foot. What was I going to do now? It was already dark outside and I had no idea where I was going to go. I couldn't stop the tears from running down my face as we left the Crown Inn.

Chapter Sixteen

The Gardener's Hut

It was getting dark and cold and I pulled my cloak around myself as we stepped out of the Crown Inn. Will handed me my violin case and then grabbing my hand started to cross the road. I wondered where he thought he was taking me. As soon as we were on the other side I pulled my hand free.

"Where are you taking me?" I said as I wiped the tears from my face.

"Where do you think? Back to the rectory."

"I can't go back there," I said shaking my head. Not that he could probably see me very well in the fading light.

"What do you mean you can't go back there?" he said. I could hear the astonishment in his voice. "I know you ran away because of me, but there's no need. I love you and I want to marry you."

"I didn't leave because of you." I groaned as I realised I hadn't told him I was expecting his baby, or that I'd told Maria and that's why I'd left this morning. God, was that only this morning? Even in the dim light, I could see the puzzlement on his face. I sighed. This wasn't how I'd imagined it would be when I told him I was having his baby – not at all. Standing on the street in the cold with nowhere to go - once again I'd made such a mess of things. "I'm...I'm having your baby, and Maria knows. She and the Reverend have been arguing about me and that's why I left."

"What?" he said clearly confused. "You're having my baby? Oh my God, Meg." He dropped my bag and swept me into his arms. He hugged me so tight I thought I'd pass out from lack of oxygen. "I can't believe it. I thought you'd left because you were so mad with me over Fanny." He released me from his bear hug but kept a hold of me. I was glad he did otherwise I might have fallen over. "I can't tell you how happy you've made me. I love you so much. A baby?"

"Yes..well I'm glad you're happy about it, but that still leaves me with nowhere to go." Tears threatened again and I swallowed as I tried to gather my thoughts. What was I going to do?

He pulled me into another hug, but this time much gentler and rubbed his hand up and down my back. "I know of someone that will take care of you, but he lives in Perth. I'll take you there tomorrow," he said. "Tonight you'll have to sleep in the loft. Come on."

He picked up my bag and still with his arm around me we started down the road towards the rectory. I was so glad to have his solid presence beside me as we trudged along. I wasn't alone. I was a little scared about how I was going to take care of myself, but as long as I had Will I knew I'd be alright. We walked up the driveway to Ardmore House and keeping to the shadows made our way around the back of the house. All was quiet as we crept into the stables and climbed up into the familiar loft.

The smell of hay and horses somehow calmed my frayed nerves. I sighed as Will fossicked around in the dark to light a lantern. A faint glow erupted moments later and I settled down on the old blanket on the floor. A minute later Will joined me after checking that all was quiet below in the stable.

He wrapped his arms around me and just held me close. I sighed and melted into him. Whatever was going to happen tomorrow could wait until the morning. For the moment I just wanted to forget about everything except for the man whose heart was thumping steadily under my hand. He brushed his hand through my hair, pushing several stray tendrils aside and began placing little kisses over my neck and face.

"I love you, Meg," he whispered before putting his lips on mine.

The kiss was long and slow and I held his face in my hands. He undid my cloak and I shrugged out of it leaving it in a pool between us. We kissed again and I moaned as he ran his hands under my skirt and pushed my chemise aside. Our lovemaking was slow and languid and later I lay wrapped in the warmth of his arms. I felt safe and loved as I snuggled into him.

I don't know what time it was when he crept from the loft and returned to the men's quarters. I missed his warm solid presence and wrapped my cloak around me as I tried to return to blissful sleep. It was nearly dawn before I finally slipped back into oblivion. I dreamt I was a prostitute in London at a bawdy brothel. The Madam was a large vulgar woman who had accused me of not paying her enough of my earnings. Her two henchmen had a hold of me and were about to throw me out into the street when I woke up with a fright.

"It's me," said Will giving me a slight shake.

"Oh, I was having a very odd dream," I said sitting up and peering at him.

"I've brought you some breakfast," he said handing me a piece of bread with a chunk of cheese. "I'm sorry it's not much, tis all I could get without being noticed."

"That's alright," I said. I was starving and in no time had devoured his breakfast offering. A cup of tea would've been wonderful, but completely out of the question.

"John's got to take the cart down to the blacksmith's today, and he said he'd give us a ride to Perth first," he said folding the old blanket and tucking it under his arm. "Sam said he'd cover for me while I take you."

"Does he know you're taking me to Perth?" I was alarmed.

"Well, yes. Don't worry. Come on, I told John to meet us down the road a bit."

I wrapped my cloak around myself and climbed down the ladder. We crept out of the stables and made our way to the road. It was a cool morning with a bit of drizzling rain, but I was glad of it. No one would likely see us leaving. We met John about half a mile down the road where he was waiting for us. Will tossed my bag and violin into the back of the cart and then helped me up. It was only about three miles to the small village of Perth, but I was anxious that someone would notice us in the Reverend's cart.

John looked nervously about as Will jumped up onto the seat beside him. He gave me a grim look before urging the horses into a trot. I wondered why John was helping us. He didn't look entirely happy about the arrangement, and I couldn't help but think it was the camaraderie among convicts that had compelled him to come to our aid. I settled back in the seat and tried not to think about what lay ahead, or who this mystery person was that Will thought would take me in. I sighed. I could think of nothing else.

Half an hour later we crossed the bridge across the South Esk River and arrived in the small hamlet of Perth. It really was nothing more than a cluster of a few simple buildings and a handful of houses. There were no substantial buildings built of stone or brick, but there was a Hotel and a General Store. Beside that was a drapers and a bakery by the looks of it.

John turned down a side street towards the river and came to a halt outside a rather squat looking timber house. It had a gable up one end, but the rest of it was single storey with one window in the front and a narrow porch over the front door. The front garden was tidy with a couple of gum trees and shrubs to one side. Will leapt down and helped me before getting my bag and violin case.

"I'll just be a few minutes while I get Meg settled," he said to John, who was looking around with an uneasy look on his face.

"This is Captain Cheyne's place ain't it?" he said turning in the seat to look at Will.

"Aye," said Will taking me by the arm. "I couldn't think of anyone else that might take her in."

John nodded and smiled at me for the first time. "Aye, he'll likely take ye in. Don't dally though, I need to get back."

Will nodded. "I'll be as quick as I can."

We went up to the front door and Will knocked. We waited. I could hear shuffling noises coming from inside and a minute later a muffled voice came from inside.

"Who is it?"

"Will Hartley. Is the Captain at home?"

"No," came the reply before the door opened just enough for them to peer out at us.

He was obviously a convict by his attire, and he looked us both up and down. "What do ye want?"

"I need to speak with the Captain," said Will. I could hear the anxiety in his voice as he tried to look beyond the man. "This is Margaret, she needs somewhere to stay."

He opened the door a little wider and poked his head out to look at me. I smiled and said hello. He was an odd little man with his blonde hair smoothed back into a ponytail. His alert brown eyes, however, seemed to take in everything, and they rested on my stomach for too long. I felt like I was being inspected and instinctively pulled my cloak around myself. Finally, he glanced at my face and grimaced.

"Aye, well I 'spect the Captain will take 'er in," he said at last.

"Good, well you can let her in then," said Will getting impatient.

"Not in the house," he said pulling the door nearly closed again. "The gardener's hut's empty, she can stay there til the Captain gets back, then he can decide."

"And when will he be back?" asked Will.

"I don't know. He's gone to Campbelltown, an' he'll be a couple of weeks I 'spect."

He shut the door with a thump and I heard the key grate in the lock. I looked at Will, who I thought was about to hammer on the door again. I put my hand on his arm.

"It's alright. The gardener's hut will do."

"I'm sorry," he said picking up my bag and heading off towards the rear yard.

"I know the Captain, he would've let you in and taken care of you. I'm sorry you'll have to wait until he gets back."

"Please don't worry, Will. Without you, I'd have nowhere to go."

We went around to the surprisingly large back yard. There was a well established vegetable garden and a small orchard. A washhouse and clothesline took up one side and a small shed was opposite. Down near the back of the yard was a small slab hut. Will opened the door and we went inside. It was just one room with a small fireplace and some simple furniture. A bed was shoved against one wall and a small table and chair were beside the hearth. It was dusty and smelled of mildew and damp, but it would do.

Will put my bag and case down and tossed the old blanket on the bed. I saw him glance around the room and wrinkle his nose in distaste.

"I'm so sorry," he said taking me into his arms. "I want so much better for you and our child."

I hugged him close and breathed him in before letting him go. "It's alright," I said before taking his face in my hands and kissing him. "It will do."

"I'll be back as soon as I can," he said going to the door. "I've got to go, John's waiting...take care, Meg."

I nodded. "I'll be just fine."

As soon as he left I closed the door and leant against it as I surveyed my new home. No matter how temporary it might be, I was going to be living here for the next couple of weeks. In the last few months, I'd learned a thing or two about cleaning, and decided that would be my first task. I'd give the place a good scrub and then it might feel better, and so might I.

Chapter Seventeen

The Gardener's Hut

It was getting dark by the time I finished scrubbing the hut as best I could. It still smelled of damp and mildew, but it would do. I was just thinking about what I might find for my supper when I heard footsteps outside the door. I opened it just as the odd little man from the house was about to thump on it – he very nearly hit me instead.

"I brought ye some supper," he said handing me a bowl of steaming stew and a piece of dry bread. "Mind it's 'ot an' Swabby might have put in too much pepper. He's a bugger for that."

"Thank you," I said taking the stew from him and breathing in the aroma. It smelled delicious. "Please thank Swabby for me."

"Aye."

He'd already turned to go when I realised I still didn't know his name. "Oh, I didn't catch your name earlier."

"Tom," he called over his shoulder.

I watched him walk back up to the house before I closed the door and settled down to eat my supper. It was delicious and I made mental a note to thank the mysterious Swabby in person if I ever got to meet him. I was sopping up the last of the gravy when the door opened and Will filled the doorway. I hadn't expected to see him again today – but I was delighted.

I put the bowl down and buried myself in his open arms. "What are you doing back here?" I said letting him go.

"I told you I'd be back," he said before giving me a quick kiss and coming into the hut and dropping a sack on the table. "I've brought you some supplies, at least enough for a few days. I see you've had supper," he said indicating to the now-empty bowl on the table.

"Yes, Tom brought it down for me. Where did you get all of this?" I said as I opened the sack and peered in. There was bread and cheese along with what looked like a heel of mutton. I removed a small sack of oats and some tea. Oh, thank goodness he'd thought to bring some tea. At the bottom of the sack were two sweet bucks along with an onion.

He grinned at me. "I don't expect you want to know where I got it."

"Oh Will, did you steal all of this?" I knew he had. He had no money and he couldn't possibly have got it from anywhere other than the rectory. "Martha will miss all of this." A part of me was shocked at his audacity, while the other half of me was grateful he'd done it.

He shrugged. "Nah she won't notice. I dug the sweet bucks myself and there was plenty in the larder."

I hugged him and kissed his cheek. "Thank you."

"Well I can't have you and our baby starve now, can I?" he said wrapping his arms around me. "I can't stay though. I'll come back tomorrow night and stay with you."

"Perhaps you shouldn't. I don't want you getting caught out when you shouldn't be," I said pulling out of his embrace. A pang of fear went through me at the thought. "Please don't, I'll be alright."

He smiled down at me and then his lips were on mine and I pressed myself against his lean body. My lips tingled and I boldly ran my tongue along the inside of his upper lip. When our lips finally parted he pulled me closer and hugged me tight.

"I can't wait until tomorrow," he said as he nuzzled my ear and kissed my neck. I felt him gently push me towards the bed. My body ached for his touch, but my mind was not so ready to throw caution to the wind.

"No," I said pushing him from me and gasping for breath. "You can't stay, you'll be missed."

He reached for me again but my resolve held and I pushed him from me. "What will happen if you're caught and sent away? It's too risky."

He groaned. I could still see the desire burning in his eyes, but he dropped his arms and stepped away from me. He nodded and sucked in a deep breath and slowly let it out. "I cannot wait until we can be together proper," he said as he opened the door. "I love you, Meg," he said turning towards me. "I'll come back as soon as I can."

"Be careful. And please don't come back tomorrow night," I said. "Not because I don't want you to, but because I don't want you to get caught. Please."

"Alright," he said nodding. "Until Thursday then?"

I smiled with relief. "Until Thursday."

And he was gone. Closing the door softly behind him he headed off back to Norfolk Plains, and I crumpled in a heap on the only chair I had. My own desires were still burning and my whole body felt like a quivering jelly. I sighed and smiled. Here I was expecting my first child and living in a gardeners hut at the bottom of someone else's yard. My life was so uncertain and I had no way of supporting myself, and yet, I couldn't recall ever feeling so content.

I hardly recognise myself as Miss Margaret of Bredgar House – and there it was, the tight spot in my heart. A pang of sadness gripped me as I thought of my mother and my dear sisters. The sadness was quickly replaced by a feeling of guilt that I'd left poor Barb to face my father after my abrupt departure. I swallowed and pressed my lips together. Poor Barb.

Bredgar House, Kent

Barb took in a deep breath as the carriage turned up the driveway to Bredgar House. She'd been dreading this day and shuddered at the thought of facing her father. Margaret had sailed on Saturday and she'd deliberately waited until today before telling her father. She hoped that after four days the William Metcalf would be so far out to sea there would be nothing anyone could do to stop it.

The carriage came to halt out the front of the house and Barb pressed her lips together and sighed. A flutter of nervousness went through her as the door opened. She stepped out into the chill autumn air and straightened herself to her full height. Barton, her father's butler was already standing by the open front door and she greeted him cordially as she entered.

"Please take the boxes and parcels up to Miss Margaret's room,' she said removing her gloves and cloak. "Be careful with the largest one, it contains my sister's wedding gown."

"Yes Mrs Hart," said Barton taking her gloves and cloak. "Sir Samuel and Lady Chambers will receive you in the dining room."

"Thank you."

She made her way down the wide hallway, pausing to peer at herself in the hall mirror. Her oval face looked pale and pinched, and her soft grey eyes appeared large and luminous - like glassy orbs. She drew in a breath and smoothed back her dark hair before continuing down the hall. She could hear murmured voices coming from the back of the house before she reached the dining room. She went through the open door and paused at the sight of her parents. Her mother looked up and smiled as she entered.

"Barbara how lovely to see you," she said, although her eyes weren't on her daughter, rather they were scanning the hall beyond. A frown creased her brow as she finally looked at Barb. "Where's Margaret?"

"Good afternoon Mamma," said Barb placing a kiss on her mother's cheek. "Papa, you're looking well," she said greeting her father similarly.

"We're just finishing our luncheon. Won't you join us for tea?" said Samuel smiling at his daughter before going back to the newspaper which was spread before him on the table.

"Thank you," said Barb settling herself in a chair at the end of the table.

"More tea," said Lady Barbara to one of the footmen before turning her attention back to her daughter. "Now Barbara, where's Margaret?"

Barb took in a deep breath and nodded to the servant as he placed a teacup in front of her. "I'm afraid Margaret won't be joining us," she said pouring hot tea into her cup.

Her mother looked confused as she stared from her to her husband. Samuel looked up from his newspaper and frowned.

"Why not?" he asked. "Good Lord, Barbara the wedding's in two days, she can't stay in London until then."

"No Papa," said Barb taking a sip of tea. She put her cup down with a clatter as it slipped from her trembling fingers. She looked at her father whose dark eyes were boring into her. She pressed her lips together and lowered her eyes. "Um, well."

Samuel pushed his newspaper aside and leaned forward as he stared at his daughter. "What's going on Barbara? Where's your sister?"

She sucked in a deep breath and slowly let it out. "She sailed on Saturday."

Samuel stared at her for a moment before her words registered. "Sailed on Saturday? What the devil are you talking about?"

"She boarded a ship and she's run away."

He swallowed and stared at her. "And you helped her?"

Samuel's accusing stare bore into her and she turned her gaze from him. "Yes."

Her father appeared to be struggling to process this information. He clenched his jaw and rubbed his fingers through his hair until it was standing on end. He glared at his daughter. "You have no idea what you've done! You've ruined us." He leapt from his chair and marched out of the dining room bellowing orders. "Barton, pack my bag we're to London."

Barb watched him leave and heaved a sigh. Good God, what did he mean they were ruined? Her mother's quick intake of breath caught her attention and she quickly turned back to her. Her grey head was bowed and her hands were covering her face as she let out a sob.

"Mamma?" Barbara got to her feet and went to her. She sat beside her and reached out to offer some comfort. "What did Papa mean?"

Barbara continued to sob for a few moments before finally raising her head and dabbing her eyes with a kerchief. She looked imploringly at her daughter. "Has Margaret truly runaway?"

"Yes Mamma," said Barb and she blew out her breath. "She couldn't face marrying Sir Owens and so she's gone to Van Diemen's Land."

"You can't be serious?" said Barbara looking aghast. "That's nothing but a penal colony."

"Well yes," said Barb with a shrug of her shoulders.

Barbara groaned and looked at her daughter. "Please tell me what happened."

"Well I don't think she started out intending to run away," said Barb taking a deep breath. "It all happened on her first visit to get fitted for her wedding gown. We were talking about Uncle James and I showed her the piece in the paper about him being sent to Bedlam. On the same page was a small advertisement offering free passage to Van Diemen's Land for domestics."

"Margaret wouldn't know how to be a servant," said Barbara staring at her daughter. "Anyway surely they wanted some sort of recommendation. I know I would."

"Well yes," said Barb nodding and pressing her lips together. "I wrote her a glowing reference which the immigration people accepted and that was that."

"That was that," said Barbara again staring incredulously at her daughter. "And you thought this was a good idea?"

"Well no Mamma of course not, but you know Margaret, she wouldn't be swayed," said Barb reaching for her cup of tea. "Anyway, I don't blame her. Sir Richard Owens of all people Mamma. Why would you agree to such a match? He's hideous."

Barbara flushed and turned her gaze from Barb's accusing stare. "I had no choice in the matter."

"So it was Papa's idea?"

Barbara delayed by pouring herself another cup of tea and taking a sip. "It was, but I can't let him take all the blame," she said casting a sideways glance at her daughter. "When he put it to me that Margaret should marry Sir Owens, I agreed. But we had no choice, Barbara. It was either that or face financial ruin." She put down her cup and groaned. "It would seem we're ruined anyway."

"How Mamma? Please what's going on?"

"It's a complicated story that I don't fully understand. What I do know is it's all got to do with your father's partnership with James," she said with a sigh.

"Alright, but what has that got to do with Margaret marrying Sir Owen? Please Mamma, maybe I can help."

"I don't think so," she said with a grimace. She reached out and patted Barb's arm. "But I thank you for the offer."

Barb knew her mother. If she was patient she'd tell her everything, although it would require some prodding. She smiled and waited.

"You remember Uncle James was declared bankrupt last year?"

"Yes."

"Well, because your father was his partner and his named heir, his debtors succeeded in claiming against him. Your Uncle Abraham did his best to untangle their affairs and he almost succeeded, but then your Uncle James was declared a lunatic."

Barb took a sip of tea and tried to follow how any of this could've ended with Margaret married to the odious Sir Owens. "And that somehow changed things?"

"Well yes of course it did," said Barbara exasperated at Barb's inability to see the obvious. She put her cup down with a loud clatter. "That made your father completely responsible. Not only for his debts but his upkeep as well. It was a nightmare. We sold off stocks and such and let a number of servants go, but we couldn't raise enough money to pay for everything."

"How much do you need? I'm sure John and I could pay some of this, and Charlotte and Osborn would surely help as well."

Barbara shook her head and waved her hand at her dismissively. "No. If it were only a few hundred pounds perhaps everyone could put in some money. I'm afraid your Uncle James has made a number of very bad business deals. He owes thousands."

"Oh," said Barb dismayed at the news. "So I gather Sir Owens was going to pay handsomely for Margaret to become his wife?"

"Well yes. Although when you say it like that it sounds like we were selling her off to the highest bidder. I assure it wasn't like that at all."

"Really Mamma?" Barb doubted her mother's sincerity.

Barbara covered her face with her hands for a moment and took in a deep breath. "It was a business arrangement," she said finally dropping her hands to her chin and looking at Barb. Her eyes were swimming in unshed tears as she searched Barb's face for some understanding. "I swear we had no choice."

"No choice but to force Margaret into a loveless marriage with a man old enough to be her grandsire?" said Barb affronted at her mother's ability to convince herself she had no other option.

"Well it doesn't matter now does it? Margaret's runaway and I expect it'll be debtor's prison for your father," she said in a shrill voice.

"Oh my God," said Barb sucking in her breath. Of course, there would be no money forthcoming now, and she shuddered at the thought of her father in prison. How could he survive in such a place? It would surely kill him. "Did Margaret know any of this?"

"Your father told her why we needed her to marry, but I expect she understood even less than me." The tears that had been threatening finally came, and she sobbed into her hands. "We're ruined, and I don't know what I'm going to do."

Barb wrapped her arms around her mother and allowed her to sob into her shoulder. What a mess. Although she refused to feel guilty for her part in helping

Margaret escape. It was disgusting that her father had tried to use Margaret in such a way. No, even if he did end up in debtor's prison. She shuddered and swallowed. God, she hoped it wouldn't come to that.

Chapter Eighteen

Perth, November 1837

Over the next few weeks, I settled into life in the hut at the bottom of Captain Cheyne's garden. Will came every other night with supplies and to check on me, and I spent my days trying to prepare for my impending motherhood. Captain Cheyne had still not returned from Campbelltown, but Tom had proven to be an immense help.

I soon discovered he'd once been a well-respected tailor in London. He'd just completed a new jacket for the Captain, and he offered his services to me. I immediately jumped at the opportunity to ask for his help in preparing a layette for my baby.

"Aye, have ye got an old petticoat ye don't need? I could cut that down into nightgowns an' such."

"Yes," I said immediately thinking of my woollen one. Winter was over and I'd get another one for next year. "I'll go fetch it." I turned and started down the path to my hut.

"Aye, an' you'll need flannel for clouts an' such," he called after me.

I turned and nodded before hurrying on down the path to the hut. I wondered how he knew so much about what babies might need. We were not so well acquainted that I could ask him, but I wondered if he had a family back in England; one that he would likely never see again. I didn't want to think about it – I was no different, and would likely never see my family again either.

I pushed all thoughts of family aside as I went inside the hut and pulled my bag out from under the bed. I was sorry I'd been forced to leave so many of my things at the rectory, but I was happy to sacrifice a couple of undergarments. I found my woollen petticoat at the bottom of the bag and also a well-worn flannel one. I held it in my hand and ran my fingers over the soft fabric. It would leave me short but it couldn't be helped, my baby's needs were far greater than my own. I shoved the bag back and went back up to the washhouse where Tom was waiting for me.

I handed the two petticoats to him and waited while he inspected them. I hoped they'd be suitable.

"Where did ye get this?" he asked looking at me quizzically as he ran the woollen fabric between his fingers. "This be quality an' expensive."

"Oh, I had it made in London," I said trying to sound as offhand as I could. "Will it be suitable for nightgowns do you think?"

"Aye, but this is fine wool, Margaret. How could ye afford such a thing? Did ye steal it? I don't mind if ye did, I won't tell."

I sucked in my lip as I wondered what to tell him. I needed his help, and I didn't want to offend him. Would he be more inclined to help if he thought I was like him? I didn't know, and his alert brown eyes weren't giving anything away. I sighed and decided it was time for some honesty.

"No, I didn't steal it," I said at last. "My father's the High Sheriff of Kent, and my mother was Lady Barbara Roper. I ran away to escape a horrid arranged marriage."

He gawked at me for a full minute. "You're a lady?"

"No. Please Tom I really need your help. I left all of that behind me when I ran away, and now I'm just plain Margaret."

"Plain Margaret?"

"Yes," I said smiling at him in what I hoped was a friendly way that would put him at ease. I'm not at all sure I succeeded.

"Ye do talk mighty fine," he said giving me a sideways glance.

He was clearly not too sure what to make of my claims, but I didn't care so long as he helped me. "All of that means nothing to me anymore."

"Ye serious then?" he said with shrug. "I ain't never met a lady afore."

"I can assure I'm nothing special."

"Well alrighty then," he said finally smiling at me. "I'll get to work."

Two days later he presented me with several baby nightgowns all cut out ready to sew. He'd cut lengths of my flannel petticoat to be used as clouts; all I had to do was finish the raw edges. I can't imagine what my poor baby would've been wearing without his help.

I paused, my needle halfway in the small nightgown I was stitching, and listened. I thought I heard footsteps approaching but I wasn't expecting Will at this hour. I put my sewing aside and was just getting up from my chair when there was a loud knock on the door. It rather took me by surprise and I jumped at the sound.

"Who is it?"

"Sorry ter disturb yer lass, it's me, Captain Cheyne."

I quickly smoothed my skirt and took in a deep breath before opening the door. I smiled widely and gave a little bow. "Captain Cheyne delighted to make your acquaintance at last."

Captain Cheyne smiled warmly back at me, his blue eyes appearing to take me in all in one glance. He was tall and must've been a handsome man in his young days. Even now, he would command a second look with his steel-grey hair and broad shoulders.

"Aye, likewise," he said in an unmistakable Scottish accent. "I ken yer needing someplace to stay?"

"Yes. I do hope you don't mind Tom letting me stay here."

"No of course not," he said, but I thought there was some reservation behind his words.

"I won't be any trouble to you Captain. My husband's been taking care of me, and I just need a roof over my head."

He nodded and rubbed his fingers through his whiskers. "Aye, there's the thing. It's not proper for a lass such as yer ter be living at the bottom of my garden, now is it?"

"Will's not got a ticket yet, and I've got no way of paying rent anywhere," I said almost pleading with him. "I promise not to be a bother."

"Och it's not that lass. I'd gladly have yer stay, but with Swabby, Tom and me, well people will talk yer ken. It's not proper."

I really didn't think anyone would even notice I was here. I kept to myself and never went anywhere. To be honest there was only the General Store which didn't have much to offer anyway. I sucked in my bottom lip and took a deep breath.

"If you're worried about my reputation, well you needn't be," I said rather boldly. "It's utterly ruined and I doubt anything could make it any worse."

To my surprise, he chuckled in a rich and musical tone. I couldn't help but smile and my shoulders relaxed a little. I didn't think I'd misread him, he was concerned for my reputation. I thought he should be more concerned about his own.

"Och lass, ye've clearly not met the town gossips yet. Yer may not think yer reputation can be further ruined, but I assure yer it can," he said still grinning at me. "I tell yer what," he said running his fingers through his whiskers again. "Yer can stay. I would not see yer in the street, but we'll be telling anyone who wants ter listen that yer my niece."

"Your niece?" I said rather surprised at his suggestion. "Surely that would ruin your reputation to have such an association with me? I couldn't have that on my head."

"Nonsense lass. My reputation doesna matter a fig," he said scoffing. "I dare say folks around here might think more of me for taking my poor widowed niece into my house. Especially as she's expecting a bairn and all."

My first impression of him had been right. At first glance, he'd taken all of me in, and hadn't missed my growing belly. I liked him immediately and felt like I'd known him my whole life. I couldn't help but smile and relax in his company.

"Thank you. I can't tell you how much I appreciate you letting me stay. I only hope you won't regret associating yourself with me like that," I said heaving a sigh. "So should I introduce myself as Mrs Cheyne?"

The name sounded strange to my tongue, and I wondered what Will would think of it. Well, it had been his idea to bring me to Captain Cheyne's in the first place, so I expect he'll just have to be fine with the arrangement. I certainly hoped so.

"Aye, Mrs Cheyne will do fine," he said looking at me thoughtfully. "We'll say you're the widow of my nephew George, newly arrived from Western Australia. That ought ter keep the busybodies quiet."

"Alright, I think I can remember that."

"Good," he said turning to leave. "Oh, one more thing." He turned back to face me and peered into the hut. "Yer canna stay here in my gardener's hut, that wouldna be right. Ye'll have ter move into the house."

"What? With Tom and Swabby?"

"Och no lass. They'll have ter move into the hut in the meantime."

I didn't like the sound of that. Not that I was concerned about being alone with the Captain, but I didn't want to be the cause of Tom and Swabby having to move into the cramped hut. I'd formed a bit of an odd rapport with Tom and I knew him well enough to know he wouldn't take kindly to being usurped by me.

I shook my head. "Perhaps it would be best if I stayed in the hut. It's far too small in here for Tom and Swabby."

He looked from me to the hut and frowned and ran his fingers through his whiskers. "Alright, yer can stay here for now. But, if anyone comes visiting get yerself up to the house and pretend like yer lives there with me."

"Alright," I said smiling to myself. He seemed rather over concerned about what people thought. I used to be like that once, but since coming to Van Diemen's Land I'd thrown all that out the window. What with lying and running away, and now expecting my first baby, and not exactly married. I hardly recognise myself as Miss Margaret of Bredgar House.

He gave me a satisfied smile before turning on his heel and heading up the garden path. I watched him go before going back to my sewing. I was relieved that I'd finally met the Captain and he'd given his permission for me to stay.

Since arriving I'd been feeling very uncertain about my circumstances, but finally, I felt settled again. I dearly wanted to see Maria and explain my reason for leaving without so much as a goodbye. A pang of guilt went through me at the thought. I hadn't even thanked her for all her kindness.

I sighed as I pushed the needle through the fabric. I would go tomorrow and see her except I didn't want to draw attention to either myself or Will. I'd lied to her about him, and it had settled uneasily in the pit of my stomach. I would go and see her and explain, I just didn't know when.

Chapter Nineteen

Perth, February 1838

Life for me had settled into a very comfortable rhythm. I couldn't remember ever feeling more content than I did right now. If only Will had his ticket and we were able to be together, then life would be perfect. We needed to be extra careful though. Will had been missed on a couple of occasions because he was with me all night. Last time he was caught missing the Reverend had admonished him, but he'd managed to convince him he'd been in the privy.

I rolled over and snuggled closer and breathed in the male scent of him. Dawn would be upon us soon and he'd have to go and I wanted to savour every moment. I gasped as I felt a flutter in my abdomen. I'd been feeling them for a few days and thought it was my baby. I lay very still and waited. A few minutes later it happened again and I couldn't help but smile and run my hand over my growing belly. How perfect life would be if it could just stay as it was right now?

Will moved beside me and I groaned and threw my arm across his chest.

"Not yet," I said pressing myself against him.

I felt his chest rumble as he laughed softly, and then I was in his arms and he was kissing me. I drank him in and ran my fingers through his hair. I was breathless when we finally parted.

"I'd love to stay, but I have to get back," he said letting me go and easing himself from the bed.

He was naked and I admired his lean muscular form in the early morning light. He was such a good looking man and I felt my cheeks warm as I watched him dress.

"When will I see you again?" I asked leaning on one elbow and tilting my face towards him.

He obliged me by leaning down and softly kissing my pouting lips. "Not tomorrow. Maybe Friday."

"What do you mean maybe? I'll expect you Friday evening," I said with a slight petulant ring to my voice. I was teasing, I knew he'd come when he could.

He grinned at me as he fastened his breeches. "Will you miss me then?"

"You know I will," I said turning serious. "Please be careful."

"I will. You take care of yourself and the babe," he said blowing me a kiss before disappearing through the open door.

I lay back down and snuggled under the covers. They smelled of him and of our lovemaking, and I drifted back into a dreamless slumber.

Friday came and went and there was no sign of Will. I knew he'd come when he could safely get away, and I just hoped it would be soon. I had enough food to last me a couple of days without having to ask Captain Cheyne for provisions, but I was starting to worry about him.

I picked up my sewing and tried to put all thoughts of him from my mind. I'd already completed several nightgowns and jackets for my baby and I was now busy hemming flannel clouts. I was so busy concentrating that it took me a moment to realise someone was knocking softly on my door.

"Who is it?" I said setting my sewing down.

"It's me, Maria."

I wrenched open the door and broke into a wide smile. She was looking rather thin but she was smiling back at me. I felt tears prick my eyes at the sight of her. I couldn't believe it was her. We fell into one another's arms and hugged each other tightly.

"Oh Margaret thank goodness I've found you," she said letting me go and holding me at arm's length. She placed a warm kiss on my cheek. "Can I come in?"

"Of course," I said stepping aside to let her inside. I looked around at the small cramped room and gestured to the chair I'd just vacated. "It's not very big. You sit on the chair," I said perching myself on the edge of the bed. "I'm so glad to see you, Maria. I can't tell you how sorry I am that I just disappeared like that, but I didn't know what else to do."

"It doesn't matter," she said dismissing my apology with a wave of her hand. "I've been worried sick about you, but I'm not here for a social visit, Margaret."

"Oh," I said staring at her with a raised brow. Now that I took a good look at her I noticed she was rather pale and drawn. "What is it then?"

"I'll get straight to the matter," she said taking a deep breath. "I suspected that William Hartley was the father of your baby even though you denied it. Please tell me if I'm wrong?"

I nodded and pressed my lips together as I wondered where this conversation might be going. "You're not wrong. I'm sorry I lied about that, but I didn't want to get him into trouble."

"I know, and believe me I understand, but you should've trusted me."

"I'm sorry, but I didn't want to cause trouble for you either. I couldn't stay and let you defend me." I couldn't change any of that and I thought she'd understand my motives.

She nodded. "Believe me I do understand, Margaret, and I'm not mad at you for doing what you thought was right. I'm not here to berate you," she said standing up. "It's William. He was caught stealing food from the larder. There was nothing I could do."

I paled as my heart started thumping hard in my chest and I sucked in a deep breath as my world tipped on its side. It was all my fault. He was only stealing food for me. Oh my God, what had I done?

"Caught?"

"Yes. Margaret, I'm so sorry. I had to threaten John to find out where you were, and I came as soon as I could," she said looking pale and scared. "I tried to convince Robert to give him another chance, but he wouldn't listen."

"Where is he now?" I jumped to my feet as the true realisation of what she was telling me dawned. Will would be punished and sent back to the Government – maybe even the chain gang. Tears welled in my eyes at the thought of what they might do to him.

"I'm not sure, but I expect he's been taken to the barracks at Launceston," she said staring at me. "You can't help him, Margaret."

"Well I can't just sit here and do nothing," I said wiping away the unwanted tears that were now rolling down my face. "There must be something I can do."

She shook her head. "There isn't anything anyone can do now," she said as she gazed around my humble abode and screwed up her nose in distaste. "Come with me back to the rectory. You can't stay here."

I shook my head while my mind raced. What could I do? I wasn't his legal wife, and anyway, they wouldn't listen to a woman. If only I knew where they'd taken him. Surely he'd be brought before a Magistrate and someone could plead his case.

"Margaret, please come with me. You can't possibly stay in this hovel. Think of your baby if not yourself."

I smiled at her. She was so kind and I knew she only had my best interests in mind, but I couldn't leave. Will knew I was here, if I left and he came looking for me, well then what?

"No, Maria I can't come with you. Apart from causing trouble for you, Will knows I'm here, and I want to be here when he gets released."

"Be sensible Margaret," said Maria with a note of exasperation in her voice. "How will you care for yourself? God only knows how long he'll be gone. It'll likely be months."

I paled at the thought, but I knew she was right. He would likely have time added to his sentence and be sent back to the chain gang for a time. What could I possibly do about it? Captain Cheyne – why hadn't I thought of him in the first place? He would help. He had something to do with roads and bridges, and the gangs of convicts that worked on them. Maybe, just maybe he would know what had happened to him.

I hugged Maria and kissed her cheek. "Thank you so much for worrying about me, but I promise you I'll be fine," I said nudging her towards the door. "I think Captain Cheyne may be able to help."

She stopped and stared at me. "Captain Cheyne? He can't help Margaret, he'd lose his job. Please come with me and we'll see what we can do."

"That's very kind of you, but no, I'm sure the Captain will know what to do," I said as I opened the door. "I can't thank you enough for coming and telling me what happened, but if I went to the rectory and didn't do something to help Will - well I'd never forgive myself."

"I promise you I'll help," she said imploring me to listen to her. "But you have to think of yourself and your baby."

"I know you're worried for me, Maria," I said with a wry smile. "But truly, I will be just fine here. The Captain should be able to locate Will for me and maybe even get a message to him or something."

Maria sighed as she finally gave up trying to convince me to go with her. "Alright, but please come to me if you need help," she said stepping outside. She turned and hugged me. "Promise you'll come to me if you need to."

"I promise," I said hugging her close. Tears pricked the back of my eyes again, not from fear or sadness, but because of her kindness. She truly cared about me and I knew she'd help me if she could. "Thank you so much for being my friend, Maria."

She smiled at me. "You need not thank me. You were my friend at a time when I needed you, even if you didn't know it. No, Margaret, it is I that will be forever thankful that you came into my life."

I pressed my lips together and sucked in a breath as I tried hard not to cry.

I finally managed to give her a smile. "Take care going home," I said kissing her cheek. "And thank you so much."

"You're welcome. Take care, Margaret, and don't forget what I said. If you need me I'll be there."

I nodded and watched her as she made her way back up the yard. She turned and gave me a wave before disappearing around the side of the house. I blew out my breath and sucked in my bottom lip. Now what? I'd have to wait until the Captain came home before I could do anything. I didn't know how I was going to wait patiently until then, but there was no point rushing off to Launceston or anywhere else for that matter.

I went back into the hut and picked up my sewing. I sat with it in my limp hands as the enormity of what had happened settled into the corners of my mind. Without Will, I was alone in the world and could barely care for myself let alone my baby when it arrived. I ran my hand over my belly and sighed. I'd made such a mess of things and perhaps the best option was to go home, back to England. I could feel panic welling up from my stomach as I thought about what that would mean. No, I couldn't return. I was a disgrace and would find no comfort there.

I sighed as I realised I had no choice but to stay. I couldn't desert Will, and I didn't want to. I loved him with all my being and I would not deprive my child of its father. No, I had to find a way to live with my decisions and find a way to help Will. I stabbed the needle through the fabric and tried to block out all other thoughts.

Chapter Twenty

Perth, February 1838

It was nearly dark before I finished my supper and made my way up to the house to see if Captain Cheyne had returned. I knocked softly before opening the door and stepping inside. I'd only been inside the house on a handful of occasions and never when the Captain had been home. I could hear voices coming from the front of the house and so I headed up the hallway in that direction. I noticed Swabby in the kitchen as I passed, but I didn't stop to speak with him.

I knocked on the solid oak door and after a momentary pause, I opened it and entered the parlour. Captain Cheyne, who had been relaxing in a chair by the fireplace immediately, sprang to his feet when he saw me. Tom gave me a nod from his position on the other side of the room where he was leaning against the sideboard.

"Margaret, this is a surprise," said Captain Cheyne smiling widely at me. "Come in, will yer not join us?" He swept an arm towards a rather comfortable looking armchair on the other side of the fireplace. "Would yer care for a wee nip?

Tom and I were just enjoying a wee sherry."

Perhaps a small nip was just what I needed. "Thank you, Captain, that would be lovely," I said as I made way over to the chair he'd proffered and sat down.

"Tom, pour a wee nip for Margaret," he said before downing the last of his sherry and holding out his glass for Tom to refill. "So for what do we owe the pleasure of yer company?" he said sitting back down in his chair.

I took the small glass of dark liquid that Tom offered and took a sip. I felt it burn down my throat and warm my stomach. I sighed before taking another small sip.

"I'm afraid I must throw myself upon your mercy once again Captain Cheyne," I said putting my glass down. I could feel a lump in my throat and I swallowed as I tried hard to not give in to more tears. "It's Will. He was caught stealing food for me, and I expect Reverend Davies has had him charged and he's been taken off somewhere. I'm hoping you might be able to speak on his behalf or something." I was on the verge of tears but determined not to dissolve into a sobbing puddle. "Please Captain I don't know what to do."

I heard Tom's intake of breath and glanced at him. His alert brown eyes flicked between me and Captain Cheyne before he gulped down his sherry. "I'll leave ye two to talk then," he said putting his empty glass on the sideboard. "I'll see ye in the morning Captain." He gave us both a nod and left the room.

"Ah that's unfortunate lass, but I canna do anything to help him. He'll be fine."

"Fine?" I spluttered on another mouthful of sherry before staring at him in disbelief. I truly thought he'd do something. Tom had told me how he'd freed him from the chain gang and he'd apparently helped other convicts. Why wouldn't he help Will?

"Aye, he'll be fine for the time being."

"Alright," I said slowly as I tried to fathom what he meant. "But you will help him?"

He sort of shook his head and shrugged his shoulders. "It's not that I willna help him, but I canna do anything right now," he said swallowing another mouthful of sherry. "Yer have to ken, Margaret. I canna interfere. He'll go before a magistrate who will decide on his punishment, and then we can see what can be done. If he sentences him to the lash or gaol there isn't anything I can do, but if he sends him back to the chain gang, then I might be able to intervene."

The sherry curdled in my stomach at the mere mention of the lash. I felt sick at the thought of Will being punished in such a way. I swallowed and tried to push the image of him stripped bare to the waist and shackled while the whip snapped and the cat bit into his flesh. I shuddered and swallowed the rising bile.

"Are yer alright lass? Yer look a wee bit pale."

"I'm fine, thank you," I said swallowing and taking a breath. "So you'll help him?"

"Aye, but we just have ter wait and see," he said putting down his now empty glass. "I canna promise that I can do anything at all, we'll have to wait to see what punishment he gets."

I nodded and sighed. Captain Cheyne was my only hope.

"Yer will need ter be patient mind. It could take a few weeks before I find out what they've done with him."

I nodded. "Thank you, Captain Cheyne. I cannot tell you how much I appreciate your help. I'll do my best to be patient."

"Good," he said smiling at me.

I presume he was trying to reassure me, but I didn't feel reassured at all. In the weeks that I would have to wait to find out what had happened to him, well anything could've happened to him. Panic threatened to overwhelm me and I gulped in a deep breath in a most unladylike fashion.

"Could you not just make a few enquiries?" I said putting down my glass.

"Twould be best not to," he said shaking his head. "We dinna want anyone to think we're interested in the outcome. Patience, Margaret. I promise yer I know what I'm doing."

I nodded and sighed. "Alright," I said standing up and smoothing my skirt. "I'll do my best to remain calm and leave it to you. Please do your best to find out where he is."

He stood up and placed his hand on my arm in a rather fatherly manner. I looked into his eyes which were full of kindness and what I thought was concern for me. "Even if I discover his whereabouts yer canna see him, yer ken? Twould only make things worse for him."

I pressed my lips together and swallowed the lump in my throat as tears threatened once again. I managed to nod.

"Good night then," he said letting go of my arm and opening the parlour door. "And try not ter worry overmuch alright?"

I nodded again and left the room. I felt numb as I headed back to my hut at the bottom of the garden. It was going to take all my resolve to remain calm and patient.

February gave way to March and still, there was no news. I'd spent the last couple of weeks trying to keep myself busy but it only took a moment of idleness for my mind to turn to thoughts of Will. I imagined all manner of ghastly things being done to him and I was driving myself mad with worry. Panic gripped me every time I thought of him and what he might be enduring. I couldn't shake the guilty feeling that this was my fault. All I could do was pray that Captain Cheyne would soon discover where he was. Then what?

I stopped walking and eased myself down beside a tall gum tree. My back ached and I leaned forward in an attempt to stretch my tired muscles. My baby picked that moment to give me a good kick.

"Ouch do you mind," I said giving my abdomen a gentle rub.

One part of me would be glad when my baby arrived, while the other part was apprehensive, to say the least. I'd introduced myself to the local midwife a few weeks ago. Her name was Mrs Mundy, and I'd been assured by several of the local women they wouldn't trust anyone else. I had my doubts. She was a small wizened old lady who looked at least a hundred.

She prodded my stomach and leaned her ear against my abdomen. "Hmm your wee un has a ways to go yet," she said straightening and giving me a toothless grin. "All's well."

"Thank you, Mrs Mundy," I said sitting up and easing myself off the bed. "How long do you think?"

She shook her head back and forth and made some odd tut-tutting sounds. "Come back an' see me in a month."

Another month or more? Surely I would know Will's whereabouts by then.

After a short rest, I got to my feet and continued down the road to Norfolk Plains. I'd estimated that it would only take me an hour or so, but I wasn't walking at my usual pace and it was taking far longer than I'd anticipated. I was relieved when the tall gables of Ardmore House finally came into view. I walked down the familiar driveway to the front porch and took a deep breath before knocking on the door. I almost held my breath while I waited.

I was anxious to see Maria and I knew she'd offer me soothing words of comfort, but I was unsure how I'd be received by the other resident's. A few moments later the door was swung wide open.

"Good Lord above," said Mrs Fitz clapping her eyes on me. "I didna expect ter see ye again. Come in." She stepped aside to allow me to enter. "Mrs Davies' will be ever so happy ter see ye. She's in the parlour. I expect ye remember where tis?"

"Yes, Mrs Fitz, thank you," I said squeezing passed her.

I heard the door close and her heavy footsteps behind me. "Tell Mrs Davies I'll get ye some tea."

I turned and smiled. "Thank you."

The door to the parlour was open and so I knocked softly to let Maria know I was there. She looked up from her sewing and a smile spread across her face. I burst into tears at the sight of her. A moment later she was by my side and I was crying into her shoulder. Great wracking sobs tore from me as I let go of the fear and despair I'd been holding in for the past few weeks.

"Oh Margaret," said Maria as she hugged me and whispered soothing words in my ear. "It will be alright, come now. Tell me what's happened."

I tried to stop crying, but my heart was breaking and I continued to cling to her until I got myself under control. I finally pulled from her embrace and wiped the tears from my face.

"It's everything," I finally managed to say in between great gulps. "I've had no news of Will, and I don't know what to do. I truly thought Captain Cheyne would've heard something by now."

"I'm sure he's doing his best. You must be patient," she said guiding me over to a chair. "I'll ask Robert to make some enquiries."

"Would you? Oh, Maria, that would be wonderful," I said sitting down.

It was only then that I noticed young Rowland standing beside the sofa. He was jiggling up and down on his chubby baby legs and looking as pleased as could be.

"Oh my goodness Maria, Rowland's grown so much."

"Yes," she said turning towards her young son. "It won't be long before he's walking, and then there'll be no stopping him."

As if he heard his mother's words he took two steps aided by the sofa before plopping down on his bottom. I couldn't help but smile at him and was truly enchanted. He proceeded to crawl across the floor to a pile of blocks, ignoring his mother and me.

"Oh he's just a delight," I said watching him as he grabbed two and began hitting them together. I didn't even mind the noise he was making.

I looked up as Martha came into the parlour carrying a tray with tea for Maria and myself.

"Hello Martha," I said smiling at her.

"I heard it was ye," she said placing the tray on the sideboard. "We were all so worried when ye disappeared. Are ye alright?"

"Yes, thank you," I said nodding.

"Thank you, Martha," said Maria pouring the hot tea into a cup and handing it to me.

"Well I'm glad to hear it," she said before departing.

I took a sip of hot tea and sighed. I was surprised at how soothing it was to be back at Ardmore House. It might've just been Maria's company, but I felt that somehow the house had also welcomed me. I took a deep breath and slowly let it out.

Maria sat down on the sofa with her tea. "Are you feeling better?"

"Yes," I said smiling at her. "I think I just needed someone to talk to. Thank you so much."

"Nonsense. You know you're welcome any time, and I'm so glad you came to me," she said sipping her tea. "I promise we'll find out about Will."

I pressed my lips together and nodded. I didn't want to start crying again, but a lump was forming in the back of my throat and I swallowed. The pain cut across the back of my windpipe and I took in several deep breaths until it passed.

Maria and I spent a lovely afternoon chatting and being entertained by Rowland. I was loath to leave. I was feeling so much better, and I trusted her to help me discover what had become of Will. I was also grateful when she insisted that John take me home in the spring cart. Once upon a time, I'd hated it, but now I was so grateful as I climbed up onto the seat beside John. I waved goodbye to her as John clicked horses into a walk and we started down the driveway. I watched her until we rounded the corner and John urged the horses into a trot. We hadn't gone far when he started up a conversation that I hadn't expected.

"I hear tell Will's back on the chain gang then?" he said glancing at me.

"What? Where did you hear that?" I was so surprised. John wasn't normally much of a conversationalist, and secondly, how did he know about Will.

He shrugged his shoulders. "Hmph, I don't know. Things get around ye know."

No, I didn't know, but I suspected he did. But if that was true, why didn't Captain Cheyne know about it?

"You mean the other convicts, they talk?"

"Aye, news always travels that way," he said with a casual tone to his voice. "I thought you knew."

"No, I've been trying to find out what they did with him," I said taking a breath and slowly letting it out. "Do you know where?"

"Aye, I hear he's at Campbelltown, working on the new bridge."

I was stunned. Campbelltown, on the new bridge? That just didn't make sense. Captain Cheyne was the Director of Bridges and Roads, he'd been down to Campbelltown just the other week. He had to know Will was on the chain gang there. How could he not? I could feel my heart thumping in my chest as a surge of excitement ran through me. I couldn't wait to tell the Captain and ask him to deliver a message for me.

"Thank you so much, John. I'm surprised that Captain Cheyne doesn't know about this."

He shrugged again. "He might."

Chapter Twenty One

Captain Cheyne's Deception

I could barely contain myself as I waited for John to help me down from the cart. If the Captain wasn't yet home I planned to wait for him in his parlour. I would have answers tonight.

"Thank you John," I said as he helped me down. "And thank you for the information about Will."

He shrugged and climbed back into the cart. "It was nothing. Bye, Margaret."

"Goodbye," I said smiling at him.

I waited for him to turn the horses for home before I headed around to the back of the house. I knocked softly on the back door before letting myself in. The backdoor opened into a narrow hallway, with a lean too bedroom on one side. Further along was the kitchen off to the left and a small dining room opposite. I noticed Tom and Swabby were in the kitchen as I passed, but there was no sign of the Captain. I presumed it was bit early for him to be home so I headed straight for the parlour. I settled myself in one of the comfortable arm chairs and prepared to wait. I didn't have to wait long before Tom came snooping.

"I thought I 'eard someone. What are ye doing?"

"I'm waiting for the Captain."

He eyed me from the doorway with curiosity clear on his face. However, I wasn't inclined to enlighten him on my reason for being in the Captain's parlour. It wasn't that I didn't trust him; I didn't trust myself to remain impassive. I suspected that Captain Cheyne knew full well where Will was, and had chosen not to tell me. I had no intention of having that conversation with Tom. I stared at him with what I hoped was a demure expression. He was waiting for me to expand on my explanation, but I just gave him a small smile and a nod. I hope I'd left him no choice but to leave.

After a long pause he gave shrug and left. I took in a deep breath and slowly let it out. Good, I wouldn't have to explain myself to him. I wasn't sure what time the Captain would be home, so I relaxed and prepared to wait for as long as necessary.

I must've nodded off, because the next thing I woke with a start. Captain Cheyne was leaning over me shaking my arm.

"Oh good yer awake lass," he said taking a step back. "Have yer had yer supper?"

I yawned and peered at him as I sat up straight in the chair. "Oh I must've fallen asleep," I said stating the obvious. I stood up and tried to clear the fog of sleep from my mind.

"Aye," he said smiling. "What are yer doing here? Tom said yer were waiting for me."

"Yes," I said plunging straight into the matter at hand. "I know where Will is. He's on the chain gang working on the new bridge at Campbelltown." I couldn't help the accusing tone in my voice. "But I think you knew that. Didn't you?"

He sighed, but didn't flinch from my steady gaze. "Aye I did."

I felt deflated. "Why didn't you tell me?"

"I dinna want yer to get yer hopes up lass. I plan to seek him out next week when I do my rounds." He paused and ran his fingers through his whiskers. "I was going to tell yer then."

I pressed my lips together while I weighed up his words. He was going to tell me - I really wanted to believe that. The Captain had never given me any cause to doubt him or his motives, but I couldn't understand why he'd kept it to himself. I sucked in a deep breath.

"Alright," I said nodding. "Well can you get a message to him for me?"

"Aye, dinna fash," he said putting a fatherly arm around my shoulders. "Come and have some supper with us and yer can give me yer message."

It was only then I noticed the enticing aroma coming from the kitchen, and my stomach rumbled in response. I headed for the kitchen with the Captain at my heels. Swabby and Tom were already sitting at the small dining table, which had been set for four. I sat down opposite Tom and waited while he recited a simple grace. I murmured amen when he finished.

Swabby lifted the lid on the pot that was sitting in the middle of table and helped himself to a large serve. It smelled really good, and when it was my turn I scooped out a spoonful of what looked like vegetable stew. I took a mouthful and savoured the flavours. Swabby had used a myriad of vegetables and herbs from the garden and had somehow turned them into a very delicious pottage.

"Now, while we're all here together, we need to discuss a few changes," said Captain Cheyne piling stew onto his plate and inhaling the aroma. "It's not proper that Margaret's living down in the hut, particularly when her wee bairn comes. So, I think she should move up into the house. Swabby can stay in the lean to, and Tom, you'll have to move out to the hut."

Swabby shrugged and went on eating his supper, and Tom looked at me and nodded.

"I don't want to be a bother," I said putting down my fork. "It would be unfair of me to expect Tom to move out."

"Aye, but you're not are yer?" said Captain Cheyne. "I am. And seeing as you're masquerading as my niece, and there won't be enough room in the hut once yer bairn comes. It makes perfect sense."

"Aye it does," said Tom swallowing a mouthful of stew. "I'll move out in the morning."

"Good," said Captain Cheyne. "Now that's settled. I'm going to Campbelltown tomorrow and I won't be back til Friday."

I was going to protest further, but I would only be making a fuss and there was no point. The Captain had clearly made up his mind, and if I was honest, I had to agree with him. There was barely any room in the hut, and there was certainly no room for a crib - not that I had one.

"Thank you Tom," I said smiling at him.

"It's nothing," he said waving his fork in the air.

"Now, Captain Cheyne, when you see Will next week will you please tell him I'll wait for him," I said turning my attention to the Captain. "No matter how long he's got to serve on the chain gang, I'll be here waiting for him."

"Aye," he said nodding. "I ken he's been sentenced to nine months."

Nine months. Oh my goodness I didn't think it would be that long. I sucked in a breath and slowly let it out. Our baby would be nearly seven months old by then. Tears pricked the back of my eyes and I blinked them away.

"Dinna fash," said the Captain placing his large hand on mine.

"He means don't worry, and I'd take that as a good sign," said Tom.

Swabby nodded as he stuffed his mouth full with the last of his supper. He'd barely said a word over supper, which wasn't unusual. He mainly just nodded and grunted, and I think in the time I'd known him he hadn't said more than two words to me. I wasn't sure if he his silence was driven by shyness or something else. I smiled at him and then at Tom and Captain Cheyne. They were trying hard to assure me that all would be well; I just wasn't sure I believed them.

The following day Captain Cheyne went off to Campbelltown to check on the progress of the bridge work. I took up residence in the front room. It was a well proportioned room with a large tester bed and a wardrobe in one corner. An almost threadbare rug took up most of the available floor space, and a hard bench stood below the front window. There was room for additional furniture if I had any - which I didn't. However, I would need to get a crib and there was plenty of room for one in the corner.

I tried to keep myself busy, and not think about Friday when the Captain would return with news of Will. At least I hoped he'd have news. I wished I had something more distracting to do other than sew. I couldn't very well visit Maria again, not so soon on the heels of my recent visit. I'd read the only two letters I'd received from home so many times that I knew them off by heart. I hadn't made any other friends since moving to Perth, and I couldn't very well pay Mrs Mundy another visit either.

I sighed as I stabbed the needle into the flannel. Thoughts of Will crept unbidden into my mind and I tried hard to push them aside. It wasn't that I didn't want to think about him, I did. But my thoughts about him invariably invoked a feeling of panic and fear as I dreaded what might happen to him; and to us. Would he still love me when he finally saw me again? I had to think of something else and stop tormenting myself.

I'd already decided that if my baby was a boy I'd name him William. The idea of having a son of my own was beyond my imagination and left me feeling like the most blessed woman in the world if it were to happen. If I have a daughter I'd name her for my two dear sisters Barbara and Charlotte, although not in that order. While Barbara was my favourite and had risked much to help me, I much preferred the name Charlotte. So, she would be Charlotte Barbara Hartley. I sighed as I ran the name over in my mind. Would she be Hartley or Penny? I'd have to see what Will thought about that.

This week seemed to take on a different way of measuring time. It crawled by at a snail's pace and no matter what I did it went no faster. My impatience and frustration was at a fever pitch by the time Friday actually arrived. I spent the day pacing up and down, which I'm sure Tom and Swabby found most annoying. I couldn't help myself. I couldn't settle to do anything and I didn't think I'd be able to stand waiting another minute.

As it neared supper time my anxiety and impatience seemed to compress into a tiny space and I thought I'd explode at any minute. I breathed heavily as I tried to calm myself and concentrate on the task at hand. I now realised that Swabby was a rather astute man. He rarely engaged in conversation and kept to himself, but he'd read my mood perfectly and asked me to help him in the kitchen. I had no idea about cooking but he'd patiently directed me to help prepare our supper. I was so glad of the distraction, and found my skill at preparing vegetables had improved greatly since I'd first helped Martha in the kitchen back at Ardmore House.

I handed the bowl of perfectly peeled and sliced carrots to Swabby to add to the pot, and was busy chopping rosemary. I didn't immediately realise that anyone else had joined us in the kitchen until I turned to give the herbs to Swabby.

"Will." My heart starting thumping madly and I launched myself into his arms. Oh my God it was really him. I buried my head into his shoulder and breathed in his familiar male scent along with the smell of stale sweat and dirt. He felt solid under my hands as I held him tight. I clung to him for what seemed like an eternity before I returned to my senses.

"What are you doing here?" I said letting him go and stepping back. He was thin and looked bone weary but he was grinning at me.

"Is that any way to greet your husband," he said grabbing me.

Then his lips were on mine and I thrilled at his touch. Our kiss was long and passionate and when our lips parted he rained kisses all over my face. I laughed, before taking his face in my hands and kissing him softly. I sighed with utter contentment.

"Come on yer two," said Captain Cheyne arriving on the scene. "Yer'll have plenty of time for that later." He gave a chuckle and looked meaningfully at us.

I felt my face warm under his teasing gaze.

"I didn't expect you to bring him home with you," I said letting go of Will and taking a step back. I couldn't understand how he'd come to be here at all. He was a convict working on the chain gang – he couldn't just leave, even if it was with the Director of Roads and Bridges.

"Aye, well I didna want to say anything in case I couldna get him away," said Captain Cheyne with a smirk. "But, as luck would have it he was working with the brick makers. Twas fairly easy to spirit him away, and I dinna think he'll be missed."

My confusion must have been evident on my face – spirit him away? Wouldn't be missed? What on earth.

"Aye lassie," said Captain Cheyne slapping Will on the back. "Will here'll be working in my garden from now on. I've been wanting a fine gardener to tend to the vegetables and such."

"You can't do that!"

"Well I can take him back if yer like," he said running his fingers through his whiskers. "But I thought yer'd be happy with the arrangement."

Will was now looking at me with a bemused expression. I wasn't sure how I felt – surely this could only end in more trouble. Someone would undoubtedly notice he was gone, and then what?

"Well of course I'm happy he's here," I said shaking my head. "I just don't understand how."

"Dinna fash lass," he said smiling at me. "We've nay been caught before."

So this wasn't the first time – well of course not. Tom had told me how the Captain had saved him from the chain gang, I just hadn't imagined it was like this - spirited away without anyone noticing. Good Lord how had they gotten away with this?

"The Captain knows what he's doing," said Will grinning at me. "And we can be together at last." He wrapped his arms around my waist and pulled me close to him. "You, me and our babe."

Chapter Twenty Two

Norfolk Plains, May 1838

Maria looked at me over the top of her sketch pad, a frown creasing her delicate brow. I did my best to sit still, but my lower back was beginning to ache and I'd have to change positions soon. As if reading my mind she put down her pencil and sighed.

"I just can't get you right," she said frustration evident in her voice. "But I cannot have you sitting any longer."

"No, my back is starting to ache," I said rubbing it with both hands and stretching my cramped muscles.

"Oh, Margaret I'm so sorry, you should've said." She came and sat down beside me on the bench under the tree and sighed.

"Not at all," I said smiling at her. "I so enjoy our time together. I'll just be glad when this baby comes." I'd been having odd contractions for a few days but Mrs Mundy had assured me I'd know when the time came – and this wasn't it. Although, I'd had this growing feeling of pressure all day and hoped it would soon go away. I continued to stretch and rub my lower back until the pain began to subside.

"I felt the same way when I was expecting Rowland," she said with a far-away look on her face. "Now look at him. He's a right little rascal. Speaking of which, I half expected Mrs Fitz to come looking for me before now."

I had to agree. We'd been out in the garden for an hour or more and it was unusual for Mrs Fitz not to need help with Rowland after so long. "Perhaps we should go and check on them?"

She nodded and got to her feet before extending her hand to help me up. I'd gotten so clumsy in the last few days and I appreciated her assistance. I'd only taken a couple of steps towards the house when I felt an intense pain ripple across my abdomen. I gasped and bent over to try and ease the cramped feeling - I groaned as the pain swept over me.

"What is it?" said Maria turning to see what I was doing.

"I think my baby's coming," I said standing up straight again as the pain eased. I took several steady breaths which seemed to relieve my discomfort.

Maria was by my side in an instant – putting her arm around my shoulders to steady me. "Come on let's get you inside."

I nodded as I sucked in another deep breath. My whole body tensed in readiness of another contraction, but after a few moments, when nothing else happened, we began walking up to the house. As we entered the rear door Maria called out to Martha who appeared almost immediately.

"Aye. It's the babe?" she said eyeing me up and down.

"Yes. Help me get her to the guest room," said Maria taking hold of my elbow and pointing me in the direction of the stairs. Martha grabbed me on the other side. I was sure I didn't need their help, but they both had such a grip on me that I went along willingly. "Annie," Maria called, as the three of us ascended the stairs.

"Please, I'm alright," I said trying to wriggle free of their grasp. "I should go home."

"No you will not," said Maria in her most commanding tone. "Good Lord, Margaret, you're having a baby."

While not very experienced with such matters, I had no doubt she was right. However, Mrs Mundy had told me that I could be in labour for many hours before giving birth. I was about to protest further when another sharp contraction made me gasp, and I nearly buckled at the knees. I was thankful the two women did have such a firm grip of me.

"Annie," Maria called out again as the three of us manoeuvred along the passageway to the guest room. I'd never been in here before but was thankful when the two women guided me over to a winged chair. I sank into it and tried to steady my breathing. Mrs Mundy's advice was to breathe in and out in a sort of rhythmic way, and I closed my eyes and gave it all my concentration.

"Aye, Mrs Davies," said Annie finally heeding her mistresses call.

"Oh, Annie go and fetch Doctor Salmon," said Maria as she and Martha began stripping the bed. "Tell him Margaret's having her baby and he's needed."

"What!" I said opening my eyes. "I need Mrs Mundy, not the doctor."

"Nonsense," said Maria waving a dismissive hand in my direction. "Go, do as I say."

"Aye," said Annie. With one more look from me to Maria, she disappeared to do Maria's bidding.

"Martha here's a fine midwife. Trust me, Margaret between the two of them your baby will be safely delivered."

"Please, Maria I'm sure the doctor's not needed. At least not..." Another contraction took my breath away and I moaned as the pain intensified in my lower back and pelvis. I leaned forward in an attempt to get some relief – it didn't really help. I eased myself out of the chair and found that standing immediately released the pressure on my lower spine.

The bed had been stripped of its quilts and comforter, and now the two women turned their attentions to me. "Let me help you out of your blazer," said Maria reaching for the buttons without waiting for me to reply.

I stood still and let her help me out of my jacket and skirt. In no time at all I was reduced to my chemise - I must admit I felt much more comfortable without my constraining clothes. Any further protest on my part was also an obvious waste of time.

"Thank you," I said smiling at her.

She gave me a warm hug and kissed me on the cheek. "You are my dear friend, Margaret and I have your best interests at heart."

"I know," I said taking a deep breath as another contraction rippled through me. I let out a long moan as my entire abdomen cramped and I was surprised by the warm wet feeling between my thighs.

"Ye waters broken," said Martha coming to my side. She placed a supporting hand beneath my elbow. "Sometimes walking can help things along. Come walk with me around the room."

I spent the next – I don't know how many hours – alternating between walking and resting. Maria and Martha both offered soothing words of encouragement, which I was most grateful for. Doctor Salmon had arrived several hours ago and after examining me announced I was unlikely to have my baby today. He'd snapped his bag shut and told Maria to call him in the morning. The news did nothing to lift my spirits, and as the day gave way to night I was forced to concede that he was probably right. My baby wasn't coming today.

However, Martha insisted that all the signs indicated it would be coming very soon. My contractions had become regular and I was starting to feel a growing pressure and stretching sensations. "I feel like I need to push."

"Push on the next contraction," said Martha feeling my protruded belly and nodding her head. "Your baby's ready to come."

I was panting and more than a little afraid. When the next contraction came I grabbed Maria's hand in a vice-like grip. I let out a long groan and pushed as hard as I could. After bearing down a dozen or more times, Martha encouraged me to push harder.

"I see your baby's head, Margaret," she said smiling at me. "One more big push should do it."

The pressure was intense and my body felt like it was stretching and tearing.

With a sudden burst of energy, I pushed with all my might. I was exhausted and bathed in sweat but still, Martha urged me on.

"Come on – push."

Maria wiped my brow with a damp cloth and gripped my hand firmly in hers. "Not long now, Margaret. You're nearly there."

I sucked in a deep breath and pushed as hard as I could. I felt something give way, as Martha guided my baby into the world. I cannot explain the myriad of feelings that happened all at once. Most of all I was relieved when I heard my baby let out an indignant cry.

"Ye have a fine and healthy girl," said Martha.

I spent the next day alternating between sleep and watching my new daughter, Charlotte. She was perfect - with a head of dark hair, rosebud mouth and a ruddy complexion. I on the other hand felt like I'd been hauled through the hedgerow backwards. My whole body felt sore and my nether regions were particularly uncomfortable. I shifted onto my side to watch her sleep.

The door opened and Maria's head poked around. "Ah you're awake," she said entering the room proper. She smiled as she bent over to admire Charlotte. "Oh she's just beautiful, Margaret," she said before settling herself down in the wing chair which she pulled up to my bedside.

I eased myself into a sitting position with a plumped cushion to lean on. "I can't thank you enough for helping me bring her into the world, and for having me in your guest room."

"It's nothing," she said smiling at me. "I'm just glad I could help." She glanced furtively towards the door before looking back at me. "Annie will be up with a tray for you in a minute, but before she gets here. I can get word to Will about Charlotte if you like. I believe he's in Campbelltown."

She must've seen the look of horror on my face. I've never been any good at hiding what I'm thinking. I quickly tried to settle my expression into one of surprise.

"What's the matter?" she said peering at me.

"Oh, it's nothing," I said trying to sound as normal as possible. "I'm just not sure that he's still in Campbelltown."

"Oh yes, he would be. Robert told me he's been sent there for nine months, so he'd definitely be there," she said in a matter of fact tone. "So I'll send John down to find him and tell him shall I?"

A thousand thoughts rushed through my mind all at once, slipping and sliding over one another. Panic nearly won through, until a little voice in the back of mind reminded me – 'remember how you felt about lying to Maria about Will being Charlotte's father?' I took a deep breath and decided to trust her with the truth. God, I hope I'm not making the biggest mistake of my life.

"He's not at Campbelltown," I said and a nervous flutter went through me. "He's at Captain Cheyne's place. Please, Maria, you must promise not to tell anyone."

"What?" she said, her pale blue eyes opening wide with surprise.

A soft knock on the open door startled both of us, and Annie looked at us with one brow raised. "Sorry," she said coming over and placing a tray across my knees. "I didn't mean to scare ye."

"Oh thank you," I said inhaling the aroma of Martha's vegetable soup. All of a sudden I was famished and my stomach gave a grumble in response.

"Oh ain't she a sweet one," said Annie admiring Charlotte who was still curled up asleep by my side.

I smiled and looked down at my sleeping daughter. Yes, she was a sweet one, and I hoped she'd stay that way until I'd eaten.

"Yes thank you, Annie," said Maria in a tone that clearly meant she was dismissed. She gave Maria a nod and left the room.

As soon as she went Maria checked the hallway for anyone else who might be passing. She stood looking at me from the doorway for a moment before taking in a deep breath and retaking her seat.

"Now, tell me what's going on. How can he be at Captain Cheyne's?"

I put down my spoon and compressed my lips. "Well, a couple of months ago the Captain brought him home to work in his garden. Of course, he's not supposed to. He should be on the chain gang at Campbelltown, but apparently, Captain Cheyne's done this before."

"Done what before?" said Maria with an incredulous look on her face.

"Taken convicts from the chain gang and brought them home to work for him," I said taking a mouthful of soup before continuing. "The other two men are also from the chain gang. Tom's a tailor from London, and Swabby's a cook. I believe he's brought others into his home as well."

"Good Lord," said Maria sitting back in her chair.

"Please, Maria you won't tell anyone? Promise me."

She nodded. "Of course I won't, you can trust me. But he can't get away with this, Margaret. He's the Director of Roads and Bridges, he'll lose his job if he gets caught." She paused for a moment. "And probably go to gaol as well."

I nodded as I swallowed another mouthful of soup. "He says no one will notice Will's missing."

"Well I hope he's right," she said looking thoughtful. "I just can't believe he's gotten away with this before. Does anyone else know?"

"No," I said shaking my head. "But I'm worried what Will might do if I'm missing for much longer. He knows I'm here, but he must be worried about me."

"Don't worry, I'll get word to him somehow," she said getting to her feet. "You finish your soup and get some rest."

"Thank you."

Chapter Twenty Three

Perth, June 1838

After spending two weeks - at Maria's insistence - tucked up in her guest bed resting, I was glad to finally be back at Captain Cheyne's. I snuggled down under the quilts and tried to ignore the soft mewling noises coming from beside me. Charlotte would start to cry in earnest soon, but I hoped to lie here a little longer. I could hear Will's steady breathing coming from the pallet on the floor where he'd taken to sleeping. I missed his solid presence beside me, but until we had a crib for Charlotte there wasn't another option.

A letter from my sister Barb had arrived at the rectory while I was there, and I couldn't get news of my mother out of my mind. She was bedridden and suffering some sort of heart condition. According to Barb, it was quite serious and she was under the care of our family doctor – Doctor Jeffrey's. There was nothing I could do, but I did wonder if it would lift her spirits to know about Charlotte. I'd been tossing the idea around in my mind for days and was no closer to making a decision.

Charlotte began to whimper and I pushed myself into a sitting position and reached for her. She felt damp and smelled of wee mixed with her own sweet smell. She immediately started to nuzzle me, seeking her breakfast - a clean clout would have to wait. I opened my nightdress and guided her onto my nipple which she immediately latched onto. I sighed as she suckled and I pushed her wispy brown hair back with my thumb. She was so perfect and a pang of sadness went through me at the thought that my mother would never see her. I would write to her and tell her. Tell her what? I'm not married and here's your granddaughter? No, I'd have to lie, but there'd be no harm in it. She would never find out it wasn't true, and anyway, it would be true soon enough.

I looked at Will sleeping on the floor and wondered when that might be. Not any day soon that was for certain. We were living a lie, with him here illegally. There was no hope of him getting a ticket any day soon, and even more unlikely that he'd be able to get permission to marry me. I didn't want to think about it, and I pushed all thoughts of my predicament aside. I bent and kissed the top of my daughter's head – I'd write to my mother.

Bredgar House, Kent, England

Lady Barbara stared aimlessly at the rain running down the large glass panes of the conservatory. The weather matched her mood which had turned decidedly gloomy since becoming invalid. She was sitting in her wheelchair with a woollen rug tucked around her knees. How had she come to this state of affairs? She sighed as her eyes flicked to the small bell sitting on the table beside her. She couldn't even move without calling for assistance. It was almost unbearable.

She looked up at the sound of footsteps coming down the hallway. It was Barton. God, what did he want? He came through the open doors of the conservatory and placed several letters on the table beside her.

She stared at them for a moment. "Thank you, Barton."

He bowed and turned to leave, but paused and lifted one of the letters from the pile. "You may want to read this one, my lady," he said handing it to her. "It's from Van Diemen's Land."

"Oh," she said taking the battered envelope from him. What a lovely surprise - a letter from Margaret. She watched him leave before turning it over in her hand and running her fingers over the familiar writing. Her first impulse was to tear it open and devour it, but she also wanted to savour it. She held it to her bosom for a moment, before reaching for the letter opener and slitting it open. She unfolded the creamy paper.

Dearest Mamma,

I do hope you are much improved and enjoying better health. I must confess, Barb wrote to me about your condition and I can only pray that it is not as bad as she described. At any rate, I hope that my news will lift your spirits considerably.

I should have written to you some time since, but I was afraid that you and Papa would not have approved. Please forgive me for not writing to you at once. Last July, I married a wonderful man by the name of William Hartley. He's from a good family in Essex. He works for the Director of Public Works here in Van Diemen's Land and we live in a modest house in Perth.

She let the letter go limp in her hand as she digested the words. Married? Margaret? She supposed things were different over there. Perhaps a spinster like Margaret could find a suitable husband. She just hadn't expected Margaret to ever marry is all.

Anyway, the next piece of exciting news is that I have a daughter. I've named her Charlotte Barbara after my two dear sisters, and you of course. She is just the sweetest thing.

Barbara swallowed as she reread the words. Tears pricked the back of her eyes and she sucked in a breath. A granddaughter, that she'd likely never see on the other side of the world. Of course, she was pleased for Margaret. Every woman needed a family and she was so happy that her daughter would never be on her own again. But, it also meant there was no hope of her ever coming back to England. She had a husband and a child of her own now. Barbara let her tears fall. They were a bittersweet mix of happiness and sadness in equal measure.

She was so engrossed with her letter she didn't hear Samuel approaching.

"What's that you're reading," he said sitting down in the nearest wicker chair. He looked expectantly over his glasses. "What's a matter?"

He gave her such a start the letter slipped from her fingers and landed on the floor. "It's a letter from Margaret," she said in a shrill voice. "She's got married and has a daughter. I just can't believe it."

"Who'd she marry?" said Samuel retrieving the letter.

"A man by the name of, William Hartley."

Samuel read the letter before looking at his wife with a quizzical brow. "Do you think he's a convict?"

"Good God no," she said snatching the letter back from her husband. "What a ridiculous suggestion, Samuel. He sounds like a fine upstanding man – working for the Director of Public Works."

"Hmm," said Samuel with a sceptical look on his face. "I can't help but wonder why she didn't write to us last year when she married him. She says herself, we wouldn't have approved of the match. If he was a fine upstanding man as you say, then why wouldn't she have told us? I think you're too trusting, Barbara."

"And you're too suspicious," she said with an air of annoyance. Why did he have to spoil everything? Why couldn't he let her believe Margaret was married to a good man and happy? "Margaret wouldn't be so foolish to marry a convict."

"Well I do hope you're right my dear," he said standing. He bent down and kissed her forehead before leaving her. He stopped in the doorway and turned. "Give her my best wishes when you write her...oh

I almost forgot. Osborn and Eleanor will be joining us for supper."

"What they're coming down in this weather?" she said surprised that they would do such a thing. Osborn hated the journey from London to Kent at the best of times.

"Yes well, Osborn and I have some business matters to discuss," he said with an air of finality. He turned and left the conservatory without offering any further explanation.

Barbara sighed as she watched him until he was out of sight. She hoped whatever business he wished to discuss with Osborn would not involve James. She pushed the matter from her mind and went back to Margaret's letter. Her lips curved into a small smile as she reread the letter. A convict indeed!

Down amongst the cabbages

I pushed a few straggling wisps of hair back from my face with the back of my hand. I was pegging the last of the washing on the line. I hate laundry more than any other chore, but with Charlotte, the amount has quadrupled. The warmer weather was at least making it easier to get things dry. For most of the winter, the kitchen had been draped in clouts and nightgowns as it was the only place I could get them dry.

Will took me by surprise. He came up behind me and wrapped his arms around my waist. I leaned into him as he nuzzled my neck.

"Ye look very enticing," he whispered in my ear.

"Really," I said turning around and putting my arms around him. "I expect I look like a washerwoman. Perhaps you find them attractive?"

"No, only you," he said before lowering his head and kissing me.

I pressed myself closer to him as we kissed and I could feel him. He wanted me, and the very thought of it made my pulse quicken. Our kiss deepened and I ran my tongue along the inside of his upper lip. I heard him groan and smiled to myself. I was glad he couldn't resist my charms. Our lips parted and he grinned down at me.

"No one's around, come with me down by the cabbages." Keeping one arm firmly around my waist he started to urge me down the garden path.

I glanced up towards the house. He was right – no one was around. The Captain was at work and Tom was out running errands. Swabby was in the kitchen baking bread, and would not likely come down the yard. I found the idea of making love in the garden both intoxicating and scandalous all at the same time. I hesitated for the briefest of moments. Charlotte was asleep, and would likely stay that way long enough for us to enjoy our interlude.

I allowed him to lead me down the path to the rear of the garden. It was quite secluded and sheltered by several large bushes. The foliage from which had recently been trimmed and left to rot – it provided a soft bed of leaves on which we settled upon. I was nervous and excited as Will took me in his arms and we kissed and fondled. My heart rate and breathing quickened when I felt his warm fingers urging my thighs apart. I gasped in delight and let all other thoughts go as my excitement grew.

"I love you," he whispered and kissed me softly.

"Yes," I said thrusting my hips forward. "I love you too."

He gave a low chuckle and continued his slow exploration. I wanted him - and I was growing impatient at his leisurely pace. I pushed him onto his back and deftly undid his breeches and helped him to wiggle free of them. I sucked in a breath as I guided him to my soft inner being and plunged him into me. I moaned as he filled me and our bodies began to move in unison. I ran my fingers down his chest and arched my back as the intensity grew.

Being on top like this was a novelty I'd only tried once before, but I loved the freedom it gave me. I leaned down and kissed him and he grabbed my bottom firmly and thrust his hips harder. I gasped and let out a long moan as we both found our release.

I was panting and bathed in a sheen of sweat, as I climbed off of him and tossed him his breeches. I grinned. He was looking even more dishevelled than me. I straightened my blouse and pushed several loose tendrils back under my cap. I didn't think Swabby would notice anything different about me. Will stood up and put on his breeches before taking me in his arms. I smiled and kissed him softly.

"You're wicked," I said letting him go. "And I love you so much."

"Aye, but don't forget you were wicked with me."

I laughed as I began making my way back up the path. "Well, I hope Charlotte's still sleeping and Swabby hasn't noticed me missing. I don't want to have to explain my wickedness."

I heard him chuckle as I turned and headed up to the house. I really did hope Charlotte was still asleep.

Chapter Twenty Four

Perth, January 1839

A haze of idyllic bliss had descended on me. The last few months had been the happiest in my life, and I look forward to every day with renewed enthusiasm. I've taken to calling Charlotte Lottie, and she's growing so fast I can't keep up with her. At nearly nine months old she's just about crawling and I think she's close to saying her first words. I hope it's going to be Mamma.

The house is quiet this morning. Captain Cheyne's in Campbelltown and the other men are down the bottom of the yard doing some repairs on the hut. A storm blew off part of the roof the other night and Will's helping Tom to repair it. I'm not sure how much help Swabby will be, but he's down there with them.

I'd finally got Lottie down for a nap, and after giving her one last look I tip-toed out of the room. I quietly closed the door, leaving it slightly ajar and slowly let my breath out. I'm hoping to get some sewing repairs done while she sleeps. My sewing basket never seems to empty. There's always a shirt of Wills or other garments that need repairing. Not that I'm complaining, it makes me feel useful and domesticated. I paused, with my needle in hand. I can't believe how much I've changed, and its simple things like sewing that remind me how different my life would've been if I'd stayed in England.

I jumped in fright as someone starting banging on the front door. Oh no, I'd only just got Lottie to sleep. I dropped my sewing in the basket and hurried to the door and swung it open. I was greeted by several soldiers who barged into the house.

"What's the meaning of this?" I said staring at them.

"Captain Cheyne?" said the one in the lead. He was tall with a shock of red hair and freckles. He looked me up and down with a sneer.

"He's not home at present," I said pushing my shoulders back and standing tall. "Perhaps I can give him a message."

"I think not," he said before turning to the others. "Search the house and the yard. Arrest anyone ye see. I'll take care of this one."

Before I could make any protest he grabbed me by the arms, digging his fingers into my soft flesh until I squealed.

"Let me go," I said struggling to free myself. I could hear Lottie – the noise had woken her and she'd started to cry. I knew she'd scream in earnest if I didn't go to her. "My baby's crying. Let me go."

To my surprise he did, and I hurried into the bedroom. I gathered her into my arms and whispered soothing words to her. Much to my relief she settled immediately.

"Get back out here."

I emerged from the bedroom with Lottie in my arms. "I don't know what you want, but I'm the Captain's niece. Mrs Cheyne." I hoped that would be enough to elicit some sort of respect. I was wrong.

"Tell that to the magistrate," he said giving me a shove towards the door. "Let's go."

There was a dray waiting outside, and I managed to climb into the back of it. There weren't any seats, and so I squatted on the floor with Lottie on my knee. My heart was hammering and I could hear shouts coming from the yard. I was so scared of what they might do to Will and the others if they resisted. I almost held my breath until I saw them being marched towards the cart with their hands shackled. I swallowed, and tried to remain calm. Lottie was fussing.

"Sh little one. It's alright." My soothing words appeared to calm her although she stared wide eyed at the soldiers.

Will climbed into the back of the cart and sat beside me. "Are you alright? They didn't hurt you did they?"

I could see the fear in his eyes, and I swallowed. "No, I'm fine," I said shaking my head. "What's going on?"

"I think the Captain's been caught."

Tom and Swabby joined us and two soldiers climbed into the back of the dray. They looked scared but resigned to their fate. Tom's alert brown eyes flicked from me to Will before he turned his attention to one of the soldiers.

"She's a free woman," he said frowning. "Ye can't arrest 'er."

"Shut up."

The dray started with a jolt and I clung to Lottie as I tried to silently tell Tom that it was no use. They wouldn't listen. I shrugged and smiled weakly. He seemed to get my message as he gave me a resigned look and said nothing further. I had no idea where they were taking us or what they would do to Will, Tom and Swabby. I expect they'll be sent back to the chain gang, I just hope that's all – and nothing worse. I pressed my lips together and tried to concentrate on keeping Lottie happy. Fear would overtake me if I thought too hard.

After a couple of hours we came into the large settlement of Launceston. I'd never been here before, and was surprised at how large it was. Its streets were lined with fine buildings and houses. The cart pulled up outside an imposing stone building which I presumed was the gaol.

Will squeezed my arm and kissed Lottie on the head. "Take care. I'll find you." He kissed me quickly before he was ordered out of the dray.

Tears filled my eyes and I managed to give him a nod before he jumped down and I was left on my own. I watched as the soldiers escorted the three of them into the gaol. I wondered what they were going to do with me. I wiped my tears away with the back of my hand as one of the soldiers climbed back into the dray and we started moving again.

We hadn't gone far when we came a halt outside another imposing building. This was obviously where I was going.

"Get out," said one of the soldiers.

I put Lottie down while I got to my feet. My joints were stiff and sore from the hours crouching in the dray. Lottie pulled a face like she was about to start crying, so I quickly picked her up and held her close. I managed to get down from the cart with her perched on one hip while I held onto the side with my free hand. The young soldier gave me a small smile before gesturing to me to go into the building. He followed me inside.

We stepped into a hallway with a rather large woman sitting at a desk. She gave the soldier a nod.

"Leave her wi' me," she said before calling for some other woman. "Lizzy, come an' get the young un."

The soldier turned and left. While I wondered what Lizzy was going to do with Lottie. I sucked in a deep breath and clung to her.

"You can't take her from me. She needs me."

The woman didn't respond, but looked at me in a, 'I've heard it all before' kind of way. A moment later a thin woman with lank blond hair came wandering down the hallway. She held her arms out expectantly for Lottie. I stared at her.

"Come with me sweetie, I'll take care of ye," she said reaching for Lottie.

I took a step back. "You can't take her. Please she's only a baby and she needs me." I could feel the panic starting in my stomach and the tears welling in my eyes. "Please."

"She'll be taken care of," said the large woman behind the desk. "Give her to Lizzy now."

I stared from one to the other and let out my breath. There was nothing I could do. I kissed the top of her head and handed her to the young woman. "Please take good care of her."

"Aye," she said before turning and sauntering back down the hall. I watched her go with absolute terror. My poor baby.

"What's ye name?" said the large woman.

I reluctantly drew my eyes from the young woman and Lottie. "Margaret Ch...Cheyne," I said stopping myself just in time from saying Chambers. "There's been a mistake, I came free – I'm not a convict."

"Ship?" she said ignoring my protests.

I stared at her bent head for a moment. Surely they'd realise I shouldn't be here. I compressed my lips. "I'm not a convict. I want my baby back."

"Look sweetie, ye'll make it a lot easier on yeself if ye just tell me what ship ye came on," she said with an exasperated sigh.

I sucked in a deep breath and slowly let it out. "William Metcalfe."

"Year?"

"Thirty-seven."

She finished writing and pushed the large ledger to one side before looking me up and down. "Mary," she called to an older woman who had been lurking in the shadows. "Take this one down to cell nine.

She can start work in the laundry tomorrow."

"Come on then lovey," she said giving me shove between the shoulder blades.

I started walking down the stone corridor towards an open door. From what I could work out the building was an octagonal shape with two central corridors. This one led passed the exercise yards and into an open area used for laundry. There were at least a dozen women scrubbing clothes in wooden tubs. The cell block was outside in a separate area. It had a veranda running the length of it with doors every few feet. Mary stopped and opened the door to number nine.

"There ye go lovey," she said standing back to allow me to enter. "Supper'll be at six, don't be late."

She turned and left the cell, closing the door on her way out. My knees were trembling and I was panting as my mind whirled and grasped, trying to make sense of this madness. My poor Lottie, what had they done with her? I swallowed as the panic threatened to overwhelm me. God, how was I going to get out of this nightmare?

The cell was small, dark and smelled of unwashed bodies and urine. I swallowed and waited for my eyes to become accustomed to the gloom. There were four beds, like bunks on a ship, two on each side which left a narrow walkway between them. I had no idea which one would be mine, and expected the current residents would quickly let me know. I sighed as I gingerly sat down on one of them.

I sat there in the gloom for a long time - trying to work out what to do. I had no idea. I could only hope that Captain Cheyne would realise where they'd taken me and come and get me out of here. I glanced up as the door opened and a young woman stepped inside. She left the door open, and I saw her face in the light - I thought I recognised her.

"Annie?" I said standing up. It was her. It was Annie from the rectory. What was she doing here?

"Well, would ye look what the cat dragged in," she said sneering at me.

I was shocked by her response and took a step back. "It's me, Margaret."

"Aye, I know who tis," she said. "An' I hoped to never lay eyes on ye again ye thieving hag."

I was now completely perplexed. I shook my head and stared at her. "I don't know what you think I've done, but I swear it wasn't me."

"Oh, it was ye alright. He was sweet on me until ye went an' threw yeself at him. Why else would he have preferred ye over me?" she said seductively swaying her hips. "Ye didn't even care that he was married. I thought ye'd back off after ye found out about his wife, but no ye had your hooks in him right proper."

"Will," I said staring at her, mouth agape. "You're talking about Will?"

"Aye ye know very well who I'm talking about," she said taking a step towards me.

I saw the hate in her eyes and I took another step back. I eyed her warily as I half expected her to hit me at any minute. I had no idea she'd pinned her hopes on Will. I remember her flirting with him and she somehow always managed to sit near him. But I had no idea she blamed me for his lack of attention. I swallowed as I tried to think of something to say that might calm her.

"What about Henry? I thought you were sweet on him?" How many nights had I noticed her missing from her bed? I was sure she'd been with Henry - and that was before Will had come to work in the garden.

She scoffed. "That was just a way to make William jealous an' take notice of me.

An' it was working until ye set yer cap on him."

"I'm sorry. I had no idea you felt that way."

Her upper lip curled back in a snarl and she let out a shrill laugh. "Well, it don't matter now. Your cosy little arrangements come to an end, an' ye an' ye bastard daughter is on yer own."

It took a moment for me to realise what she'd said. Cosy little arrangement? I stared at her - she couldn't have known. Maria would never have betrayed my confidence.

I shook my head. "No."

"Oh aye," she said with a laugh. "Except it worked out better than I thought. Yer in here with us croppies."

My breathing was laboured and I felt the panic starting to build in my stomach. She was responsible for this nightmare. It was her.

"You reported Captain Cheyne? But how did you know?"

"Oh ye always did think ye was so clever," she said flopping herself down on one of the bunks. "I overheard ye an' Mrs Davies talking, an' I just bided my time."

Another young woman came into the cell and glanced at us both, before sitting down on the other bunk.

"Oh, Alice this is Margaret," said Annie smiling at the woman. "She's the hag that stole my husband."

"I did not," I retorted with some intensity.

Alice gave me a cursory glance before giving a shrug of her shoulders. She looked exhausted and I didn't think she had the energy to get involved, for which I was thankful.

"You're better off without him." She screwed up her face and gave another shrug. "I was glad when my Harry pissed off."

Our conversation, if you could call it that, was interrupted when Mary arrived back on the scene. My heart leapt – Captain Cheyne must've come for me. I smiled at her and waited for her to speak my name.

"Well, Annie, it looks like ye free to go," she said rolling her eyes in mock surprise. "The Matron herself's assigned ye to work for Mrs Burnett in Glenorchy. Ye have friends in high places."

Annie smirked and jumped from the bunk. "Well, I expected as much. Goodbye, Margaret. I do hope ye enjoy ye stay." She laughed as she followed Mary from the cell.

I stared after them. The growing feeling of panic spread from a lump in my stomach to my extremities. I swallowed and tried to stop the tears that were now dripping down my face. It dawned on me that Annie was being rewarded for betraying Captain Cheyne. He'd probably been arrested as well, and wouldn't be rescuing me. My poor, Lottie. Fear gripped me. I had no idea where they'd taken her or if she was being cared for. I couldn't see any way out of this nightmare.

⁂

I spent the next three days scrubbing and washing soldiers breeches and shirts. There was an endless supply and the other women and I worked all day. It was hot and heavy work and my whole body was aching. My hands were rubbed raw and I was utterly miserable.

I pushed my hair under my cap with the back of my hand as I finished wringing out the last shirt. My basket was full of clean laundry ready to hang on the makeshift lines. I groaned as I lifted the heavy basket onto my hip and picked my way among the other women to the line. I'd just put the basket down when I heard someone call my name.

"Cheyne," said Mary coming up to me. "I've been callin' ye name for a good five minutes. Leave that, come wi' me."

I nodded and followed her into the main building and down the hall. Normally

I would've been curious as to what was going on, but I was beyond caring. I was exhausted and didn't think my situation could get any worse. We were nearly at the Matron's office when I saw a familiar figure standing at the end of the hall. My heart leapt and I sucked in a breath – Maria.

She rushed towards me and I collapsed into her arms and burst into tears. I clung to her like my life depended on it and buried my face in her shoulder.

"Hush," she whispered as she held me close. "It's alright, you're safe now."

I gulped in a lungful of air and tried to brush aside my tears. Finally, I managed to regain enough control of myself to speak. "Charlotte?"

"She's fine. She's with me," she said smiling at me. "Martha and I retrieved her from the nursery earlier. Are you alright? You're not hurt or anything?"

I shook my head. "No, I'm fine."

"We're so sorry Mrs Cheyne," said the Matron emerging from her office. "It was a terrible misunderstanding, but Mrs Davies has explained everything."

I stared at her as I tried to get myself under control. I finally managed to give her a nod. She smiled benignly at me.

"Well, you're free to go. We're so sorry, but you must understand we had no idea."

I wasn't about to protest or argue with her. I wanted nothing more than to get out of there and hold Lottie in my arms. If they'd listened to me in the first place of course this wouldn't have happened.

"Thank you," I said and I pressed my lips together so that I wouldn't say anything else.

"Come, Margaret," said Maria pushing her hand on my lower back and guiding me towards the main door.

I sensed she was worried about what I might say. I turned and allowed her to lead me from the horrid place. As soon as we stepped outside I saw John and Martha waiting for us in the spring cart. I could see my daughter's head of brown hair in the crook of Martha's arm. My heart leapt and I hurried over to her. She was asleep and looked perfectly alright. I brushed aside my tears of joy at seeing her and gently kissed her cheek.

Martha smiled down at me. "She's worn out poor thing. I'll hand her to ye when ye get up into the cart."

"No," I said with a shake of my head. "I don't want to disturb her." My arms were aching to hold her, but I knew she was safe. I climbed up onto the seat beside Maria and John urged the horses forward. I couldn't wait to get home, have a bath, to sleep and to forget.

Chapter Twenty Five

Safe in my own bed, January 1839

I stretched and yawned as I came out of my sleepy cocoon. Then the events of the past week came screaming back into the forefront of my mind. Lottie! I dived out of bed and arrived at the side of her crib in two steps. She was fast asleep and looking angelic. I sighed and padded back to bed. The morning light was only just starting to creep in under the blind. I climbed back into bed and snuggled down under the quilt.

Sleep wasn't likely to come as my mind was awake and alert. I hadn't given Will much thought since being arrested - not that I wasn't concerned for him - I was. But I'd had other things to worry about. Now, my mind turned to him and I was gripped by fear and anxiety. Maria hadn't had any news of him, and until Captain Cheyne returned I knew I'd have to be patient. I had no idea where he was either. He must've been arrested as well, or else he would surely have returned home by now. I groaned - I wish I could stop thinking.

After much protest last night Maria had brought me home to Captain Cheyne's. I wanted to be where Will could find me, and that was in Perth. Martha had immediately set to work preparing a hot bath for me. It was bliss to sink into the warm water and wash away the dirt and grime. I'd dressed in my own clean clothes and the three of us enjoyed a simple supper before I fell into bed from utter exhaustion. Maria had wanted to stay, but she'd done so much for me already and so I insisted she go home. I knew she'd want to get back to Rowland. She promised she'd come and check on me in a couple of days.

Lottie began to babble away happily and I smiled. It wouldn't be long before she'd start to complain and want her breakfast. I sucked in a breath and slowly let it out. What I needed most was to calm my thoughts and be patient. Perhaps some music would soothe my frayed nerves. I hadn't played my violin in months – I could definitely do with the practice.

Over the next few days, I spent every moment I could with Lottie. I'd been so terrified when she'd been taken from me, and I never wanted to be separated from her again. She gripped my hand as she pulled herself onto her feet. She thought she was so clever as she bounced up and down, testing how well her legs would hold her.

"Clever girl," I said laughing. "Who's a Mamma's girl? Mamma?"

She looked at me and giggled, before letting go and slumping to the floor. She put her fist in her mouth and went on babbling to herself – ignoring me, content with her own company. I stood and stretched and turned just as the front door opened.

"Captain Cheyne."

"Och lass, thank God ye here," he said marching over to me and embracing me in a tight hug. I was more than a little surprised. He'd never hugged me before. "And the bairn. I dinna ken if Mrs Davies got my message or no."

He let me go and I took a step back as I regained my balance. "Yes," I said smiling at him. "Thank you for sending her to my rescue. But I've been worried about you as well. Did they arrest you?"

"Och no," he said running his fingers through his whiskers. "They dragged me afore the magistrate and gave me a fine tis all. I lodged an appeal in Campbelltown, but I wasna successful."

I presume he meant he still had to pay the fine. I thought he ought to be grateful he hadn't been arrested and thrown in gaol. "Have you any news about Will, Tom and Swabby?"

"Not really," he said throwing himself into one of the comfortable chairs. "I expect they'll be back on the chain gang. I dare not make any official enquiries ye understand."

I nodded. I understood well enough. They would be in enough trouble without him trying to find out their whereabouts. I hoped they were alright. I knew Will would get word to me if he could. He knew where I was, and the last thing he'd said to me was – I'll find you.

"I just dinna understand how they found out," he said running his fingers through his hair. He'd obviously been doing that a bit because his hair was sticking out in all directions. He tried to smooth it back down and gave me a perplexed look, with what I thought was a tinge of sadness. "I've had croppies working for me for years, and we ain't ever got caught afore."

I swallowed and hoped he couldn't read my thoughts. I was never good at hiding what I was thinking, and I tried to put on an equally perplexed expression. I had no intention of telling him about Annie. It was my fault he'd got caught. I was desperate to stay here until Will came back. Captain Cheyne might not ask me to leave if he found out, but then again he might. I couldn't take that chance, so I shrugged my shoulders.

"No, I don't know how they could've found out."

He shook his head. "Well lass it's just the two of us now, and the bairn of course," he said getting to his feet. "You'll have to take care of yeself for the next week. I've got to get back to Campbelltown to see about my position."

I glanced at him. "Surely you won't lose your position?"

He raised his eyebrows and shook his head back and forth. "They stood me down pending an investigation. But no, I dinna think so. Dinna fash lass." He gave me a lopsided grin. "They willna find it so easy to be rid of me."

He disappeared down the hall, and I heaved a sigh. I hoped he was right. It was bad enough that the men had been arrested and sent back to the chain gang. I would be guilt-stricken if the Captain lost his job as well. I pushed all thoughts of Annie from my mind as I turned my attention back to Lottie. She was on her stomach with her knees pulled up beneath her, rocking back and forth with her bottom in the air. I smiled – it wouldn't be long before she was crawling.

Captain Cheyne came back wearing a clean set of clothes and a bag slung over his shoulder. "I'll see ye in a week or so.

Take care lass," he said giving me a peck on the cheek.

"I will. And good luck," I said putting my hand on his arm. "I truly hope you can work it out."

"Dinna fash," he said with a grin as he went out the door.

I watched him go, before closing the door and leaning against it. I slowly let out my breath. All I could do now was wait - wait for news of Will and pray the Captain would be reinstated.

February 1839

The weeks went by, and still, I had no news of Will's whereabouts. Captain Cheyne had resolved his employment with the Department of Public Works. I was so relieved. Life for me had settled into one of domesticity. I was thankful Swabby had taught me how to cook a few dishes, and so I was at least able to take care of myself and the Captain. I smiled to myself as I lifted the lid on a pot of corned beef. It was bubbling away nicely. I hardly recognise myself these days – cooking and cleaning - like I know what I'm doing.

A knock at the door took me by surprise. I wasn't expecting visitors. I hurried up the hall and opened it. A wide grin came across my face.

"Maria," I said hugging my dear friend and placing a warm kiss on her cheek. "What a lovely surprise. Come in, come in." I stood back to allow her and Rowland to enter. He toddled in and looked at me with his big blue eyes.

"Ottie?"

"Oh, she's asleep darling. She'll be awake soon," I said smiling at him.

"Run along and play Rowly," said Maria giving him a slight push towards the parlour. He headed for Lottie's toys without another word. "Let's talk in the kitchen," she said giving her son one last look.

I eyed her quizzically, but her face remained passive and unreadable. I couldn't help the feeling that she had something important to talk to me about. We settled ourselves at the table and Maria leaned across and took my hand.

"I have news," she said with a warm smile. "I'm so excited. I'm expecting another baby." Her smile widened and her face was alight with obvious excitement.

"Oh, Maria that's wonderful news," I said taking a better look at her. She was thin as usual but glowing with inner vitality. I hoped for her sake that everything would go well. "A little brother or sister for

Rowland by Christmas. I'm so pleased for you and the Reverend."

"Thank you. I've also got news for you," she said letting go of my hand and sitting back in her chair.

I stared at her. She could only mean one thing – news of Will. I swallowed and held my breath while I waited for her to continue.

"I've heard that Will's working for John McDowell in Norfolk Plains."

I let my breath out. "McDowell? I don't think I know him. But that's wonderful news. He's not on the chain gang." Tears pricked the back of my eyes, and I compressed my lips as I tried to hold them back. "Oh, Maria thank you so much. I've been worried sick about him,"

"I know you have," she said as she reached across the table for my hand again. She squeezed it gently. "You'd remember McDowell. He comes to our Church. A short dumpy sort of man with a big chin. His wife always looks exhausted."

I nodded. Yes, I remembered him. He had a reputation for being quick-tempered and thinking himself superior to most other people. His poor wife always looked worn out, and I'd always suspected he might hit her. The idea of a man like him having control over Will sent a chill through me. I shuddered and gripped Maria's hand.

"I hope Will doesn't do anything to antagonise him," I said taking my hand from hers. I ran my fingers down my skirt and gripped the folds of fabric. I prayed he wouldn't do anything to give McDowell an excuse to punish him. God, I hated this. I just wanted Will to be free so we could live our lives in peace.

"I'm sure he won't, Margaret," she said with a tone of reassurance. "Will's not stupid."

No, Will wasn't stupid, but he was a proud man who would stand up to a bully like McDowell. That's what really worried me. "I hope you're right," I said with some doubt in my voice.

Lottie's cries reached me. "I'll tend to Lottie then I'll make us some tea," I said standing up. "Will you stay for supper?"

"No. John's waiting for me with the cart," she said smiling. "Tea would be nice though."

"Alright, well just give me a few minutes to tend to Lottie."

I changed Lottie and took her into the parlour. Rowland was delighted to have her join him in the parlour to play. And I smiled with pleasure at seeing the two of them together. Rowland was such a sweet child.

Maria and I enjoyed another hour of gossip over a pot of tea before the children started to complain. I bid her farewell and set to preparing supper for Lottie and myself. I thought the Captain might not return home tonight. I couldn't help but wonder if Will would sneak out of McDowell's and come to see me. My heart thrummed at the thought, but my stomach clenched in fear. I wouldn't want him to give McDowell any reason whatsoever to punish him. I sighed. Would we ever be together and free?

Chapter Twenty Six

Perth, February 1839

It was the end of February, but already the evenings were getting cool. I wrapped my shawl around my shoulders and closed the door quietly behind me. Lottie was finally asleep and I had no desire to disturb her. She'd been fussy and grizzly all day, and she'd finally gone to sleep from sheer exhaustion. I think the reason for her irritability is she's teething. Lately, she's been sucking her fist and dribbling far more than usual. She also had a slight flush to her cheeks. I sighed as I sank into one of the comfy chairs in the parlour.

The Captain was away and I hoped to finish knitting a new jumper for Lottie before the weather got any cooler. I picked up my yarn and had just begun clicking my needles together when I heard an unfamiliar noise. I stopped and listened. A second later another sound reverberated down the hall. It sounded like someone was at the back door. I put down the knitting and with my heart thumping, I made my way towards the kitchen.

"Who's there?" I called as I peered into the gloom.

"Meg. It's me," came the reply.

I swear my heart stopped beating altogether. "Will."

In the pale evening light, he just appeared in front of me. He was grinning and I could see tears in his eyes. And then I was in his arms. I buried my face in his shoulder and breathed in the scent of him. His presence was so warm and solid and familiar. I melted into him and ran my fingers down his back. I felt him stiffen and I pulled myself from his embrace.

"What is it?"

He replied by pressing his lips to mine. I ran my tongue along the edge of his lip and pressed myself into him as our kiss deepened. I was breathless when we parted.

"I've missed you so much," he whispered in a hoarse voice.

"I've been worried sick about you," I said reaching for him. He took a step back and I stared at him with a raised brow. "What's wrong?"

He looked sheepishly at me and the silence stretched between us. "It's my back," he finally said. "I was flogged."

I pressed my hand to my mouth in shock. Flogged? Oh my God. It was like my worst fears had come to life. That bloody McDowell. Tears welled in my eyes as I thought of him tied up and beaten.

"When?"

"Last month," he said taking my hands in his. "Before I was sent to McDowell's. It's alright, it's nearly healed. It's just a bit tender is all." He bent down and kissed me softly again.

I nodded and stared at him. I could feel large wet tears slipping down my face and I wiped them away with the back of my hand. "I'm so sorry."

"I'm alright as long as you and Lottie are alright," he said looking into my eyes. "I was so scared when they took you and Lottie away."

"I know, I was as well, but Maria rescued us," I said and quickly filled him in. I told him about the Captain and how Maria had come for me. I very deliberately left any mention of Annie out of the telling. Now was not the time to tell him about her vengeful actions.

"I'll thank her when I see her next," he said smiling at me. "She's been such a good friend to us."

I nodded. "Yes, she has." I pressed myself against him and held onto his shoulders. "Hug me, I promise to not touch your back."

He wrapped his arms around me, and I felt safe for the first time in weeks. I sighed and breathed him in. I knew he couldn't stay for long and I just wanted to stay in his embrace forever. We finally parted and tiptoed into the bedroom so he could see his daughter. He kissed her gently before we quietly retreated.

"I'll come back and visit for longer next time," he said as he stood in the doorway ready to leave. "Stay safe."

I stood on tiptoes and kissed him. "I will. You stay safe too. And don't come if you can't. I know you want to and that's all that matters."

He smiled down at me. "I need to see you, Meg."

I knew what he meant, and I blushed. I needed him too.

Will managed to visit us several times over the next few weeks. On his last midnight escape, we'd made love and talked into the small hours. I told him how Annie had betrayed us.

"But there was nothing between us," said Will astounded at the news. "A bit of flirting was all."

"I know, but she was obviously hoping for more," I said snuggling closer to him. "Do you remember how she always found a way to sit beside you at mealtimes?"

"I do. And how can I forget the day she decided to drop news of Fanny." He wrapped his arm more firmly around me and kissed the top of my head. "I'm so sorry about that."

"It doesn't matter," I said, and I meant it. I knew how much he loved me and Lottie, and I was sure that one day we'd be together – maybe even married.

"So do you know where the bitch is? I'd have a word with her for meddling in our lives." His voice was gruff with anger.

"No," I lied. Should I have told him about Annie? It was too late now, but I had no intention of telling him she'd been assigned to work for Mrs Burnett. I could see nothing but trouble for us if he confronted her. "Forget about her, she's not important."

"No, but she's caused so much trouble for us and Captain Cheyne. All because she was jealous," he said in a voice edged with disdain. "She's due her comeuppance."

I nodded and ran my fingers down his chest. "She'll get hers. Forget about her, we have so little time." I wriggled my hips closer to him and nibbled his ear.

I heard him groan as he reached for me. We made love slowly as we explored each other and I committed him to my memory. It was nearly dawn before he crawled from my bed and started on the walk back to Norfolk Plains.

⁓

It would seem that John McDowell didn't deserve the reputation he had. According to Will, he was a firm but fair taskmaster. He grew a variety of vegetables on his small farm, and as long as the men did their work he had no complaint. He turned a blind eye to anyone missing from the huts at night – which was just as well. Will generally spent a couple of nights a week with Lottie and me.

To my surprise – and I'm sure Captain Cheyne's as well – in early May he was promoted to the position of Director of Public Works. He was now home most evenings and expected me to provide supper. Luckily my expertise in the cooking department had improved significantly.

Lottie marked her first birthday with Will and me singing happy birthday. She thought the whole affair was most peculiar, however, she did enjoy the cake.

I soon found the days and weeks starting to merge into one. I busied myself with cleaning and cooking, although I spent most of my time alone with Lottie. I looked forward to the nights when Will came and I had someone to talk with. Captain Cheyne had descended into a rather gloomy depression, and rarely engaged in conversation. I thought he'd be more than pleased with his new position in Launceston, but something was very wrong. I had no idea what.

I visited Maria and found her bedridden. I left Lottie in the company of Rowland under the watchful eye of Mrs Fitz. Maria had lost her baby and Doctor Salmon insisted she needed bed rest. She was pale and thin, and I thought some fresh air would benefit her.

"I'm so glad you came, Margaret," said Maria smiling wanly at me. Tears still clung to her eyelashes from telling me of her loss. "I just don't understand what happened."

I shook my head. "There's never an answer, these things just happen," I said and I squeezed her hand. "The main thing is that you recover your strength."

She smiled at me. "I think Doctor Salmon is being over cautious." She paused and stared out the window. "I'm just sad."

My heart wrenched for her, and I wished I had some words of comfort. I couldn't think of anything to say that would alleviate her sadness. We sat in silence for a while. It wasn't an uncomfortable silence, but more one of companionship. Finally, Maria turned to me with a small smile.

"Did you hear the stone for the new church was laid?"

I was so grateful for a new subject, and one that I knew was close to her heart. "Oh, that's wonderful news," I said sitting back in my chair. "I'm surprised the old church hasn't fallen down."

"I know," she said with a laugh. "It was such a wonderful affair. The Governor and Mrs Franklin came and he laid the stone. Now, we just have to be patient until it's finished."

"That must've been quite an affair," I said impressed that Governor Franklin had made the trip to the small hamlet. "Has the Reverend raised enough funds?"

"Not yet," she said with a shake of her head. "Actually, he's preaching at St John's in Launceston this Sunday, and I'm sure he'll be hoping for a good collection afterwards."

We chatted away amiably about the new church, and some local gossip. It was late in the afternoon before I had the heart to end our visit. I hoped I'd distracted Maria from her melancholy for a few hours at least, and I promised to visit her again the following week.

With the end of winter came the realisation that I was pregnant again. Morning sickness persisted for a month or more before finally dissipating. However, I wanted to be absolutely sure before I told Will. I wasn't sure how I was going to go on pretending to be the widowed Mrs Cheyne – not that anyone believed that story anyway. And I couldn't see how Will and I could marry any time soon.

Everything was going really well for Will working for John McDowell. However, it didn't seem like there was much hope of him recommending Will for a ticket of leave. He couldn't apply for permission for us to marry until then. I sighed as I pushed my vegetables around my plate with my fork. Captain Cheyne was equally disinterested in his supper, and sat staring into space.

"I'm sorry it's nowhere near as good as Swabby's," I said in an attempt to engage him in conversation.

The Captains head snapped as he looked at me in surprise. It was almost like he hadn't realised I was there until I spoke. "I think it needs more salt," I said before taking another mouthful.

"Och no lass, it's fine," he said waving his fork in the air. He unenthusiastically shovelled another forkful of supper into his mouth.

I swallowed and smiled. "Is everything alright?"

He sighed and ran his fingers through his whiskers. "Oh aye. Tis naught for ye to worry about," he said giving me what was supposed to be a reassuring smile. It didn't quite reach his eyes. "I think I'll retire."

"Oh, alright."

He rose from the table and left the room. I stared after him. I shook my head and with one final look at my supper decided I'd had enough as well. I collected the plates and prepared to clean up the kitchen. Whatever was bothering the Captain he didn't want to talk about it. I wasn't sure if I should continue to try and pry it out of him or not.

Chapter Twenty Seven

The Sewing Circle 1839

The local midwife, Mrs Mundy, was a sweetheart. She was monitoring my pregnancy and I think she must have realised I was lonely. She invited me to join her sewing group of local women. I wasn't much of a sewer but I needed the company.

I stabbed my needle into the dress I was sewing for Lottie, and allowed the women's chatter to wash over me. The children were playing happily under our watchful gaze, and I started to relax. Although, I expected it was just a matter of time before the gossip turned to me. I wasn't wrong.

"So, Margaret I hear you're from Western Australia. What brought you here?" said Mary Muller. Her needle was poised as she smiled at me in expectation. She was a rather plain young woman but her hair was the prettiest color. It was a pale blonde with reddish highlights through it.

"My husband died," I said taking a deep breath. I was sure they'd all heard my story and I expect I'd been the subject of their gossip. "I really had nowhere else to go. His Uncle Alex had always been so kind, and he insisted I come and stay with him here in Perth."

The women nodded and gave me piteous looks, and I tried my best to remain calm and poised. "I'm so grateful to he him for taking care of Lottie and me."

"Well of course you are," said Ivy Perch giving me a condescending smile. "But I hear you've remarried? How wonderful. What does your new husband do?"

I smiled and tried to put on my most demure face. "Will's a gardener," I said pushing the needle through the fabric as I tried to calm my growing nerves. "He works over in Norfolk Plains."

"Well congratulations," put in Charlotte Pert. "You're still living with your Uncle though?" Both her dark eyebrows were arched on her questioning face, and I shifted uneasily in my chair.

I smiled and nodded. "Yes, I think he enjoys our company."

"The Captain's such a fine man," said Mary cutting her thread with a pair of small scissors. "Ye know he always takes in the croppies and cares for them."

"I don't think so," scoffed Ivy. She turned her inquiring brown eyes in my direction. "Didn't you get caught up in the last raid my dear?"

"Yes," I replied. "But he was only trying to help." I was desperate to change the subject. I was squirming under their scrutiny and knew it was only a matter of time before I gave them more to gossip about.

"Well of course you'd wish to think the best of him," said Ivy putting her needle work in her lap and looking around the room. "But, I hear tell he's in a lot of trouble."

"Enough ladies," said Mrs Mundy standing and stretching. "Come and help me with the tea, Margaret."

"Of course," I said putting my needlework aside and standing up. I smiled at Mrs Mundy as I followed her from the room. I was glad to escape the other women, but I would've also liked to know what sort of trouble the Captain was in. I knew there was something amiss, and I was burning with curiosity.

December 1839

I received a surprise invitation to spend Christmas with Maria and Robert. I wouldn't normally have accepted such an invite, preferring to spend Christmas with Will and Lottie. But, there was little to no chance of seeing Will, and so I accepted. It was a warm day, and I appreciated Maria sending John in the spring cart to collect me.

The rectory had a festive appearance with a wreath of intertwined leaves on the front door. Garlands of pine adorned the hall table and the dining table had been set with the best crockery. Mrs Fitz immediately took charge of Lottie and the last I saw she was leading her out into the garden to play with Rowland. I smiled as I watched them go.

"Please come and join me in the parlour," said Maria putting her arm around my thickening waist and guiding me into the front room. "I'd have a private talk before luncheon."

I smiled and squeezed her in return. She was even thinner than she'd been last time I'd seen her, and the dark smudges under her eyes stood out in contrast to her pale skin.

"Are you alright?" I enquired as we sat together on the sofa. "You're so terribly thin, Maria. Unlike, me," I said with a laugh as I ran my hands over my growing belly. I was only two months off having my baby.

Her face settled into serious lines as she looked at me. "No, I'm not very well."

"What is it?" I said, my voice rising in pitch as I searched her face. "Are you expecting again?" I hoped not. She'd not recovered fully form the last miscarriage, and by the look of her she'd be unlikely to bring a child to full term.

"No, no," she said shaking her head. "Quite the opposite. I've been having terrible women's problems with cramps and bleeding."

I drew in a breath and slowly let it out. "I'm so sorry. Is there anything Doctor Salmon can do?"

"No," she said with a note of finality in her voice. She sighed and then gave me a weak smile. "He's suggested I return to England and seek medical treatment."

I swallowed. "England? But that would be such an arduous trip."

"I know," she said taking my hands in hers. "But, Robert has agreed and so we're leaving in the New Year."

I felt my breath leave my body, and I just stared at her. She was my rock, had been my best friend and supporter, and I didn't know what I'd do without her. I felt hot tears prick my eyes.

"No."

"I know. I'm going to miss you like mad," she said with tears welling in her eyes. "But I must try and get help from the best Doctors if I hope to have more children. And I desperately want more children."

I grabbed her in a tight hug and held onto her for dear life. "Of course you want more children, and I so hope you do," I said kissing her cheek and letting her go. "But must you go so soon?"

She smiled and wiped her tears away with a clean handkerchief. "Robert's booked passage for us, we sail in three weeks. I'm sure we'll come back though. He's taking a leave of absence."

"Of course you must do what you must, but I'm going to miss you so much," I said with a tremulous smile. "But more than anything, I hope it's successful for you."

"Thank you, Margaret. I know you want the best for me. And you'll be fine. You've got Will and before you know it you'll have a new baby to keep you busy."

I ran my hand over my belly. How could I deny her the same happiness? I couldn't. I just prayed she'd get the treatment she needed, and would come back safely. The joy of Christmas was bittersweet knowing we'd part in a few weeks, and may never see each other again. Lottie and I stayed as late as we could, and Maria and I clung to one another as we said our goodbyes.

March 1840

Will sat in the chair under the window nursing his new son. I'd gone into labour in the early hours, and our son William was born at dawn. He looked so tiny in his father's arms. Will had a rapturous look on his face as he watched his son sleep. I smiled and lay back against the pillows, exhausted but content.

"Who will you ask to be his godmother?" he said looking wide eyed at me. "Maria won't be back this year, I wouldn't think."

I shook my head. "I don't know," I said closing my eyes. I was glad when I heard him sigh but he didn't say anything further. I wanted nothing more than to snuggle down under the covers and sleep. All thoughts evaporated as I drifted off into a dreamless slumber.

I was woken an hour later by the hungry cries of my new son. I smiled sleepily as Will placed him in my arms. I peered down at his screwed up face and kissed the top of head before guiding him onto my breast. After a bit of fussing he latched on and I sighed as he began to suckle.

"Are you alright?" said Will kissing me on the forehead before relaxing in the chair by the window again. "Can I get you anything?"

"No, I'm fine, and Mrs Mundy will take care of me for a few days. You needn't worry," I said with a yawn. "Shouldn't you be getting back? McDowell will be missing you."

"Not yet. I would spend a few hours with you and my new son."

I nodded and ran my thumb over William's head. He was nearly bald with only a few wisps of dark fluff covering his head. It was enough to tell me he'd probably have my wayward locks. I smiled at Will, who was looking adoringly in my direction. I was anxious for him, and would've preferred him to go. John McDowell had proved to be a fair taskmaster, but he wouldn't take kindly to Will being absent for the day.

William stopped suckling and I put him over my shoulder and began rubbing his back. I'd forgotten how small new born babies were. He let out a soft belch and I cradled him in my arms. His eyes were half closed and I expected he'd be asleep again in no time.

Will stayed with us for most of the day, and I was glad when he finally bid me farewell. I was sure he'd be in trouble. Mrs Mundy stayed with me for next four days, sleeping on a pallet in the lean to where Swabby used to sleep. She was a godsend.

Captain Cheyne had been away in Hobart for the past two weeks, and arrived home just as Mrs Mundy was leaving.

"Congratulations lassie," he said as he peered at William asleep in his crib."Och he's a fine big lad."

"Yes he is," I said smiling as we tiptoed out of the room and cautiously closed the door. "How was Hobart?"

He ran his fingers through his whiskers and sighed. "Och it was as I expected," he said in a resigned tone. "I dinna think Governor Franklin is such a supporter of mine as he used to be."

"Oh," I said raising my brows. Perhaps this had been the cause of his melancholy of late. "I'm sorry to hear that." I didn't know what else to say without sounding like I was prying.

"No matter," he said with a shrug. "Oh, I brought ye a copy of the Hobart Courier. I thought ye might like to catch up on the latest gossip and such."

"Thank you," I said with genuine enthusiasm. The small town of Perth was such a backwater, and it took months for news to reach us. Having a copy of the latest newspaper from Hobart Town was a real treat. "I'll look forward to reading it," I said as I headed for the kitchen to prepare supper. I would find time tomorrow to savour my treat.

Chapter Twenty Eight

Perth 1840

My entire day now evolved around Lottie and William. I barely had time to do the necessary chores in between changing and feeding them. It was a week before I found time to do more than just skim the newspaper from Hobart Town. I sipped on my tea as I relaxed in the chair and turned the page. William was asleep, and I expected he'd remain that way for at least another hour. Lottie was playing happily with her doll, and would not require my attention. At least I hoped not.

I was perusing the lists of advertisements and was amazed at the diversity of goods on offer. I could only dream of being able to purchase such a variety here in Perth. I was halfway down the page when a name jumped out at me – William John Hatley Penny otherwise known as William Hartley.

My heart leapt into my throat and I put my teacup down with a clatter. It was an advertisement for him to contact some solicitors in Hobart Town. I was sure it was about Will. I reread it several times.

If William John Hatley Penny, otherwise William Hartley, who, in or about the year 1836 left England for Hobart Town in the ship Lord Lyndoch, be living, he may hear of something to his advantage. He was a native of Essex and related to Frances Elizabeth Penny. Any person furnishing information about him will be rewarded. Apply to Mr G Butler, Solicitor, Butler and Son, 4 Harrington Street, Hobart Town.

Fanny! Oh my God, it was his wife. I felt sick. What could she want? The only thing I could think of was that she hoped to reunite with her husband. Maybe she'd come looking for him? My stomach clenched and I felt panic rising from my belly, which was about to overwhelm me. I was breathing heavily and coming out in a cold sweat as I shoved the newspaper aside and got to my feet. What was I going to do? I paced up and down the small parlour as I tried to calm myself and gain control of my thoughts. Will would never read the newspaper, I could simply not tell him. I eyed the newspaper as I weighed up my options.

I groaned. Who was I kidding? I couldn't keep something like this from him. I sucked in a deep breath and slowly let it out. If only Maria were here. She'd know what to do. But she'd only sailed for England two months ago, and wouldn't be back until – well I didn't know when or even if she would be back.

I picked up the paper and reread the advertisement. I was sure it was about Will and knew it could only mean trouble. I'd keep it to myself. A pang of guilt shot through me as I came to the awful decision. I had too much to lose. I tiptoed into the bedroom and slid the newspaper under the edge of my mattress. I compressed my lips as I quietly closed the door and leaned against it. Tears pricked my eyes as I thought about what this would mean to Lottie and William. I blinked them back and sucked in a deep breath.

I spent the next few days in a constant state of anxiety which was making me feel quite ill. It was well after supper time when Will called in unexpectedly. I never knew when he might be able to escape McDowell's unnoticed. I'd just got Lottie settled for the night and I'd changed William ready to put him down.

"Ah I've missed you," he said wrapping his arms around us both and nuzzling my neck. "How's my lad?"

"As you can see, just about ready for bed," I said handing him his son. "You can put him down if you like."

He cradled him in his arms and kissed his forehead. "He's growing so fast Meg. Look at the size of him already."

I smiled at them both. He was right. William had put on weight since he was born, and was a picture of health with his rosy chubby cheeks. I watched Will quietly go into the bedroom. He returned a minute later and quietly closed the door on our sleeping children.

He took me in his arms and our lips met. I was hungry for him and clung to his broad shoulders. He ran his tongue along my top lip and I pressed myself closer as our kiss deepened. I sighed with contentment when we parted. He hugged me close and ran his hands down my back.

"I cannot wait to make love to you," he said kissing my neck and nuzzling me.

I arched my back and snuggled into him. I couldn't wait either.

"It won't be long," I said pulling back from him and smiling.

His mood turned serious, as he ran his thumb across my cheekbones. "Are you well? You're pale and there are dark smudges under your eyes."

"I'm fine," I said turning away from him. I was hopeless at hiding anything, and

I was sure he'd read my face. "I'm just tired. A baby and a toddler are a lot of work."

"Of course," he said nodding. "I'm so sorry I can't be here to help you."

"It's alright," I said trying to fix my face with a look of nonchalance.

He peered at me with concern etched in his hazel eyes. "You'd tell me if there was something wrong?"

"Yes, of course," I said sucking in a breath. I could feel a flutter starting in my stomach, and I was sure he'd see it in my eyes. The panic I'd been trying to control was rising like acid in my throat. I needed to change the subject, but I was floundering to think of anything except that damned newspaper.

He crossed his arms and stared at me. "I know something's amiss. It's written all over your face."

Damn. I compressed my lips and groaned inwardly. I should never have tried to deceive him, but what if he left me? What would I do? I suppose I could return home and tell more lies to my family. I was just so bad at lying. I took a deep breath and slowly let it out.

"Yes, you're right."

"Whatever it is I'm sure it's not as bad you think," he said taking my hands in his and squeezing. "What is it then?"

I lowered my eyes and breathed in. "It's about as bad as it gets. Wait here."

I tiptoed into the bedroom and slipped the newspaper out from under the mattress. Lottie and William's rhythmic breathing assured me they were both asleep. I left the room and quietly closed the door behind me. I crossed to the parlour and looked at Will. He was looking at me with raised brows and worry clear in his eyes.

"What is it?"

I handed him the paper which was folded in such a way as to show the advertisement clearly. "See the advert. Someone's looking for you."

His eyes flicked from me to the paper as he read the article. "Fanny," he said looking at me with astonishment.

"Yes, Fanny." I could feel the tears pricking my eyes as I watched him. He reread the advertisement before putting it aside and reaching for me. I took a step back from him and stared. "She's come for you."

"Don't be ridiculous."

"Well, what else would this be about?" I said as I tried to hold back my tears. "Why else would she be looking for you? You're her husband." My words shot through me like a bolt of lightning. Her husband - not mine. The ache of unshed tears tore across my throat, and I swallowed.

"No, Meg. You're my wife. I love you," he said reaching for me again and enveloping me in his arms. I sobbed against his shoulder.

"But..but she's."

"Hush," he said squeezing me. "I don't know what she wants, but she can't have me. I promise you."

I shook my head and pushed him away. "She's your wife."

"No. You're my wife, and I don't care what she wants. I'll ignore this..this advertisement. She means nothing to me."

I wanted to believe him. I wanted so much to be his wife, but ignoring this wouldn't make it go away. I wiped my tears aside with the back of my hand.

"We cannot ignore this. I don't want to be haunted by your wife and forever looking over my shoulder."

"Aye," he said with a sigh as he slumped into the nearest chair. "You're right. We cannot be forever looking over our shoulder."

"What will you do?" I said sliding into the other chair.

"I'll write to this solicitor and find out what he wants," he said running his fingers through his hair. "And then I'll deal with it, whatever it is."

I pressed my lips together and breathed in through my nose. I was scared I'd lose him, but I knew it wouldn't be because he didn't love me, or our children. I just prayed Fanny hadn't arrived in Hobart Town already. I wiped away my tears that were running down my face.

"Whatever it is, we'll face it together," I said getting off my chair and kneeling at his feet. I looked into his worried face and knew he'd do everything to keep us together.

He took my face in his hands and kissed me softly before wiping my tears away with his thumb. "I promise you, Meg nothing, not even Fanny, will drive me from you."

I believed him.

The wait for news from Mr Butler in Hobart Town was agonising. The weeks went by, then a month and still, there was no reply. I oscillated between feelings of optimism and hopelessness. I was grateful for William and Lottie, who kept me so busy and occupied. It was only in the evenings once they were both in bed that my thoughts dwelled on Fanny.

Will was constantly optimistic that everything would be fine. I knew he was putting on a brave face for me, but the fear of losing him didn't leave me. It was nearing the end of November before Will arrived one evening clutching an envelope from the elusive Mr Butler.

I stared at him and held my breath as he opened the envelope. Inside was a short note from Mr Butler, and another envelope addressed to Will.

"It's from Fanny," he said slitting open the envelope.

I heaved a sigh of relief. She hadn't come at all but had only sent a letter. I felt my whole body relax for the first time in weeks. "What does it say?"

15th October, 1839
Margaretting, Essex

Dear William,

I write to you in the hope that this letter finds its way into your hands. It has been three years since you departed, and in that time I've come to believe that you will never return. Your family have been most kind, but it is time for me to live my own life. I am still a young woman, and I would marry and have a family of my own.

Will stopped reading and looked at me. "What did I tell you? There's nothing to worry about, she doesn't want me back."

I was grinning like a loon, as the realisation that Fanny wasn't going to interfere in our lives hit home. "I'm so glad," I said brushing a wayward tear of happiness aside. "I'm so relieved. What else does she say?"

I beseech you, do not return to England. I am to be married to a fine man who loves me and cares for me deeply. He believes me to be a widow, and I would ask that you do nothing to enlighten him. By the time you receive this letter, I will be Mrs Henry Whittington. Please do not seek me out, but rather let me find some happiness in this world.

I pray for your redemption and your wellbeing. I hope you will acquire your freedom and find some solace in your new life. Goodbye, William and God bless.
Fanny.

Will dropped the letter on the table and scooped me into his arms. We hugged and kissed as our tears of joy intermingled. What I had perceived as a threat to our happiness could not have been further from reality. Will was mine, and he was all I needed.

Chapter Twenty Nine

Perth January 1841

Reflecting on the year just ended has left me feeling hopeful for our future. I have my little family, which is growing by the day, and although life isn't perfect, I'm happy. Christmas was a quiet affair this year, with just me, Captain Cheyne and the children.

I received a letter from home with news of my family. My brother Philip, who I've not seen for many years is now with the Madras fusiliers in India. According to mother, he's married to the army and never likely to find a woman who would put up with his life on the road. Barb had yet another miscarriage and seems destined not to be blessed with a family. Charlotte and John are enjoying the London life, and John's association with Uncle Abraham has worked to both their benefits. I know my sister Charlotte will be enjoying the prestige of her husband's position.

I sighed as I folded the last of the washing. I could hear Lottie's raised voice coming from the parlour. I would need to intervene if I wanted peace. I arrived in the doorway of the parlour just in time to see

Lottie smack William's hand away from her tower of blocks.

"No Willie," she said trying to push him away. She turned to me, "tell him no Mamma." The frustration with her young sibling was clear in her soft grey eyes.

William turned his large hazel eyes in my direction to see what I would do. I smiled at my cheeky ten-month-old son. He was a rascal and delighted in annoying his older sister.

"Leave her be," I said scooping him into my arms and kissing him. "Come out into the garden with me." I tickled him and he squealed as I made my out to the rear garden.

The afternoon was warm, but not too hot, and the vegetable patch needed my attention. I put Willie down beside me and we began pulling weeds together. We were so engrossed in our work that I didn't hear Will approaching until he spoke.

"What are you two doing?" he said dropping down beside us. He kissed Willie on the cheek before pulling me into his arms. "You smell like dirt," he said kissing me and nuzzling my neck.

I laughed and pushed him away. "I'm surprised that's all I smell like."

"How are you my rascal?" He scooped him into his arms and swung him into the air, much to Willie's delight. He put him down and got to his feet, stretching his back. "I have news. Good news."

It was only then that I realised Will was grinning from ear to ear. I wiped my hands on my apron and eased myself off my knees. I raised my brows at him. "What?"

"I've got my ticket," he said waving a piece of paper under my nose. "I can hardly believe it."

He grabbed me and swung me around. I wasn't sure that I'd heard him correctly. He stopped spinning and put me down and I gazed up into his smiling face. "Your ticket? You mean your ticket of leave?" I could hardly believe what I was hearing.

"Aye. McDowell gave me the paperwork this morning. Apparently, he recommended me for it last year, and it's only just come through. I'm free. We're free." The excitement in his voice was unmistakable and I could see the tears of joy welling in his eyes.

I grabbed him and hugged him tightly. "Oh my God, Will. You know what this means?" We had hungered for it for so long, that it was hard to comprehend he finally had it. He was free. We could go wherever we wanted, he could get a job and earn a living. We could live a normal life. I burst into tears – tears of joy.

"Yes I know what this means," he said letting me go.

He stooped down on one knee and took my hand in his. "Will you marry me? In a church, proper like, before God?"

A wide smile spread across my face and I stared at him. "Yes. Oh my goodness of course yes."

He swept me into his arms again and our lips met. This time it was a lingering kiss, and I ran my tongue along the inside of his lip. His tongue darted into my mouth and I groaned as I pressed myself against him. It was only Willie's insistent pulling on my skirt that broke us apart. I laughed and lifted him into my arms.

"Do you know what your Papa just asked me? Do you?" I said kissing him. "We're going to be married."

"I'll seek permission as soon as I can," said Will grinning at us.

That evening over supper we told Captain Cheyne our good news. He was delighted for us, of course, but it was a double-edged sword. I'd been living with him since before Lottie was born, and he'd become like a father to me. Now that Will was free, we'd be making our own way in the world.

"I can't thank you enough for all you've done for me and Margaret," said

Will putting down his cutlery. "But I also can't wait to leave this place and Norfolk Plains."

"Och laddie, Margaret's like my own daughter," said Captain Cheyne waving his fork around. "I can understand that ye want to leave here, but dinna rush."

I reached out my hand and squeezed the Captain's arm. His words had touched me, and I felt the same way about him. I would miss him. "We won't be leaving right away," I said smiling. "Will plans to go and get settled first."

"Well, that's a fine idea. Send for Margaret and the bairns once you're settled. Where do ye plan to go?"

"Down Hobart way," said Will swallowing a mouthful of pork. "I reckon New Norfolk might suit us."

The Captain nodded. "Well I canna deny that I'm going to miss ye all, but a new start will do ye the world of good." He took a mouthful of ale and wiped his mouth with the back of his hand. "Matter of fact, I know someone down that way who may be of help to you, Will. James Triffett. He runs the pound and has a farm of about eighty acres where he grows all manner of things."

Will raised his head and grinned. "Aye, well I could do with a recommendation. Triffett you say. I'll look him up."

"Do," said the Captain nodding. "Tell him I sent ye." He raised his glass and looked at us both. "Here's to new beginnings then."

I clinked my glass with his and Will's and sighed with contentment. Finally, things were going our way. I was sure we'd make a go of it in New Norfolk, away from Will's convict past. I planned to teach music if I could attract a few clients. It was like life for us was starting afresh, and I couldn't wait.

A week later Will set off for New Norfolk. We wouldn't be seeing each other for at least a month, and I'd clung to him when we'd said our goodbyes. The memories of our lovemaking last night would have to stay with me until I saw him next. I smiled to myself as I remembered being cocooned in his arms. The wait would be worth it. We'd be free, and I hoped – married at last.

In the meantime, I busied myself with caring for the children and keeping house for Captain Cheyne. Surprisingly his mood had improved, although he was tight-lipped about the work he was doing in Launceston.

The aroma coming from the stew I was cooking was making my mouth water. I gave it a stir and had a taste. It was delicious, but it wouldn't be cooked for another hour.

I peeked in on Willie and Lottie, who were playing happily in the parlour. I wondered how long it would before a disagreement broke out between them. I settled myself at the dining room table and prepared to write. I hadn't had any word from Maria since she'd left Van Diemen's Land last January, but I thought she and Robert would return at some point. By then I'd be gone, and I didn't want to lose touch with her. I determined to write her a short letter, letting her know we'd gone to New Norfolk.

I spent the best part of an hour musing over what to tell her, making sure I filled her in on all the local news. Not that there was much to tell. I realised on rereading the letter that it was mostly about Lottie and Willie. I smiled as I signed it and folded the creamy paper and carefully slid it into the envelope. I planned to ask Mary Muller to mind the children this Sunday so I could go to Norfolk Plains and deliver my letter.

Sunday morning dawned bright and sunny, and I dressed in my Sunday best. I put on a straw bonnet and tied the ribbons under my chin. Peering in the polished mirror I thought it suited me. My dark unruly hair was confined in a snood and I thought the lines of my face had softened and looked more rounded than they used to. Motherhood had softened my features, although my mouth was still too wide to be considered pretty.

I gathered Willie in my arms and told Lottie to hold onto my skirt as we went down the street to Mary's house. I dropped them off at the front door into her care. Lottie barely said goodbye as she skipped inside. She always enjoyed playing with the Muller twins, Katie and Mary. They were just six months older than her. I handed Willie to Mary and kissed his cheek before handing her a bag of clean clouts and clothes.

"Thank you so much for doing this," I said smiling. "There's a clean set of clothes for them in there just in case." I turned and set off down the path.

"Ye are welcome, Margaret," she said putting a wriggling Willie down. He immediately set off on all fours after the girls. "Have a good day, and don't worry about the younguns, they'll be fine with me."

I turned and waved. "Thank you."

I set off for Norfolk Plains unhindered and I set a good pace. I hoped to be there before Church service started. I reached the outskirts of town an hour later and headed for the rectory. The driveway and front of the house looked just how I remembered it, but it had a deserted feel to it.

I made my way around the back passed the stables and followed the path down to the back gate. The garden looked overgrown and in need of attention. Weeds were sprouting out between the rocks that edged the path and the whole place felt neglected. The gate creaked in protest as I pushed it open and headed for the Church.

The congregation were filing inside as I approached I scanned those ahead of me for anyone I knew. I was hoping Mrs Fitz or Martha would be here today. I introduced myself to the Reverend Browne and shook his hand as I entered the Church. Nothing much had changed inside. The props holding up the roof were still in place. I smiled to myself as I remembered how on rainy days we'd placed pots around to catch the drips from the leaky roof.

The Church was crowded and noisy, and although I craned my neck to see, I didn't see anyone I recognised. I decided to settle myself in the back row and enjoy the service, and afterwards, I would find someone to deliver my letter for me.

As soon as the service ended I filed outside and positioned myself near the door. I didn't have to wait long before I spied Mrs Fitz. I waved and called out to her, and she turned and caught sight of me. A wide smile spread across her face as she picked her way over to me.

"Oh Lordy be, Margaret how lovely to see ye," she said as we embraced.

"I was hoping to see you here," I said letting her go and smiling. "Have you had any news of Mrs Davies?"

"Och I was about to ask ye the same. No, nary a word," she said folding her arms across her ample bosom. "But I dinna expect to really. I'm sure they'll be back afore too long."

"I hope so," I said reaching into my pocket and retrieving my letter. "I wonder if I could ask a favour? Would you mind giving this letter to her when you see her? I'm moving to New Norfolk soon and I wanted to let her know."

"Aye of course," she replied taking my letter and putting in her pocket. "I dinna know when that will be, but I expect I'll know all about it when they do get back. How's that wee lassie of yours?"

"Growing up faster than I can keep up with. She'll be three this year, and I also have a son, Willie. He'll be one come March."

"Well, ye have your hands full. I can only hope that Mrs Davies will have a new bairn when she gets here."

I nodded and smiled. "Yes I hope so as well."

"Would ye like to join me for dinner afore ye head back? It won't be much, but ye'll at least need a cup of tea."

"Thank you, that would be lovely."

I hadn't realised until she mentioned it, that I would be starving before I got back. I was grateful for her kind invitation and looped my arm in hers as we left the churchyard.

Chapter Thirty

The Cottage New Norfolk, May 1841

It had taken far longer for us to make the move to New Norfolk than we'd anticipated. Will had secured work with James Triffett, and we were most grateful for Captain Cheyne's recommendation. Suitable accommodation had been somewhat more difficult to obtain. We had no furniture to speak of, and any of the affordable houses for rent were unfurnished. Finally, Will had found us a small furnished cottage to rent for a reasonable ten shillings per week.

The children and I had spent three days travelling by coach down to New Norfolk. It had been cold and uncomfortable for the most part, and Willie had shared his discomfort and grumpy disposition with our fellow passengers. I'm sure they are glad to be rid of him. The coach only went as far as the north side of the Derwent River. Although there is a newly opened bridge across, it's only open to foot traffic.

Will was waiting for us at the toll booth. A rather odd beehive-shaped building situated on the north side of the river. I collapsed into his waiting arms. I was so relieved to hand Willie over to him, along with our baggage.

"How was your trip down?" he asked picking up our portmanteau.

"Cold and uncomfortable, but Willie was the real trial. He hated it," I said taking Lottie by the hand and picking up my violin case. "I'm just glad we're finally here."

I smiled at him as we headed for the bridge. I'd missed him so much, and couldn't wait for a proper reunion later tonight. I felt my cheeks flush as I watched him walk ahead of me, and I admired his muscular form.

The river Derwent was narrower here than it was in Hobart Town where we'd crossed by the ferry. Its grassy banks were lined with gum trees, and the settlement of New Norfolk was nestled at the base of sweeping hills. The main street went straight ahead from the bridge, and from this distance, I could see several shops and businesses. It was far bigger than Perth had been.

"You'll find we've a general store, butcher and baker," said Will over his shoulder. "Our place is just down here." He pointed down the road which ran along the river's edge. "And around the corner. It isn't far."

"I must say New Norfolk's busier than we're used to," I said as a carriage and two men on horseback passed us. I pulled Lottie over to the side of the road and held her firmly until they'd passed. She looked at them wide-eyed.

"Aye, well tis only twenty miles to Hobart Town from here," he said stopping and waiting for me and Lottie to catch him up. "Although some go by river, the road is busy."

I nodded. It was going to be different living down here. It was more populated and so close to Hobart Town, which I found quite exciting. I wondered if we'd be able to go for a visit and see the shops and the market. Will turned the corner and about a hundred yards down the street came to a halt outside a modest cottage. It had a very small frontage with only two windows with a front door between them. There wasn't any garden to speak of, just a weepy looking gum tree hanging over the front of it.

"Well, what do you think?" said Will walking up the dirt path to the front door. He opened it and stood aside with a look of uncertainty.

I smiled and kissed his cheek as I went inside. "I love it."

The cottage was small with only two bedrooms which were sparsely furnished, On the whole, the furniture was shabby and worn, but it would suffice. It was clean and it was ours. I couldn't have been happier if it had been a grand castle complete with moat. The main room consisted of the parlour and dining room. I dropped my case and let go of Lottie's hand before exploring the rear of the house. A lean-to kitchen was tacked on the back with a wash house set just outside the back door. A quick glance of the rear garden took in a few trees and a small vegetable patch. I headed back inside.

"It will do nicely," I said turning around and taking in the whole place.

"I know it isn't much," said Will wrapping his arms around me from behind. He rested his chin on the top of my head. "But, we're free...and," he said spinning me around to face him. "We have permission to marry."

He was grinning like a loon, and he lowered his head and pressed his lips to mine. I leant against him and returned his embrace, mindful that we were being watched by our young offspring. I sighed as we parted – content with life and our future together.

"I can hardly believe we're finally going to be married. When?"

"Soon," he replied before heading off into one of the bedrooms and returning a moment later without our baggage. "I'll speak with the Reverend about having the banns read. As soon as that's done, we'll be married."

A warm contented feeling spread from my midsection outwards, until I felt a tingling in my toes. I just knew everything was going to work out for us. New Norfolk was going to be a new beginning, and I couldn't wait.

The next morning after breakfast I gathered Lottie and Willie and headed for the main street. I was anxious to explore our new home and buy some much needed supplies. I have no idea what Will's been living on because our larder was almost bare. There were a few basic items like flour, sugar and oats, but not much else.

I retraced our walk from yesterday and headed up the main street towards the shops. We were not the only ones out and about, and I couldn't help but notice people stopping and talking in the street. I smiled and looked forward to the day when I would know someone to talk to. I continued along Blair Street until I came to the general store.

"Margaret. Margaret is that ye?" came a woman's voice from behind me.

I turned to face the woman, no doubt with a quizzical expression on my face. She looked vaguely familiar, but I had no idea from where. She was rather short and plump with her blonde hair pulled back into a tight bun. But her smiling brown eyes were very familiar.

"Ann?" The last time I'd seen Ann Chapman was on board the William Metcalf. I never expected to see her again and was delighted.

A wide smile spread across her face. "I wasn't sure if it was ye or not. I never thought to see ye again. How are ye?" she gushed and wrapped me in a warm embrace. "Are these ye children? Hello," she said bending down slightly to better see the children. "I've got a little one about your age, his name's Johnny."

"Yes, this is Lottie and Willie," I replied. "Say hello to Ann."

"Hello," said Lottie before hiding behind my skirts.

Willie was even less enthused and scowled at her.

"It's so nice to see you again. Are you living here in New Norfolk?"

"Yes, with my husband John. He works for old Henry the smithy," she said straightening and smiling at me. "Well, actually we live with his mother, but we hope to get our own place one day. What about ye?"

"Oh, the children and I only moved here yesterday," I said lifting a grumbling Willie into my arms.

"Oh well, I can show ye around if ye like. Have ye got many messengers to do?"

"Yes, our larder is bare," I said with a laugh.

"Well how about ye call around for tea tomorrow? I'd so love to have a proper chat with ye, I don't know too many people here meself."

"I'd love to. Where do you live?"

"Oh just around the corner in The Avenue," she said waving her hand in the general direction. "Number twelve. How would ten-thirty suit ye?"

"Perfect. Thank you, Ann, I'll look forward to it."

"Tomorrow then," she said with a wave as she headed off down the street.

I watched her go before stepping into the general store. It was well stocked and after introducing myself I handed over my list of items. Mr Brownell offered to open an account for me and to have my order delivered for a small fee. I couldn't have been happier with the arrangement.

After a visit to the baker and the butcher, I headed back home. I planned on unpacking and settling into our new home proper. Some cleaning would definitely be needed, and if time permitted I'd set to work in the vegetable garden.

The following morning I set off in search of the Avenue. It was just around the corner from Officer Street, and I had no trouble finding number twelve. The house had a wide veranda and was set back from the street with a well maintained front garden. I opened the gate and led Willie and Lottie up the path to the front door and knocked. A moment later it swung open and Ann greeted us.

"I'm so glad ye came, come in," she said standing aside to allow us to enter.

"Thank you." I stepped into a narrow hallway with Lottie and Willie close on my heels. A young boy with a mop of blonde hair, not much older than Willie, was leaning against the wall, peering at us. "Hello, you must be Johnny."

"Yes, say hello," said Ann bustling past me. "He's a bit shy, but he'll come round. Come this way." She grabbed Johnny by the hand and headed down the hall.

I followed her and soon found myself in a large kitchen. An older woman was busy rolling out dough on the kitchen table. She looked up as we entered and smiled warmly at us.

"Ye must be, Margaret," she said in a gravelly voice.

I was momentarily taken aback. Her voice didn't match her rosy complexion and rotund shape. With her greying hair pulled back in a loose bun she looked like the most motherly person imaginable.

"Yes," said Ann as she headed for the stove and placed the kettle on. "This is my mother-in-law, Elizabeth. Everyone calls her, Bessie."

"Very nice to meet you," I said gathering my children in front of me. "This is Lottie and Willie."

"Ah, very nice to meet ye," she said reaching for a scone cutter. "Would ye like to help me make some scones?" She held the cutter out to Lottie, who after a moment of hesitation took it and sidled up to the table.

"Ye'll have to wash ye hands first," said Ann taking the cutter from Lottie and leading her over to the trough.

"I can do it," said Lottie taking the proffered soap.

"Aye, of course, ye can," said Ann stepping aside. "Johnny, why don't ye take Willie outside to play?"

"Awright Mamma. Come on."

Willie wasted no time in letting go of me and scampering after Johnny. I smiled as I watched them disappear out the back door.

"I'll make us some tea then," said Ann lifting cups and saucers from the dresser. "Sit down Margaret." She paused and looked around the kitchen. "Take the chair at the end there."

"Thank you, Ann," I said pulling the chair out and sitting down. I smiled as Bessie gave Lottie a box to stand on so she could reach the table. She looked so serious as she began cutting out scones under the watchful eye of Bessie.

We spent a wonderful morning with Ann and Bessie. I hadn't realised how much I'd missed the company of other women. With Maria gone, I'd only had the sewing circle in Perth. They had been nice enough and had included me in their group, but I hadn't formed a true friendship with any of them. Being back in Ann's company, even after so many years, was a reminder of how close we'd become during the voyage from England. I sighed with contentment as I sipped my tea and watched my daughter.

Chapter Thirty One

July 1841, Married at Last

No sooner had Reverend Robinson pronounced us husband and wife, than I was in Will's arms. He gave me a modest kiss that held the promise of a more passionate one to come later. The Reverend indicated for us to sign the register, and Ann and her husband John witnessed for us.

"Congratulations," she said giving me a tight hug. "I'm so glad you asked me to stand with you today."

"It's me who is so thankful that you agreed," I said letting her go. "And I'm so glad we have reconnected our friendship."

"As am I."

We'd made arrangements to have a small wedding feast following the ceremony, back at our house. Bessie, who I was fast learning was worth her weight in gold, was watching the children and preparing luncheon for us. I looped my arm in Will's as we walked from the church to our house. I was just elated at finally being married. After lying to my family for so long, I felt like a great weight had been lifted. I was Mrs Margaret Hartley, and I couldn't have been happier.

Life soon settled into its regular rhythm. For the very first time in our lives, we were living like regular people. Not in someone else's house, but on our own, and under our own steam. Will's job with James Triffett was working out very well, and Mr Triffett was happy with his work. He grew a variety of different vegetables which he periodically took to market in Hobart Town. During those times Will would stay over at the farm and I always missed him like mad.

I was delighted to receive a letter from Maria in August with news they had returned home from England. I had missed her more than I would've imagined. I'd never had a friend like her, and I was anxious to visit, but I was loath to leave Will. Finally, Ann convinced me to go. She and Bessie offered to keep an eye out for Will, and I promised to be back in just over a week. I wrote to Maria telling her of my plan to visit and made the necessary arrangements.

I snuggled into Will and pulled the quilt up over my shoulders. "I'm already missing you."

He ran his hand down my side to my rather round hip. "I think you've got rounder, Meg."

I pushed my hips into him and ran my hand down his stomach. "Do you? I think you've got fatter as well. What's this?"

He chuckled. "I might've got a bit content. But is there a reason you might be rounder? Hmm?"

"No," I said nibbling his ear. "Perhaps you ought to do something about that." I giggled as he scooped me into his arms and began kissing me. I felt like I was melting and thrust my hips into him. I wanted to be sure he knew my intentions. This would be our last night together for at least a week. I moaned as he ran his fingers down my bottom and began lifting my shift. I wanted him, and I wanted him now.

Our lovemaking was fast and furious, and as he gave one final thrust and collapsed on top of me, I moaned with pleasure. Our bodies were slick with perspiration but I clung to him as our lips met. I ran my tongue along his lip and he moaned with delight. I could feel my body beginning to respond to him again, but my eyelids were already drooping. Sleep would win out.

September 1841, Norfolk Plains

Three days later I stood on the threshold of the rectory in Norfolk Plains.

There were signs the garden had been tended to, and the house had that feeling that it was once again loved. The door opened and to my surprise, Mrs Fitz's filled the doorway.

"Margaret," she said smiling widely at me. "And the bairns as well. Wee Rowland will be beside hi'self to see Lottie again. Come in." She stood aside as best she could to allow us to squeeze past her.

"Thank you. I didn't expect to see you here, Mrs Fitz."

"Well I didna expect to come back either, but Mrs Davies begged me," she said grinning. "Leave your bag there an' I'll get John to take it up to your room for ye." She continued down the hallway, ushering the children ahead of her. "Mrs Davies' out in the garden with Rowland. Why don't ye go an' surprise her?"

"Alright I will," I said as we reached the end of the hall. "Is John back working here as well?"

"Oh aye. He's a ticket of leave man now."

I was pleased to hear it and found myself looking forward to meeting up with him again. We headed out the back door and down the path past the kitchen garden. I could hear Maria before I saw her sitting under the arbour. I couldn't help the wide grin that came across my face.

"Maria."

She looked up, and smiled widely at me, her pale blue eyes dancing in her face. From here I could see she had a healthy glow and even her cheeks appeared to be rosy. As she stood up I could tell she was nowhere near as thin as she used to be.

"Margaret!" she exclaimed as she came up the path towards us. A moment later I was in her arms and we were clinging to one another. I felt the hot salty tears sting my eyes and I was surprised. I hadn't expected to cry, it just happened.

"Oh, Maria I've missed you so much," I said pulling out of her arms. "You look wonderful."

"So do you," she said looking into my teary eyes. "And I see you have a son. What's his name?"

"This is Willie."

Rowland came sauntering up the path with a serious frown on his face as he eyed us. Lottie who was still hanging on to my skirts peered at him.

"It's Rowland. Don't you remember?" I said pushing her towards him. She pushed back against me and shook her head.

"Do you remember Lottie?" said Maria turning to Rowland. He continued to stare at us and shook his head.

It was no surprise they didn't remember each other. It had been a year and a half or more since they'd last met, and Lottie had only been Willie's age.

"Well this is Lottie and Willie," said Maria smiling at her son. "I'm sure they'd love to meet the chickens. Why don't you show them?"

"Alright," he said slowly, still eyeing them with some suspicion.

"Go on," I said urging them to go with Rowland. "Go and see how many there are."

Lottie and Willie started down the path hand in hand following Rowland. I was confident they'd be the best of friends when they returned.

Maria sat down on the seat beneath the arbour and invited me to join her. "So tell me everything. What's been happening since I left?"

I held up my left hand with its thin gold band around my ring finger. "Well, Will and I finally got married. It's official, now I'm Mrs Hartley."

"Oh congratulations, I'm so happy for you. Does that mean Will's now a ticket of leave man?"

"Yes. He got it back in January, and now he's working for a market gardener down in New Norfolk. What about you? How did everything go in England?"

"Quite well. The physician I saw believes I'll be able to have more children. So Robert and I are just hoping he's right." She smiled but there was sadness in her pale blue eyes. "I think the more I worry about it the less likely it is to happen."

My heart went out to her. I knew how heartbreaking it had been the last time she'd miscarried, and I prayed the physician in London knew what he was talking about. I reached out and squeezed her hand.

"I can only imagine how hard it is for you not to worry. But, Maria you are looking so much better. You have a glow about you and you've put on some weight," I said looking her up and down. "I'm sure you'll be expecting in no time."

"I hope you're right."

"Where're the bairns?" said Mrs Fitz coming down the path. She stopped by the arbour, breathing heavily and holding her hand to her ample bosom. "Martha says she'll give them early supper."

"They're down seeing the chickens. Would you like me to fetch them?" said Maria getting to her feet.

"No, I wouldna hear of it," she said continuing down the path. "I'll fetch them."

The children and I spent the next three days with Maria and Rowland. By the time we left, they were the best of friends, and I promised to visit again soon. For me, it had been wonderful seeing Maria again. I'd missed her so much, and a part of me was sorry that Will and I had moved so far away. I would've loved to have been able to visit her more often.

By the time we arrived back in New Norfolk, Willie was grumpy and irritable and I couldn't wait to hand him over to his father. He hated travelling, and while I had to agree with him, his demeanour made the journey worse. I promised myself I'd leave him home next time.

Spring slid into summer as we settled into life in New Norfolk. I was almost able to forget all the time Will and I had been forced to live apart. I loved his solid presence breathing rhythmically beside me every night, as I snuggled into him. Life was blissful.

I received a letter from Barb. It arrived shortly after Christmas and was full of family news. My mother's health had deteriorated further, and she was now receiving constant care from Doctor Jeffrey's.

I commissioned a small painting to be done of the children which I was now sliding carefully into an envelope addressed to my mother. I hoped it would bring her some joy to see her grandchildren's likeness. I was kicking myself that I hadn't asked Maria to paint them on our last visit. I know she would have. I'd included snippets of our family life in my letter that I thought might interest her and lift her spirits.

My thoughts were tinged with sadness as I sealed the envelope. I would never see her again, and my heart ached at the thought of it.

Chapter Thirty Two

Bredgar House February 1842

The carriage rumbled up the driveway to Bredgar House, and Barb peered out at the frosty landscape. She'd packed hurriedly as soon as she'd received news that her mother's health had deteriorated and she was unlikely to last. She prayed she'd made it in time to say her final farewells. She sighed with impatience while she waited for the groom to open the door and lower the steps.

She stepped down from the carriage and hurried to the front door. Barton was waiting for her, and she wasted no time in divesting herself of cloak and gloves.

"How's my mother?"

"Weak, but still with us," he said catching her outer attire as she threw it in his direction. "Sir Samuel and the rest of the family are in the drawing-room."

"Thank you, but I would see my mother first," she called over her shoulder.

"I'll tell your father you've arrived," he said following her down the wide hall. "The blue room has been prepared for you."

Barb gathered her skirts in her hand and started up the stairs. She paused at the top and sucked in a breath before walking along the corridor to her mother's room. She slowly turned the handle and went into the dimly lit bedroom. The curtains were drawn and the only light was coming from a lamp and the glowing embers in the fireplace. She could see her mother's frail form lying back on several large overstuffed pillows. The pale pink counterpane engulfed the rest of her slim body.

"Mrs Hart, I'll leave you alone with Lady Barbara if you'd prefer," said a young maid appearing from the shadows.

"No, please stay." She approached the bed and leant over and kissed her mother's forehead. She was so pale and her skin looked stretched across the bones of her face. Her rasping breath sent a shudder through Barb. It sounded like the death rattle, and she swallowed the hot tears that came unbidden.

"There's a chair if you'd like to stay awhile," said the maid pushing a wing-backed chair closer to the bed.

"Thank you." Barb sat down and took her mother's frail hand in hers. She felt so cold and every breath came with difficulty. There was a long pause between the next rasping breath, and Barb held hers. "Please put some more wood on the fire, my mother's freezing."

"Yes, Mrs Hart."

"Oh Mamma, I'm here. It's Barb." She smoothed her hair back with her free hand and continued to watch her mother's laboured breathing.

She looked up as the door opened and her father slowly made his way to the bedside. "She's been like this for days, and every day I pray it will be her last."

"You don't mean it," said Barb looking sharply at him. He looked tired and drawn, and she thought - defeated.

"Yes, I mean it. I can't bear to watch her suffer like this," he said resting his hand on Barb's shoulder. "She's been the love of my life."

Barb sucked in her bottom lip as she watched her mother struggle to breathe. She understood how her father felt, but she was a daughter, not ready to lose her mother. "I would like a chance to say goodbye."

"Of course. Dr Jeffreys has given her a draft of laudanum. Let her sleep. You'll have your opportunity in the morning," said Samuel moving to the end of the bed. "Come, Barbara, come and join us in the drawing-room."

"I'll be there in a minute."

"Alright," said her father before heading for the door. He gave her one last look before stepping out into the hallway and closing the door behind him.

Barb sat there for another five minutes, willing her mother to open her eyes. She didn't. She sighed as she got to her feet and kissed her forehead. "I'll see you in the morning, Mamma."

"I'll call you if there's any change," said the maid appearing by her side. Her soft brown eyes looked at Lady Barbara with kindness tinged with sadness. "I'll be here."

"Thank you." She paused at the door, giving her mother one last glance before she headed down to the drawing-room.

Lady Barbara Chambers lingered for two more days. Barb gripped her mother's hand and allowed her sobs to mix with those of her father and siblings. Her sister Charlotte and brother Osborne sat on the other side of the bed, their heads bowed. Her father had retreated to a chair in the corner of the room in his private grief. A part of Barb was relieved her mother was finally at peace, the rest of her was grief-stricken. Life was unimaginable without her. She had been the glue that bound them all together.

Her funeral was held the following day. It was a freezing February morning, and Barb pulled her cloak closer and clung to her father's arm as they left the family crypt. He had been in a daze ever since

Barbara had died, and Barb was worried for him. What was he going to do once they all returned home? He had Barton, and she knew he'd take care of him, but it wouldn't be the same.

Her news, however, would have to wait. John wouldn't be happy with her for delaying, but she couldn't tell her father now. She sighed as they went back into the house. All she could do was hope John wouldn't go to New South Wales without her.

Barton greeted them at door. "A message has arrived from your Uncle Abraham. He requests you all remain at Bredgar House until he arrives."

"When will that be?" said Charlotte removing her cloak and handing it to Barton. "I must get back to London in the morning." She didn't try to hide her annoyance, and Barb wondered what could possibly be so important.

"The message didn't say I'm afraid."

"Well, I can't possibly stay beyond tomorrow."

"Thank you, Barton," said Osborne frowning at his sister. "I'm sure Uncle Abraham wouldn't ask us to remain if it wasn't important."

Barton gave them a short bow before retreating, loaded with cloaks and hats.

"What's so important?" said Barb looping her arm in Charlotte's. "Surely John can take care of things for a day or two."

"No, he cannot. I have a very important engagement with Lady Somerset on Thursday, and no, John can't go in my stead," she said with indignation. "It's all very well for you, but I have my position to think of."

Barb smiled inwardly as they made their way to the dining room. Charlotte had always thought herself more important than the rest of them. "Of course. Well, let's just hope he arrives tomorrow then."

Much to Charlotte's annoyance, he didn't arrive until late the following day. They were all relaxing in the drawing-room after supper when Barton announced his arrival.

"Mr Abraham Chambers has arrived and makes his apologies for not arriving sooner," said Barton from the doorway. "He requests you join him in Sir Samuel's study."

"Well it's about time," said Charlotte marching to the door. "I won't be able to return to London until the morning now." Her annoyance was obvious as she flounced from the room.

Barb rolled her eyes at Osborn as they followed her from the drawing-room. Sir Samuel's study was crowded when they'd all jammed themselves inside. Samuel's brother Abraham was sitting behind the large oak desk, and he looked at them over his spectacles. Charlotte perched herself on the edge of a leather wingback chair, while Barb and Osborne squeezed onto the sofa with their father.

"I apologise for the lateness of the hour," said Abraham clearing his throat. "Business has kept me in London these past few days. I'm so sorry I couldn't be here for Barbara's funeral."

Samuel waved his hand in a dismissive manner. "Not to worry Abe, you're here now. I know you would've been here if you could."

"Yes, I would've. Words seem so inadequate at a time like this. Mary and I were devastated by the news, and I can't begin to imagine how you're all feeling after such a loss."

Barb nodded and Charlotte let out a sob from behind her handkerchief. Samuel ran his hands down his breeches and sighed. Barb looped her arm through his and smiled sadly.

"The reason I've gathered you all today is in the capacity of being your mother's lawyer," he said unfolding a crisp parchment. "As I'm sure you're all aware, any property owned by your mother automatically became your father's upon their marriage. What you may not be aware of, is that an estate in the Welsh marches was bequeathed directly to her by her mother Lady Barbara Roper from the Lyttleton estate. She has in turn bequeathed that property to her eldest daughter, Barbara Hart, and to each of her other children fifty pounds, and to each of her grandchildren, ten pounds. These monies are to be paid directly from the said estate, and will be held in trust for any children under the age of twenty-one."

Charlotte's intake of breath was audible, and Barb glanced at her sister. She was as surprised as Charlotte and had not expected such an inheritance. She suspected Charlotte was disappointed her mother hadn't singled her out for any special mention. "What if I don't wish to accept it?" said Barb letting go of her father and leaning forward.

Abraham Chambers looked at her with his steely blue eyes, his bushy brows raised in a quizzical expression. "Your mother has made no provision for such an occurrence. May I ask why you would refuse?"

Barb shifted uncomfortably. She hadn't intended to reveal her plans at such a time, but what else could she do? She pressed her lips together and sucked in a breath. "Well, I was going to tell everyone at a later time, but I suppose I must speak now," she said licking her lips. "John has received a fine offer to go to New South Wales, and it's just a matter of finalising our affairs before we leave. I'm so sorry to mention this now. I hadn't intended to do so."

"What?" said Samuel swivelling around to face his daughter. "When did this happen? You can't be serious?"

"I'm sorry Papa, I never wanted to tell you like this..today," said Barb swallowing the tears which unexpectedly stung her eyes.

"So if Barb doesn't want it, what happens?" said Charlotte ignoring the conversation going on between her father and Barb. "Will it go to the next daughter, to me?"

"That would depend," said Abraham looking at Barb expectantly.

"Charlotte can have it," said Barb dismissing Abraham and Charlotte with a look of disdain. "Papa we don't have to go right away. I'm sure John could delay for a few months until you got used to the idea."

Samuel shook his head and ran his fingers through his whiskers. "No. If you must go, then you must. I'm glad your mother didn't know. However, I would ask a favour of you."

"Anything Papa."

"Would you go to New Norfolk and see Margaret? I would like to know she is safe and happy."

"Yes, I'd love to see Margaret, so that's not really a hardship for me. I'll write you and let you know how she is."

"Thank you," he said taking her hand in his and squeezing.

"Well that's settled then," said Charlotte bringing the conversation back to her mother's inheritance. "So the estate is mine?"

"It may not be that simple. I will investigate the legality of transferring it to you if that is truly what Barb wants," said Abraham pinning Barb with his stare. "However, there are a couple of other matters I wish to discuss. The first being Philip. Samuel will you write to him and ask if he would like his inheritance forwarded to India, or if he would prefer I hold it until he returns."

"Of course," said Samuel nodding. "And Margaret?"

"Yes, she is the subject of the second matter. I will forward the funds for her to a lawyer in Hobart Town. If you could write to her advising her to contact them to collect it. The funds for the two children will be held in trust until they reach their majority."

"I'm sure Barb could take care of that," said Samuel.

"Yes of course. I'll just need the name of the lawyers."

"I'll advise you within the next few days."

Osborn had sat silently squeezed onto the sofa up until this point. He stood and stretched. "Well it would appear you have no need of me," he said as he walked towards the door. He turned before opening it. "I make no claim on the estate in Wales unless Barb truly doesn't want it. I am the eldest after all." He opened the door and exited.

Barb couldn't help but notice the daggers that Charlotte shot after him. She sighed. She had no wish to take the estate, but she also had no desire to cause a fight between her siblings. "Perhaps I've acted too quickly Uncle Abraham. I'll think on the estate," she said rising from the sofa. "Now if you'll excuse me, I wish to retire."

She swept from the study and headed for the conservatory. Osborn would no doubt be there amongst the roses, that reminded them so much of their mother.

Chapter Thirty Three

March 1842, Mrs Burnett's Berridale Inn

I sighed as I stopped sewing and let my work go limp in my lap. There was nothing I could do until the morning, but I couldn't squash the gnawing feeling in my stomach that told me something was very wrong.

Will should've returned from his trip with Mr Triffett yesterday, but there was no sign of him. I hadn't been too concerned at first. I expected they'd been held up. Maybe the sale of the produce hadn't gone as planned. Either way, I was sure he would've arrived home today. But no. It was nearly time for me to retire for the night, and there was no sign of him or Mr Triffett. That was the one thing that gave me some solace – Mr Triffett hadn't arrived back either. I just hoped they were both alright.

My mind wasn't concentrating anymore, so I put my sewing away and checked on the children. I could just make out their silhouettes in the lamplight, but their steady breathing told me they were asleep. I tiptoed from the room and headed for my own bedroom. I put the lamp on the tallboy and fossicked in the top drawer for a nightgown. The nights were starting to get cooler and I shivered as I changed into my night attire.

I climbed into bed and snuggled down under the quilt. I tried to slow my breathing and calm my mind which was going around in circles. I tried hard to convince myself that Will was alright. Of course, he was; it had just taken longer than they'd anticipated to go downriver to Hobart Town. The image of the dark waters of the River Derwent swirling around a barge loaded with vegetables, and Will falling overboard swam before my eyes. I sat bolt upright and sucked in a deep breath. I swallowed the rising bile which stung the back of my throat and lay back down. He would be alright.

I must've fallen asleep because the next thing I awoke with a start. The grey gloom of early morning was illuminating my bedroom and someone was banging on my front door and making enough noise to wake the neighbourhood. I dived out of bed and threw my shawl around my shoulders before heading for the parlour. I swung open the front door and James Triffett stumbled across the threshold.

"Oh, Mrs Hartley I'm so sorry to wake ye so early," he said gasping for breath. "I came as soon as I could."

I paled and stared at him. "What? Where's Will?" Fear gripped me as I stared at him in horror. He was dishevelled and I searched his face for any clues.

"He's been arrested. I assure ye I had no idea of his plans or else I would've stopped him."

"Arrested?" I realised I must've sounded like an imbecile, but my mind was slipping and sliding over a thousand thoughts at once, and none of them made any sense.

"Aye. He's been taken to Hobart Gaol, and I expect he'll be tried before a Magistrate before too long." He sighed and ran his fingers through his greying hair. "I'm so sorry, I cannot imagine what he was thinking."

I took James Triffett by the arm and led him through to our lean-to kitchen and sat him down at the table.

"I just need to see to the children, and then I want you to tell me everything."

"Alright," he replied putting his head in his hands.

I walked back through to the parlour and was greeted by a sleepy Lottie.

"Where's Papa?"

"He's not back yet. Come on back to bed, it's too early to be up," I said putting my arm around her and guiding her back to the bedroom.

Willie was awake and sitting up in bed. He stared bleary eyed at me. "Papa?"

"No, darling. Come on back to bed," I said as I tucked Lottie back in under the covers. "It's Mr Triffett, and Mamma needs to talk to him. Back to sleep you two."

I closed the door quietly as I left and leaned against it for a moment. I prayed they'd go back to sleep so I could concentrate on Mr Triffett. I sucked in a deep breath as I made my way back to the kitchen. I stoked the fire and threw on another log before sitting down at the table.

"Now, Mr Triffett if you please. Why was my husband arrested?"

"Oh it's a long story, but enough to say that the sale of my vegetables didn't go as well as we hoped. So on the way back upriver, we stopped in at Glenorchy," he said looking at me with his pale watery eyes.

I sucked in a breath and slowly let it out. Glenorchy? I felt a shiver go down my spine at the mention of it. I sucked in my bottom lip and nodded while I waited for him to continue.

"It was late when we arrived and so we took lodgings at the local inn, with every plan to sell my produce at the market the following day," he said running his fingers through his hair. "We had a few ales and I retired. Will stayed on talking with a few of the locals. It was only later that I found out he'd gone off in the middle of the night."

I stared at him while my mind whirred and scrambled to make sense of what he was telling me. "Where did he go?"

He took a deep breath. "Well, it would seem that he went to see a woman." His cheeks reddened and he dropped his eyes from my piercing gaze.

"A woman?" This made absolutely no sense whatsoever. "Are you sure?"

"I'm afraid so. I'm so sorry to have to tell ye this, Mrs Hartley."

The sinking feeling I'd had in the pit of my stomach since last night now gripped me in its vice-like grip. I felt ill, as realisation dawned on me. It couldn't be - Annie. And yet I could not think of any other woman that he might know in Glenorchy. He'd never been there before, and I didn't even know how he knew that she was there. I was sure I hadn't told him. I'd told him that it was her who had caused us to be arrested, but I know I didn't tell him where she was.

I pressed my lips together while I thought about how much Mr Triffett might know. "Do you know who accuses him?" I finally said. "And what he's accused of?"

Mr Triffett squirmed uncomfortably before pinning me with his gaze. "Aye.

He's accused by a servant belonging to Mrs Burnett. A young woman by the name of Annie Watson."

I gasped. It was her, and I couldn't believe it. She had obviously not given up on getting her revenge against us. "And the accusation Mr Triffett?"

"Please Mrs Hartley." He stood up and began pacing the tiny kitchen. "Ye understand this is a most delicate matter." He wiped his brow with a handkerchief as his pale eyes pleaded with me not to ask anything more.

I sucked in a deep breath and slowly let it out. I could well imagine what she'd accused him of and it turned my stomach. Poor Mr Triffett looked like he might have an apoplexy if I pressed him further, but I had to know.

"Has she accused him of rape?"

His shoulders slumped in defeat and he turned to face me. "Aye. But ye must not believe it, Mrs Hartley. I know ye husband to be an honourable man, and he would not do such a thing."

"Thank you Mr Triffett. I appreciate your belief in my husband. This young woman believes Will scorned her some years ago and has sought revenge ever since," I said walking over to him and putting my hand on his arm. "This is not the first time she's caused trouble for us."

"Then ye must go to the constable and make a complaint against her," he said with fervour. "Your husband will surely go to gaol for this otherwise."

"I fear no matter what I do that's likely to happen, but I will go to Glenorchy and see if anything can be done."

"Well I wish ye every success," he said as he made to leave. I followed him to the front door and held it open. "God speed Mrs Hartley."

"Thank you." I watched him walk up the path before closing the door. I leaned against it and sighed. My mind was in a jumble as so many thoughts flitted around it at once. I needed a plan, and I needed to find Annie Watson and somehow make her retract her allegation. I compressed my lips as I formulated a way forward.

Later that morning I dropped the children off with Ann. She'd kindly agreed to take care of them while I was away. I could only imagine what she was thinking of me – running off to Hobart Town to defend my husband. I hoped she wouldn't think too ill of me for abandoning my children.

"Be good for Aunt Ann," I said as I knelt down and hugged them both.

"Mamma's going to miss you." I kissed their cheeks and let them go. "I can't tell you how much I appreciate this," I said to Ann clutching her in my embrace.

"It's the least I can do," she said hugging me in return. "And don't worry, Bessie will help me."

"Aye of course I will," said Bessie arriving in the parlour. "Come on let's go see what Johnny's doing." She took them both by the hand and they happily went off in search of Johnny.

I felt tears prick my eyes as I watched them go. The last time I'd been parted from Lottie was because of Annie's vindictive actions, and now it was happening again. At least this time I knew my babies were safe. I swallowed the ache in my throat as I turned to leave.

I made my way down to the Bush Inn which was situated on the main road to Hobart Town. The coach was due to depart from here this afternoon and I had every intention of being on it. I entered the inn and found myself a quiet corner to sit and wait. A million things were running through my mind, and the one that kept surfacing was how was I going to find Annie? And then how would I convince her to drop her allegations? I was convinced they were false. I knew in my heart of hearts Will would never do such a thing. But why had he gone anywhere near her? I was driving myself mad.

The coach arrived early, and I heaved a sigh of relief as I climbed aboard. With any luck, we'd be in Hobart Town late tomorrow morning. I had only been to Hobart Town on the day I'd arrived in Van Diemen's Land, and I had no idea where the gaol was. However, I was confident someone would point me in the right direction.

We spent the night at an inn near the Austin's ferry crossing, and continued on to Hobart Town the following morning. The coach pulled up near the docks in Davey Street and I stepped down and waited for my portmanteau to be unloaded. A cool breeze was blowing up from the river, and I wrapped my cloak more firmly around myself. It was a grey overcast day and I hoped it wouldn't rain before I secured accommodation.

I picked up my bag and crossed Davey Street. Campbell Street ran uphill from here and I made my way along it until I came to the George and Dragon Inn. It looked respectable, and I thought it would only be a short walk to Brisbane Street where the gaol was located. At least, I had it on the best authority that it was situated on the corner, and I just hoped the coach driver knew what he was talking about. I arranged my lodgings for the night and after freshening myself and having a bite to eat I set out in search of the gaol.

I made my way up Campbell Street for a couple of blocks until I came to Brisbane Street. A large imposing red brick building stood on one corner. It seemed to cast its ominous shadow over the whole area. I sucked in a deep breath before pushing open the large heavy oak door. I found myself in a large foyer with a long timber counter taking up one wall. I made my way over and waited until the guard behind the counter noticed me.

"How can I help ye?" he asked as his beady eyes looked me up and down. A look of disdain crossed his face and a flutter of nerves washed over me.

"Good afternoon. I'd like to see my husband. I believe he's being held here awaiting trial. His name's William Hartley." My voice sounded confident and assertive to my ears, even if my stomach felt like a bucket of squirming worms.

"Take a seat," he said indicating several hard benches set against the other wall.

"Thank you." I went across and perched myself on the edge of one of the benches. It was only then that I noticed two other guards standing by another heavy door. I sighed - I prayed they'd let me see Will.

I waited - and I waited. The longer I sat the more nervous I was becoming. I'd almost convinced myself they weren't going to let me see Will when one of the guards called to me.

"Follow me, Mrs Hartley." He opened the door and gestured to me. I quickly crossed the room and followed him through the door and down a gloomy corridor. There was a set of prison bars with a similarly barred door about halfway down the hall. The guard unlocked them and as soon as I'd passed through locked them behind us. He proceeded down the hall a little further before unlocking a door on the right-hand side. He stood aside to let me pass. I smiled weakly at him as I entered a small cell.

"Knock when yer ready to leave," he said closing the door. I heard the key grate in the lock before I turned to survey the room. There was a table and a small barred window set high in the wall and two chairs. Will was sitting with his back to me.

"Will," I cried as soon as I saw him. He was on his feet and in my arms a moment later. "Oh my God, are you alright?"

"Aye I'm fine," he said hugging me close. "What are ye doing here?" He let me go and held me at arm's length as he searched my face.

"I had to come. Mr Triffett told me what happened. We can't let her get away with this. I know you're innocent of this ghastly accusation."

He let me go and shrugged. "I don't know how we can do anything to stop her," he said slumping onto one of the chairs. He put his head in his hands and then ran them through his hair. "I'm so glad you believe I didn't touch her."

"Of course I do," I scoffed as I sat on the other chair. "But what were you thinking? Why did you go anywhere near her?"

He groaned and his haunted hazel eyes pleaded with me to understand. "We were at the Berridale Inn, and I noticed her. She was serving food, and I didn't think she'd seen me. I was drinking with a couple of local lads, and I asked them about her."

Henry grinned at Will. "Aye, she's a nice bit o' crumpet that one."

"Does she live around here?" asked Will taking a mouthful of ale. He watched her as she swayed her hips seductively. He could feel his anger rising. It had been three years since she'd reported Captain Cheyne and they'd all been arrested, but his desire for retribution hadn't faded. He wanted her to pay for what she'd done to Meg.

"Aye, ye could say that," said Henry eyeing her appreciatively. "She's got a room upstairs. Second floor, second on the right." He grinned stupidly. "I've sampled those delights a couple of times. Just leave the money on the nightstand."

"Really?" said Will staring at Henry with raised brows. "She's a whore then?"

Charlie, who had been sitting quietly drinking his ale up until this point, coughed and spluttered and put down his drink. "Don't listen to 'im," he scoffed. "That one's more trouble than she's worth."

"Aye I think ye might be right," said Will with a laugh. "I don't think I'll bother."

"Suit yeself," said Henry grinning. "If I hadn't had so many ales I might see her meself tonight."

Will spent the rest of the evening drinking and enjoying Henry and Charlie's conversation. It was ten o'clock when he finally climbed the stairs and retired for the night.

Sleep evaded him, and he lay awake with thoughts of Annie going around and around in his mind. He might not get another opportunity to confront her. He rolled over and tried to push thoughts of her from his mind.

After another half an hour or so he gave up and got out of bed. He lit the lamp and ran his fingers through his hair while he contemplated what to do. He groaned inwardly as he reached for his breeches and shirt and quickly dressed. He opened the door and tiptoed out into the hallway. He thought it was probably nearing midnight as he climbed the stairs to the second floor. Second, on the right, Henry had said. He paused outside the door and listened. All was quiet. He tried the handle – it turned. Without another thought, he opened the door and went inside.

An oil lamp was burning low on the nightstand. It gave off just enough light for him to make out the form of a woman asleep in the bed. A sliver of light entering the room from the open door illuminated a chaise lounge and tallboy. He paused as his eyes became accustomed to the dim interior. He'd only taken one step towards the large bed when the woman rolled over and waved her arm at him.

"Bugger off Henry."

"It's not Henry," he said as he dived for her and grabbed her by the arms. She squealed and he clamped his hand over her mouth and pressed his body into hers. "You must remember me and my wife Margaret who you had carted off to gaol," he snarled as he glared into her wide frightened eyes. "If you ever come near us again, so help me you'll be fucking sorry."

Recognition dawned in her eyes, and the fear was replaced with contempt. Will yelped and pulled his hand away from her mouth as she sunk her teeth into his palm.

"Get off me ye bastard," she screamed at him as she pummeled him with her fists and wriggled to be free of him.

"You little witch." He tried to grab a hold of her again, but she was quicker than he'd anticipated. She squirmed out from under him and scuttled away to the head of the bed. She grabbed hold of the neck of her nightgown and ripped it from her shoulders. Her firm young breasts spilled out and she glared at him, her chest rising and falling as she gasped for breath.

"Help," she screamed before launching herself at him.

Will did his best to fend her off as she tried to rake her fingers down his face. She screamed again, and he flung himself at her and pinned her to the mattress. He'd just clamped his hand over her mouth again when he was grabbed from behind.

"Get off her," said a man's gruff voice and Will was tossed from the bed. He rolled onto the floor and was accosted by another man who landed on top of him.

"I've got 'im," said the younger man as he wrenched Will's arms behind his back.

"Get off me," he said through gritted teeth as he tried to free his arms.

"He raped me," he heard Annie say in a panicked voice. "I couldn't stop him." She began to sob and wail.

Will groaned as he realised no one would believe him. He was an intruder in a young woman's bedroom in the middle of the night. Shit, he hadn't thought this through at all.

"I know it was a stupid thing to do," said Will looking at me with pleading eyes. "I just got so angry when I saw her." He ran his fingers through his hair. "I'm so sorry Meg."

I pressed my lips together and breathed out through my nose. There was no point in berating him. I nodded. "I understand, Will but she's dangerous. Look what's she's done now. Promise me you'll never go near her again."

"I promise you I won't. But I want you to promise me you won't go near her either."

I thought about that for a moment. I really wanted to try and get her to change her story, although I had no idea how I'd do that. If Will went to trial he'd be found guilty for sure, and our lives would once again be in upheaval. He'd lose his ticket, not to mention he'd get time in gaol. What was I going to do? Tears pricked my eyes as I considered our future. It looked bleak. But I found myself nodding and giving him my promise. I wouldn't go near her.

Chapter Thirty Four

April 1842, Twelve Months Gaol

I felt numb as I left the court room with our lawyer, Gamaliel Butler. Will had been sentenced to twelve months in gaol for the rape and assault on Annie Watson. I knew from the start he'd most likely be found guilty, but to hear the sentence handed down had shocked me. My mind was whirring but I was in a daze. Mr Butler's calming voice came to me as if from afar.

"We'll lodge an immediate appeal for leniency," he said taking me by the elbow and guiding me out the door. "I don't want you to worry, Mrs Hartley. I have every reason to believe we'll succeed. I'll write to you as soon as we have a result."

I let his words wash over me, all the while my mind was trying to comprehend life without Will. I had some money, not a lot, particularly after I'd paid Mr Butler. I'd have to get a job of some kind. Perhaps I could get a position teaching music or something? I wasn't sure how long I'd be able to pay the rent and put food on the table without working. Tears stung my eyes and then ran down my face.

Mr Butler pressed a handkerchief into my hand. "Do you have any family you can turn to?"

I shook my head as I dabbed my eyes. "No."

"Friends perhaps?"

"Yes," I replied. Not that I could throw myself and the children on their doorstep. Ann had been kind beyond words. She'd taken care of the children on numerous occasions while I was in Hobart Town. I couldn't ask her for more help. She certainly couldn't take us in. She didn't even live in her own house. Maria? Of course Maria would offer if she knew, but I wouldn't abuse my friends in such a way.

"Well then, Mrs Hartley I suggest you seek assistance from that quarter," he said coming to a halt on the corner of Campbell Street. "This is where we part. Please write to my office if you change your address."

"Of course. Thank you, Mr Butler."

I watched him walk away from me down the street towards his offices. I felt so lost and abandoned but I had to keep going. I'd go home tomorrow and try and work out a plan from there.

❦

May 1842, New Norfolk

The last few weeks have been a blur. After paying Mr Butler for Will's legal fees I have the grand sum of six pounds left to my name. I applied for a position at the local school to teach music, with no success. It would appear the finer art of music isn't a necessity in New Norfolk. There's absolutely no point in me applying for any positions as a domestic servant. I shuddered at the thought. Three days of doing laundry in the female factory in Launceston had nearly killed me.

I ushered Lottie and Willie ahead of me as I went into Mr Brownell's General Store. I could at least afford a few basic supplies to keep us going. It was busy, with two other women waiting ahead of me. I did my best to prevent Willie from touching everything in sight. I grabbed him by the hand and held him firmly beside me. He could be such a trial.

"Oh," said the woman in front of me as she turned and saw me standing there. I smiled. I didn't know her, but from the look on her face she knew me. She looked down her nose and took a step closer to the counter. I compressed my lips and tried to hold myself together. News had travelled fast.

The women gave me a wide berth as they left the store twittering behind their hands. I wished the ground would open up and swallow me whole. I blinked back unwanted tears and swallowed the ache that stretched across the back of my throat. I'd better get used to being the wife of a rapist. It was so unfair.

I stepped up to the counter and handed my order to Mr Brownell. He looked at me over his spectacles with an apologetic look in his eye. Perhaps not everyone was unsympathetic to my situation.

"I'm sorry, Mrs Hartley. You'll need to pay your account before I fill your order," he said flipping through his box of accounts. "That will be three pounds ten shillings and sixpence." He looked at me expectantly, while I lost the last of my self control.

I burst into tears and if I hadn't needed provisions I would've fled. My outburst only lasted a minute before I got myself back under control. I wiped my tears away with the back of my hand. "I'm so sorry Mr Brownell."

"Quite understandable," he replied. This time I wasn't mistaken, his eyes softened with kindness and concern. "Perhaps you should consider seeking assistance from Reverend Robinson. He's well known for his charitable works."

"Thank you," I said reaching into my purse. I put the money on the counter and pushed it towards him. "I'm not quite destitute yet." I will be soon I thought to myself.

He smiled awkwardly as he collected the money and wrote paid on my account. I handed him my order which he promised to fill that very day. I thanked him and hurried from the store before I ran into anyone else.

I was so glad to get home and shut myself inside my humble cottage. People in the street had shied away from me and stared, and I was unused to being the centre of their unwanted attentions. I'd collected the mail from the box on my way inside, and was surprised to find two letters addressed to me. One from my sister Barb and the other was from our lawyer, Mr Butler. I put them on the kitchen table until I had a moment to open them.

"I'm hungry Mamma," said Lottie sidling into the kitchen and flopping herself down in a chair. Her soft grey eyes, so like my own, stared hopefully at me.

"Yes sweetheart, I'll get something for you and Willie right now. Go and wash up."

She slipped from the chair and went off yelling Willie's name. "Come and wash up."

I smiled to myself as I watched her go before busying myself with dinner.

There was a bit of cold mutton and some corn bread left over from yesterday, which would be perfectly fine. I made myself a pot of tea to wash it all down with. Lottie and Willie arrived a few minutes later and sat down at the table. I put their dinner down in front of them, and was about to settle myself when there was a knock on the door. I froze. I wasn't expecting visitors.

"You two stay here and eat your dinner," I said getting up from the table. I pressed my lips together as I went through to the parlour. "Who is it?"

"Mr Fenton," came the muffled reply.

Mr Fenton was our landlord and he usually called on a Friday to collect the rent. Today was only Tuesday, and I was sure the rent was up to date. I opened the door and smiled at the short dumpy man on my doorstep. It was hard to say how old he was. His pale blond hair was thinning on top and he had a few wrinkles around his eyes. But he certainly wasn't old.

"Mr Fenton this is an unexpected surprise."

"Ah well yes, Mrs Hartley," he stammered as he held a piece of paper out in my direction. "It's all in here."

I took the proffered page and unfolded it. I scanned the small neat writing and gasped. "You can't be serious!"

"Yes, well I'm afraid I am. Good day to you, Mrs Hartley," he said turning to leave.

"Wait just one minute," I said flying out the door after him. "I'm not behind in my rent, and I assure you I can pay."

"Be that as it may," he said stopping and turning to face me. His small beady eyes flitting from left to right, anywhere but at me. "You will be out by the end of next week. I've been more than fair."

"More than fair," I spluttered. "You're evicting me without any proper cause or reason, Mr Fenton."

"Good day to you." He doffed his hat and hurried down the street.

I stared after him. What was I going to do? My situation had just gone from somewhat precarious to downright dire. I sucked in a breath as I went back inside. I closed the door and leaned against it. My options were dwindling fast, and unless I wanted to land myself on Maria's doorstep, which I didn't, I had to think fast. The only thing that came to mind was Reverend Robinson. If Mr Brownell was right, he might be able to offer me some assistance.

By the time I arrived back in the kitchen, Lottie and Willie had finished eating and I sent them out to play. I slumped in a chair and pushed the food around on my plate. All of a sudden I wasn't hungry. I pushed the plate aside and put my head in my hands. I allowed my tears of fear and frustration to run freely. Will was counting on me to take care of our children while he was in gaol, and I had no idea how I was going to do that.

After several more minutes of wallowing in self pity I pulled myself together. I straightened my hair and wiped the tears away. I could do this. I reached for the two letters I'd brought in earlier. I decided to save Barb's letter for later. I slit open the one from Mr Butler. I hoped it was good news – that Will's sentence had been reduced.

17th May, 1842

12 Officer Street
New Norfolk

Dear Mrs Hartley,

I write to you with the utmost haste concerning the latest accusations against your husband Mr William Hartley. We were able to provide him some representation, although the evidence against him was overwhelming.

Yesterday he was found guilty of larceny before the bench of Magistrates in Hobart Town and sentenced to two years imprisonment at Port Arthur. There is no hope of appeal in this case, and it would be most unlikely to succeed.

Miss Annie Watson accuses your husband of stealing from her a gold locket and chain. This was found to be on the person of a fellow prisoner of Mr Hartley's. When questioned, the prisoner informed the authorities that your husband had traded the item with him for extra rations. The evidence was beyond question.

I enclose my account for professional services rendered in this case.

Regards Gamaliel Butler
Butler and Sons

I let the letter slip from my numb fingers as my mind went into freefall. I couldn't comprehend anything. Port Arthur? It was the harshest gaol in the country, and Will was going to be imprisoned there for two years. It just didn't seem real. He was innocent. It was too much for me to deal with today. First I'd borne the brunt of the towns gossip, been evicted from my home, and now this. I cried and I wailed and I didn't care if the children could hear me.

Chapter Thirty Five

Good news generally follows bad

I finally sat down for the evening. The children were both in bed, and asleep, at least I hoped so. I'd had such a whirlwind week that I hadn't had a chance to open Barb's letter. What with Will being sentenced to gaol for two years, instead of one, which had been bad enough for something he didn't do, and me being evicted. I'd been so busy trying to sort out my life that her letter had been forgotten.

Reverend Robinson had proven to be a most charitable and understanding man. Of course, he'd conducted our wedding us last year, but I don't think he remembered me. I'd gone to seek his help last Friday, and he'd been so kind. He said he'd ask his parishioners if anyone could help me. Then today he'd arrived on my doorstep with wonderful news.

"People are generally kind, Mrs Hartley," he said sipping his tea. "Mrs Harrison's been widowed for many years, and she lives with her son Matthew. He's a most amiable man, and they would be more than happy to give you and the children a roof over your heads."

"That's wonderful news. I can't tell you what a relief it is to me," I said smiling happily at him. "What would Mrs Harrison expect of me in return?"

"Oh, nothing too onerous I can assure you. As I say, she's been on her own for many years, and I think she's really just looking for some companionship," he said putting down his cup. "You'd also be expected to help with the cooking and other household chores."

"Of course, I'd be more than happy to." I hoped they weren't expecting me to be a live-in servant, although, at the moment I had very little choice. I would have to accept any situation that put a roof over our heads and food in our bellies. "Thank you so much Reverend, I don't know what I would've done without your help."

The final arrangements had been made and the children and I would move in with the Harrison's on Monday. Mr Fenton would just have to put up with me over the weekend. I had no intention of leaving until I had somewhere to go.

I slit open Barb's letter and unfolded the crisp parchment.

Bredgar House, Kent
18th February 1842

Dearest Margaret,

I so wish I was there with you when you receive this letter. I can only hope that your dear husband is with you as you read this. Our dear mother passed away six days ago. She slipped peacefully into a deep sleep surrounded by us all. In the end, it was a blessing. She so hated being an invalid.

Tears came unbidden and blurred my vision to the point where I couldn't read my dear sisters flowing words. I dabbed my eyes with my handkerchief as the full force of my loss hit me. I had always known I would never see my mother again, but now it was final. My heart wrenched at the thought of never hearing her voice or feeling her comforting arms around me. I could only imagine how my father would cope without her. Although he'd always been the head of the family, I knew he couldn't have done it without her.

I dried my eyes and continued reading Barb's letter.

Papa has asked me to write to you on another matter. Mother has bequeathed fifty pounds to each of us, to be paid from her dowager estate. Uncle Abraham has made arrangements for the monies to be

*made available to you through an attorney
in Hobart Town.*

Fifty pounds! I put my hand over
my mouth as I reread her words. Oh my
God, this couldn't have come at a better
time. "Oh, Mamma thank you," I said out
loud. I compressed my lips as I tried to bite
back the tears that threatened again. I
sucked in a breath and wiped my eyes with
the back of my hand. Tears of happiness
and sadness intermingled as I once again
lost control of myself. It took me several
minutes to stop crying enough to read the
rest of her letter.

*The lawyers will write to you I'm
sure, but Uncle Abraham thinks you may
have to go to Hobart Town in person. The
attorney to contact is - John Dobson,
Attorney at Law in Bathurst Street, Hobart
Town.*

*Mamma also left ten pounds each to
Charlotte and William. I believe Uncle
Abraham will hold this in trust until they
reach their majority.*

*Now onto my news. I don't know
when, mainly because I don't want to leave
Papa right now, but John and I will be
moving to Sydney. John's been offered a
wonderful position and as soon as our
affairs are in order we'll be on our way.*

Papa has asked me to come to New Norfolk to see you before I settle in Sydney, and I can assure you, it was no hardship to agree. I have missed you so much, and look forward to seeing you, and meeting your husband and children. I'll write to you again before we leave England.

I am truly sorry I'm not there with you and that you had to hear this news from a letter. Dear sister, I pray that you are well and I count the days until I see you again.

Your loving sister Barb.

I reread the letter several times before I finally folded it and slipped it back into the envelope. I hadn't yet received anything from the attorneys that Barb mentioned, and I prayed it would be soon. I felt a pang of guilt at the thought. If my mother hadn't died then what would I have done? I pushed that thought from my mind as I made my way into my bedroom.

I slipped the letter into the top drawer of the tallboy where I kept all the letters from home. I slid the drawer shut and paused. Barb was coming to visit. I didn't know whether to be happy or sad about it. She would soon discover my husband was in gaol, and I was living in a very modest and shabby cottage. I looked around my small bedroom with the paint peeling from the doorjamb and the faded patched curtain on the window. I shrugged. I had more important things to worry about than what my sister might think of me.

⁂

The next day I landed myself and the children on Ann's doorstep. I was in desperate need of an ear and someone to tell me that everything would be alright. I was so thankful she hadn't shunned me since Will had gone to gaol. I suspect her husband John would prefer she had nothing to do with me, but at least for now, she welcomed me into her house. And so did Bessie.

"So what will ye do now?" said Ann gawking at me with her mouth agape. "Are ye still going to move in with the Harrison's?"

"Well, I'd prefer not to. It just depends if Mr Fenton will change his mind."

"Oh he's bound to," said Bessie pouring me a cup of tea. "Fifty pounds is not to be sneezed at. Ye best show him the letter ye got from yer sister."

I nodded. "I will. I just hope he lets me stay. It may not be about the money." I told them how people in the store and down the street had gossiped about me. "I can't blame them really. But I swear Will is innocent of the accusations."

"Not everyone's like that, Margaret," said Bessie sipping her tea.

"I know. And I really appreciate you standing by me."

"Well of course we would," said Ann raising her brows at me. "So why don't ye leave Lottie an' Willie with us while ye go an' sort this out with Mr Fenton?"

"You wouldn't mind?"

"Not in the least," said Ann with a wave of her hand. "Johnny an' Willie are becoming fast friends, an' Lottie's such a sweetheart."

"Thank you," I said with a smile. I sipped my tea and sighed. It was so good to know I wasn't on my own. Bessie and Ann were a tower of strength to me.

I finished my tea, and after giving Lottie and Willie strict instructions to behave themselves, I set out to visit, Mr Fenton. He lived in a nicer part of town at the top of the Avenue, in a large house with a well-tended garden. I opened the gate and walked up the path to the front door. My heart started hammering in my chest as I prepared to knock on the door. I sucked in a breath and slowly let it out before rapping soundly. I prayed he was home.

A minute later the door was swung open and Mr Fenton stood there glaring at me. "I've nothing more to say to you, Mrs Hartley. Good day." He went to close the door but I stepped forward pushing my foot in between the door and the jamb.

"Now wait just a minute," I said grabbing hold of the door so he couldn't close it any further. "I've come into some money, Mr Fenton and I can pay you several months rent in advance if you like."

He paused and looked at me speculatively. "Really?"

"Yes, I received a letter from my sister saying that the money will be sent to me from an attorney in Hobart Town."

"So you don't actually have the money?" His disdain for me was clearly written on his face. "Good day." He pushed the door and I let go, but I kept my foot firmly against it so he couldn't close it all the way.

"Here, read it for yourself," I said shoving the letter into his hand. "It's fifty pounds, and I'll have it in a few days."

He let the letter fall from his fingers. "I've been more than patient. Leave or I'll call for the constable and have you removed."

I scrambled to retrieve the letter and he took the opportunity to slam the door shut in my face. I stared mouth agape at the closed door, before I came to my senses – and banged loudly on it.

"Mr Fenton!"

There was no reply.

I could feel the adrenalin coursing through me as I stepped from the porch. My heart was racing and my hands were trembling as I opened the gate and started down the street. Tears started streaming down my face as I hurried away. I wiped them away, but I couldn't stop them. I had no choice now but to leave my home and go and live with the Harrison's.

So many thoughts were tumbling one over the another in my mind. How would Barb find me? I was expecting another letter from her, and would likely not receive it. The attorney's letter would also likely miss me and go astray. I'd have to go to Hobart Town and see the attorney's myself. I had a couple of pounds left which should be enough to get me to Hobart Town and pay for some modest lodgings. Once again I would have to call on the charity of my friends to take care of Lottie and Willie. I'd make it up to them – not just Ann and Bessie, but my darling children as well.

I straightened my shoulders and dismissed my tears as I neared Ann's house. I had to be strong and fearless for my children. Oh, Will - how I yearn for you.

Chapter Thirty Six

The Widow Harrison and her Son

I sucked in a deep breath and slowly let it out, as I opened the gate and walked up the path to the large brick house ahead of me. Lottie and Willie were hanging onto my skirts, and I had my violin case in one hand, the portmanteau in the other, and a bag slung over my shoulder. They contained all the worldly possessions I could carry.

I put down my case and lifted the heavy door knocker. It rapped loudly as I let it go.

"Me do," said Willie letting go of my skirts and reaching for the ornate knocker. I grabbed him just as he was about to wrap his fingers around it.

"No."

"Mamma," he said wriggling to be free of my grasp. "Me doo."

"No, stop it," I said sternly pulling him away from the door.

Moments later it was opened by a portly man with the bushiest sideburns I'd ever seen. He smiled showing a row of crooked teeth as he looked from me to the children. "Mrs Hartley?"

"Yes," I replied holding out my hand to shake his proffered one. "Mr Harrison I presume. These are my children Lottie and Willie." I was relieved when he released my hand and I tried hard to refrain from gripping my skirt with it. A shudder went through me which I hoped he hadn't noticed. Mr Harrison had been nothing but polite and civil, and yet his whole demeanour made my skin crawl.

"Nice to meet you," he said nodding. "Please come in. My mother is anxious to make your acquaintance."

"Thank you," I replied collecting my case and urging the children to follow Mr Harrison into the house. He led us down a wide hall and into a well-appointed sitting room. A fire was burning in the hearth and sitting beside it was a plump middle-aged woman with a head of riotous blond curls. She was rosy-cheeked and looked almost girlish. I thought she had to be at least sixty, but she didn't look it.

Upon seeing us she heaved herself out of her chair and came towards me with her arms outstretched. "Oh you poor dear," she said clasping me to her bosom. "What a trial. What a trial. Rest assured, Mrs Hartley," she said letting me go and smiling warmly at me. "You've naught to worry about now. Don't just stand there like a

.

411

dolt, Matthew, take Mrs Hartley's bags to her room."

"Yes mother," he said taking my luggage and disappearing down the hallway with it.

I watched him go before turning my attention back to my benefactor. "I can't thank you enough, Mrs Harrison. You have been most kind to provide us with lodgings in our hour of need."

"Nonsense my dear," she said easing herself back into her chair. "When the Reverend told me of your plight I was more than happy to help. Anyway, why don't you go and get settled and then we can get to know one another." She dismissed me with a wave of her hand, and I took the children by the hand and went in search of Mr Harrison.

I was near the end of the hall, wondering which way he might have gone, when he stepped out of a room just behind me. I spun around to face him.

"Oh, Mr Harrison I was just looking for you. Your mother suggested I settle in."

"Yes, of course," he said opening the door behind him. "We thought you and the children would be most comfortable in here."

"Thank you." I smiled as I passed him and entered the small bedroom. There was a large bed pushed against one wall and a smaller one on the opposite wall. Lottie and I would have to sleep together, but it would suit us just fine. My case and bags had been dumped in the middle of the floor, and I noticed a single tall boy in the corner. There was no wardrobe or other furnishings, but I was most grateful that it looked clean. "This will suit us admirably."

Mr Harrison looked around the room with a distasteful look on his face. "Once you're unpacked I'll give you a tour so that you may acquaint yourself with the house."

I thanked him once again and sighed with relief when he closed the door and left. Lottie helped me unpack our meagre belongings and stow them in the tallboy. Willie was too busy exploring the small room to bother us. Not that there was much to see, and we were unpacked and settled in no time.

Matthew Harrison gave us a tour of the back garden, which Lottie and Willie stayed to explore. I followed him back into the house to continue the tour. On the ground level was a large kitchen and larder, along with one bedroom, the dining room, study and the sitting room. Upstairs were two more bedrooms and an attic.

It didn't take long for me to learn that Mrs Harrison ruled the roost. She barked orders from morning to night and required my assistance with everything. Within days I was doing all the cooking and household chores. This included the laundry, which I hated with a passion, but in all honesty, I couldn't complain. The children adored her and she was generous in many other ways. At any rate, I didn't see that I had much choice.

I pulled the joint of meat from the oven and placed it on the hob and breathed in the aromas. It smelled delicious. Mrs Harrison insisted on having the main meal in the middle of the day, which I must admit I had quickly gotten used to. I lifted the roast from the pan and put it on a plate. There were enough pan juices to make a rich gravy and my stomach rumbled at the thought. I headed into the larder for the flour. It was on the top shelf and as I reached for it Matthew Harrison filled the doorway.

"Do you need some help?"

He pushed himself up against me as he reached for the flour. "I'm fine thank you," I stammered as I moved away from him and to the back of the larder. It was only a small room, and I was mere inches from him as he removed the flour and stared at me. I could feel the heat emanating from him - I swallowed.

"You're very pretty," he said reaching his hand out to touch my face.

I recoiled and pressed my back into the shelves at the rear of the larder. "I have to get back to the kitchen." I hoped he'd hand me the flour and leave.

Instead, he put the flour down on the bench and looked at me with unmistakable lust in his eyes. My heart was racing as I realised I couldn't get out of the larder. His bulk was blocking the doorway and I couldn't even squeeze passed him.

"You won't be missed," he said as he grabbed me and pressed his lips to mine. I struggled against him and tried to wrench myself free, but he pressed himself hard into me. I gagged as he thrust his tongue into my mouth and ran his hands roughly over my breasts. He hugged me hard up against him so I could barely move. Panic gripped me when I felt his warm fingers against my thigh as he roughly lifted my skirts. I was jammed up against the shelves and my efforts to push him off were utterly useless. My mind was in a whirl as I tried to think of what to do.

"Get off me," I finally managed to yell and I kicked his shin with my boot as hard as I could. He let out a yelp and loosened his grip enough for me to bring my knee up hard into his groin. He let go of me and doubled over in pain. He let out an awful groan, but I didn't hesitate. I squeezed passed him and ran out the door.

"You witch," he yelled after me.

My heart was hammering madly in my chest as I ripped off my apron and ran to my bedroom. "Willie, Lottie, come quickly," I called as I went. I was terrified he'd come after me. I wrenched open the drawers of the tallboy and began madly tossing everything into my portmanteau.

"What Mamma?" said Lottie sauntering into the bedroom with a bewildered expression on her face. "What you doing?"

"We're leaving. Go get Willie and hurry."

She just stood there staring at me as though I'd lost my senses. "Go. Now," I said pushing her towards the door. I watched her leave before going back to packing our belongings. It didn't take long to shove everything in. I grabbed my violin case and hurried from the room. I had no intention of being in there if he came after me. I looked up and down the hallway, it was empty. I heaved a sigh as I made for the front door. I prayed Lottie and Willie wouldn't be long. I opened the front door and waited – ready to run if I saw Harrison coming.

A moment later Mrs Harrison poked her head out of the sitting room and stared at me. "Whatever's going on, Mrs Hartley? Is dinner ready?"

"Ah...no." I didn't know what else to say. I was on the verge of tears and knew I wouldn't be able to hold them back if she showed me any kindness.

"Why have you got your bags? Please, what's amiss?" she said waddling towards me with an expression of genuine concern on her face. She reached me and put her hand on my arm. "Whatever it is I'm sure we can fix it."

"No, Mrs Harrison. I'm sorry, I have to go," I blurted out as the tears that I'd been holding back spilled down my face. At last, I saw Lottie and Willie coming down the hallway towards me. "Hurry, and say goodbye to Mrs Harrison," I called to them.

Mrs Harrison's grip tightened on my arm as she looked from me to the children in alarm. "It's Matthew, isn't it. What did he do?"

"Bye Mrs Harrison," said Lottie with a confused look on her face.

"Bye," said Willie skipping out the front door with Lottie at his heels.

"Please...I can't stay Mrs Harrison. I'm so sorry," I said pulling my arm free and following the children up the path to the gate. I turned as I closed it. Mrs Harrison was staring after me, and I swallowed as Matthew Harrison joined his mother at the door. The last I saw before I turned to leave was Mrs Harrison hitting her son about the head. I hurried to catch up to Lottie and Willie, who had already started down the street.

"Are we going home now?" asked Lottie looking up at me with her large grey eyes.

"Papa, Papa," chanted Willie as he skipped down the street.

"I don't know." What was I going to do? We had no home to go to, but I wasn't about to tell them that. Thoughts were whizzing around my mind as I tried to think of what to do. I could probably afford one night in the Bush Inn, but then what? My stomach grumbled as I hurried down the street away from the Harrison's. I was sorry we hadn't had dinner before we left. I couldn't think of anyone who might help me except for Ann and Bessie. I was sure they'd take care of the children for a few days while I went to Hobart Town. All I could do was pray the money from my mother had arrived.

I stopped as I thought I heard someone calling my name. A spring cart pulled up beside us and for a moment I thought it was Harrison come after me.

Panic gripped me until I realised it was James Triffett and his son.

"It is ye, Mrs Hartley," he said peering at me with concern etched on his face. "Are ye alright?"

I burst into tears. "Oh, I'm so sorry, Mr Triffett," I sobbed as I tried to wipe my eyes with the back of my sleeve. "I've been evicted and then Mr Harrison attacked me, and now I don't know what I'm going to do." I sounded hysterical even to my own ears, and I was sure the poor man didn't know what to make of me.

"John, take Mrs Hartley's bags and put them in the back of the cart," he said taking me by the elbow. "Come, Mrs Hartley, let's see what we can do to amend the situation."

He helped me into the cart before lifting the children up beside me. Lottie took my hand and squeezed, her young face full of worry. It broke my heart to see it. I wrapped my arms around her and pulled her close. "It's alright sweetheart."

I hoped my words would give her some comfort. For myself, I prayed James Triffett might be able to offer me some assistance. He was a great supporter of Will's, and as we headed off down the road

Margaret

I felt myself relax for the first time in weeks.

Chapter Thirty Seven

Mr Triffett to the rescue

We'd spent the last two nights sleeping in James Triffett's bed. He'd vacated it for us and from what I could tell, was sleeping in the barn. We couldn't stay here forever, and I was anxious to sort out a permanent solution. I had to depend on myself with Will away, and every time I thought of him my heart wrenched and I had this awful feeling of injustice take hold of me. I was angry, but I was also scared.

I took another mouthful of porridge and gave Mr Triffett my undivided attention. He had finished his breakfast and was looking at me intently.

"John and I are going to Hobart Town, and we'll be gone at least a week. Ye are welcome to stay here until we return," he said straightening his waistcoat. "In fact, I insist ye remain here until I return. I'm also hoping ye will allow me to visit the attorney, John Dobson on yer behalf and discover if any monies have arrived for ye."

"You are too kind Mr Triffett. I would much appreciate your assistance. If it isn't too much trouble for you to make enquiries on my behalf, then please do."

"I assure ye it will be no trouble whatsoever," he said smiling warmly at me. "If ye have no objection, I plan to pay Mr Fenton a visit before I go. I believe he may be persuaded to change his mind concerning yer accommodation."

I raised my eyebrows. "I have no objection to you paying him a visit, however, I must warn you. Mr Fenton was most adamant and I think unlikely to change his mind where I'm concerned."

"I can be most persuasive," he said standing and putting on his jacket. "Please make yerself at home until I return."

"Thank you, I'll stay until you return, but then I must make other arrangements."

"Let's wait and see shall we?"

I nodded. I watched him leave before going back to my breakfast. The children weren't awake yet, and I hoped to finish my porridge before they got up. I

sighed as I swallowed another mouthful. I was going to have to come up with some way of surviving the next two years on my own, without relying on the kindness of Mr Triffett.

I was on tenterhooks for the whole week waiting for Mr Triffett to return with news. I prayed it would be good news. I'd spent a considerable amount of time thinking about my situation, and I'd come to the only conclusion I could. I would write to Maria and ask for her help. I knew she'd do all she could, and I hoped she may be able to offer me a position. I would not rely upon her good nature and charity alone.

I sighed as I looked out into the empty yard yet again. There was no sign of Mr Triffett returning, and I went back to my mending. Lottie and Willie were happily playing outside, at least I hoped they were. All was quiet, and I took that as I good sign.

I prepared a simple supper of cold lamb with rice and peas and put the children to bed soon after. I hadn't long settled down to darn my hose when the sound of men's voices filled the yard. My heart started hammering as I put my darning away and went to the door. I opened it and looked out. Sure enough, in the fading light, I saw James Triffett and his son. I was anxious to hear what news he had.

"Mrs Hartley," said James Triffett smiling wearily at me. "I'm glad to see ye are still here then."

"Evenin' Ma'am," said John doffing his hat. "I'm straight to bed Pa."

"Alright, I'll see ye in the morning," he said before turning to me. "I'd have a word before I retire."

"I hoped you would," I said stepping back to allow him to enter. "Shall I make us some tea?" I closed the door and looked at him expectantly.

"Thank ye."

He settled himself at the table while I busied myself in the kitchen. Ten minutes later I placed a pot of tea and a plate of oat biscuits on the table before him. I poured us both a cup before taking the seat opposite him.

"I have good news," he said without any preamble. "I was able to speak at length to the attorney, John Dobson. He's received the funds from yer Uncle, and his agent, Mr Elliot will deliver them to ye next week." He took a biscuit and dunked it in his tea before putting it in his mouth whole.

I nearly cried with joy. I would have enough money to survive while Will was away without having to rely on charity. I pressed my lips together while I composed myself. "I don't know how I can ever repay your kindness. Thank you so much," I said heaving a sigh. "Am I to stay here until he comes? I've already relied too heavily on your good nature, Mr Triffett. I don't wish to burden you further."

"Nonsense," he said with a wave of his hand. "What has happened to yer husband is a travesty of injustice. While I'm unable to alleviate his situation, I can ensure that ye and the children are cared for."

"Well I appreciate that, but in all conscience, I can't remain here."

"And I don't suggest ye do," he said taking a sip of his tea. "That brings me to the next piece of news.

"Oh."

"I paid Mr Fenton a visit, and it seems he's had a change of heart." He reached into his pocket and pulled out a ring of keys. Taking my hand he placed them in my palm and closed my fingers on them. "The keys to yer house."

"Did you hit him?" I asked as my eyebrows shot up towards my hairline. I couldn't believe Mr Fenton would've just agreed to rent the house back to me. He'd been so adamant. Mr Triffett didn't strike me as the kind of man to have put up a good argument on my behalf either.

"No not me, Mrs Hartley, I didn't hit him."

Not him. John then? I hoped not. Not because he didn't deserve it, but I wouldn't want either of them to get into trouble on my behalf. Tears flooded my eyes as I opened my fingers and stared at the keys. "Thank you."

"Yer most welcome," he said getting to his feet. "If ye'll excuse me, I'm rather weary. I'll see ye in the morning then."

"Of course," I said blinking back my tears and standing up. "Sleep well."

He opened the door and I watched him walk across the yard to the barn before going back inside. I leaned against the door and sighed – I was so fortunate to have James Triffett on my side.

The following morning I cooked eggs and sausages for us all for breakfast. Lottie and Willie ate with gusto, as did John Triffett. I don't think he could've had any supper last night by the way he was shovelling sausages into his mouth. There was a buzz of excitement in the air. I sipped my tea and smiled contentedly at my two darling children. I was so blessed to have them, even if Willie was a trial at times.

"When yer done there, John, go hitch up the horses," said James Triffett putting down his knife with a clatter. "Perhaps ye'd like to help him, Willie?"

"Aye," said Willie clambering down from his chair.

"After breakfast," I said grabbing him by the arm as he made to head off. "Come and finish your eggs."

He scowled at me as he wriggled to free himself from my grip. "No."

"Yes," I said getting up and lifting him back onto the chair. "John will wait for you. Won't you John?"

"Oh aye, eat yer eggs, Willie."

He settled back onto his chair and scooped more egg into his mouth. I heaved a sigh as I sat back down beside Lottie. She was solemn and I was worried that she'd seen too much in the last few weeks. She wasn't quite four and a half, and too grown up for her age.

"Are you alright sweetie?"

"Aye Mamma," she said looking at me with her soft grey eyes. "Will Papa be there?"

"No, not today," I said putting my arm around her and kissing her forehead. "Soon. I promise you'll see him soon."

She nodded and went back to eating her breakfast. I noticed James Triffett look at her with sadness in his eyes. I felt it too, but I couldn't bear to tell her the truth. Two years would seem an eternity to her.

An hour later John helped me into the cart. Our bags were in the back, Lottie was sitting by my side and Willie was up the front on James' knee. It was only a couple of miles into town from the Triffett farm, but I was anxious to get there. It had been two weeks since we were evicted, and I couldn't wait to see our shabby little house.

It was a fine spring morning with a cool breeze blowing up from the river. I pulled my cloak around Lottie and myself as John turned the horses up Officer Street. A few minutes later he brought them to a halt outside our humble little cottage. For some reason, I'd expected it to look different, but it was exactly the same as when we'd left.

John helped me down and I took Lottie by the hand as we walked up the dirt path to the front door. I unlocked it and sighed as I stepped across the threshold. It was as though we were coming home after a morning of shopping. Everything was just as we'd left it. Tears pricked my eyes, as I wandered into my bedroom.

I sighed. We were home. The only home I'd ever known with Will was this one, and this is where he'd find me. He'd come to me when he was released from Port Arthur, I knew he would. And I'd be here waiting.

The End

The Blurry Lines of Fact and Fiction

So how much of Margaret' story is factual, and how much have I invented? Well, to be honest with you, this is a work of fiction, based around a few loose facts.

I have no idea why she decided to pose as a domestic servant and travel to Van Diemen's Land in the first place. The whole story of her running away from an arranged marriage is pure fiction. The facts are that her father Sir Samuel Chambers was the named heir of his brother. James Chambers did go bankrupt, and he was declared a lunatic. I've used these bare facts to build an entire fabricated story about why Margaret ran away.

When she arrived in Hobart Town, she was supposed to go and work for Mrs Hector of Coal River. However, I couldn't find Mrs Hector. I searched the records and the newspapers, but I found no mention of a Hector family. I can only presume that whoever wrote down the details on the passenger list, either wrote down the wrong name, or only wrote down part of the name.

So, I decided to have Margaret go and work for Reverend Davies and his wife. This worked in well with the story, because William Hartley was assigned to work for the Reverend. Whether he seduced her, or they fell in love – I don't know. But in no time at all Margaret found herself pregnant. William was still a convict and couldn't take care of her, so she ended up ensconced in Captain Cheyne's garden shed. This is true.

Captain Cheyne had two other convicts working for him, a cook and a tailor. Both were supposed to be working on the chain gang, but he'd taken them home to work for him. As unbelievable as this is, it's all true. And then he got caught, and the convicts were taken back to work on the chain gang. I thought it likely that Margaret would've got caught up in this, but I don't actually know. So, her being carted off to the female factory in Launceston is fiction.

So, after the raid, William was reassigned to work for McDowell in Norfolk Plains, and I don't know where Margaret went. So, I decided she might have stayed with the Captain. Will and her must have been seeing one another during this time, because she fell pregnant with their second child. Fact.

So then William got his ticket of leave, and they moved to New Norfolk where they were finally married. All true. The witnesses at their wedding were John and Ann Brown. I made up the bit where this was Ann Chapman who Margaret shared a compartment with on the William Metcalf.

So, things were just looking up for Will and Margaret when he got caught in Mrs Burnett's female servant's room one night. This is true, but I made up why he was in there. I didn't like to think that he was cheating on Margaret, but he might have been. Poor Margaret.

Will was sentenced to twelve months gaol, and then he was found guilty of larceny. I have no idea how that could've happened, because he was in gaol. So the bit about him being wrongly accused of stealing a locket is fiction. But, he was then sentenced to two years in Port Arthur – that's true.

Margaret was left to fend for herself and the children. Her mother did die, but once again I've made up the bit about her leaving money to Margaret. I thought the poor woman needed some help.

Was she evicted? Did Matthew Harrison accost her in the larder? Did James Triffett save her? All made up.

Will and Margaret's story isn't over. There's so much more to their story that it's going to require a second book. The sequel, Burnt Bridge is out now.

Author Notes

Thank you so much for reading Margaret. I'm an Australian indie author. As such, I maintain complete control of my work and self publish. That also means I have to market and promote my work, which I'm not very good at. I find it hard to self promote.

So, I'm taking this opportunity to not only thank you for taking the time to read my book, but if you liked it, would you mind leaving a rating or review on Amazon. It's the best way to show any author that you appreciate their hard work. It also helps other potential readers to decide if they should invest their time and money.

You already know that I write historical fiction, and you may have also realised that my stories are based on the lives of my ancestors. I've been passionate about family history for many years, and I've discovered so many amazing ancestors who led such interesting lives. So, I blend fact with fiction and bring their stories to life, and I'm so excited to be sharing them with you.

If you enjoyed this book, please consider reading one of my other titles.

Thank you

Jacob's Mob

How did one fateful decision land Aaron Price in New South Wales as an assigned convict?

He and his mate James were best described as petty criminals until they decided to try their hand at breaking and entering. What started as a grab for easy money, ended with them being sentenced to transportation to the colonies for life. Aaron may be lamenting his fate and the fact that he won't be seeing his sweetheart again, but is he content to serve his sentence?

Aaron knows only too well that bushranging is a hanging offence, and yet he once again allows himself to be persuaded. On the run and eager for revenge, he and his new mates wage terror on their previous master and the other settlers of the Hunter Valley.

However, Aaron isn't content to just wreak havoc - he's got an escape plan. If only he could find a way to get himself on board a ship bound for America. The British have no jurisdiction there, and he would be free.

Based on the true story of Aaron Price, who arrived in New South Wales in 1825 on board the convict transport Guildford.

Pioneers of Burra

From Cornwall to an untamed South Australia...

Based on the true story of the Bryar family, who left their homeland in search of a better life. Richard and his son Thomas secure free passage to South Australia, where they dream of a new beginning working in the copper mine of Burra.

After months at sea and a perilous journey from Adelaide to Burra, their families are finally reunited. Can they overcome the hardships of living in a dugout on the Burra Creek to carve out a better future for their children? Will a disaster in the mine finally bring them together with hope for the future?

Burnt Bridge

Margaret's sister, Barb comes for a visit and convinces her to join her in Sydney until Will is released from prison. Before she leaves New Norfolk, the local storekeeper, Samuel Brownell makes her an offer she can't refuse. She prays it will keep her husband safe.

Meanwhile, Will still has a year to serve in Port Arthur, but his life becomes much easier when Doctor Brownell requests his services. A friendship soon develops and when an opportunity presents itself to go into partnership, Will can't believe his luck.

Margaret and Will embark on a new endeavour on the Snug River with their new found friends and partners. They acquire a property and build a thriving farm, but all is not as it seems. What secrets are the Brownell's keeping that will leave Margaret and Will reeling?

Join My Readers List

I love to connect with my readers and share updates with them. I don't send emails too often – but you'll be the first to know about promotions and upcoming releases.

Subscribe on my website.

www.cjbessell.godaddysites.com

Follow me on Facebook

I post regularly on my Facebook page, and it's a great place to connect and stay up to date with all things in my author world.

I'd love to connect with you.

https://www.facebook.com/CJBessell/

Margaret

Margaret

..

Printed in Great Britain
by Amazon

36205971R00247